Terra Firma

Special Agent O'Malley, FBI

By

Colin Setterfield

COLIN SETTERFIELD © 2016

ISBN 978-1-988719-13-9

Contents

PROLOGUE

Jon Shepard walked into the 7-Eleven on Columbus Street, New York, and scanned the variety of bottled beverages in the upright cooler. The cool air in the store brought instant relief from the hot humid sidewalk outside, which thronged with people. He slid the cooler's glass door open, selected a bottle of purified water and turned toward the counter to pay for it. A patron in the lineup ahead waited for the till-attendant to complete a transaction and Shepard noticed a peculiar mole on the back of the man's neck. A thought crossed his mind. How odd—I have a mole in exactly the same spot.

The man placed his purchase on the counter and handed the attendant a five dollar note, received his change and turned to leave but accidentally dropped the purchase which landed at Shepard's feet. The man turned around, knelt down to retrieve it but Jon had already picked it up. He handed it to the stranger with a smile.

"Thanks," said the man. For a brief moment, their eyes locked and Shepard's jaw dropped. The stranger seemed just as surprised when he looked into Shepard's face. An awkward moment passed before the man tore his eyes away, swiveled on his heel and strode briskly out of the store.

Jon stared at the door until the till attendant spoke. "Are you going to pay for that, Sir?"

Shepard blinked his eyes and handed over a banknote. The attendant gave him change and caught the eye of the next customer in the lineup but Shepard did not move.

"Do you mind, please, Sir. We're very busy," said the attendant.

Shepard apologized and left the shop. Outside, on the sidewalk, the throng of people pushed him up against the store window as he tried to catch sight of the stranger but the man had disappeared. For a long while, he stood in contemplation of the event. He couldn't get over the sudden shock of looking into what he recognized to be his own face.

✳

1

Alan McHale

Alan McHale donned a pair of dark glasses and focused on the Statue of Liberty in the distance. The approach to New York City harbor would take forty minutes plus another twenty minutes to dock before he could step out onto dry land and firm footing again. The journey from the Triangle had taken a while but at last his new home was in sight.

"Ready, Sir?" asked the boat's captain.

"As ready as I will ever be," said McHale.

"You will find everything familiar—just a few different names," said the captain.

McHale snorted. "I'll be fine. Don't worry about a thing."

"Of course you will, sir. You know how to contact us if something goes wrong, so don't hesitate."

"I won't. I'm sure everything will go off as planned."

An hour later the Lady Gray, a fishing trawler, nudged up against the jetty. Ropes were thrown out onto the quay for the vessel to be made fast and the gangway put in place for the crew's disembarkation. McHale, with a single bag in hand, stepped up onto the gangway and walked down the steps onto the dock. He stopped for a brief glance at the surroundings and noticed that the color schemes of some buildings appeared different, however, most of the dock area seemed exactly the same as he remembered it. All the smells and noises, combined with the cries of seagulls and the sound of a train shunting its load, plus the honk of an incoming ferry, all coalesced nostalgically in his mind.

McHale took a deep breath and walked off the dock in the direction of the terminal where his contact awaited him. In consideration of their task, a sudden twinge of nerves caused the muscles around his mouth to tighten. McHale had trained long and hard for this day. Ten people knew why he had come and only three of them knew the extent of his mission. The others had been in place for at least three years to establish the foundation for the plan and were all well acquainted with the city and the sea. They had learned the lay of the land, so to speak, and the major steps of the plan were already in place. The next step in the mission awaited McHale's leadership.

He entered the busy terminal and looked around for Elias Stilwell, his contact. He knew Elias well. They had trained together for Operation Terra

Firma but Stilwell had done all the initial work. A new company called Terra Enterprises had been established in Atlantic City, New Jersey, as a front for the operation. The venture masqueraded as a social event planning business but was always fully booked whenever inquiries for its services were made. McHale would steer the operation through to its culmination and ultimate success.

Stilwell stood near the exit and when he spotted his boss he waved. They embraced and exchanged pleasantries before moving out into the carpark to the waiting car and driver.

"How was your journey?" asked Stilwell.

"As turbulent as always," answered McHale.

Stilwell opened the car door for his boss. "...and, how are things back at home?"

McHale greeted the driver and sank into the soft leather of the back seat with a sigh. "It's getting worse."

"How much longer do you think we have?"

McHale gave the question some thought. "Four to five years, maybe."

Stilwell pulled out a handkerchief and blew his nose. "We have all the relevant replacement plans and the timeline ready for your scrutiny."

McHale looked through the car's side window at the traffic and buildings. "I can't get over how familiar everything is—but in a vague sort of way it's all different."

"Don't worry. You'll get used to it very quickly. When will Hastings be arriving?"

"In two days. He'll arrive with Francis Bowman. The Captain will pick them up from the arrival zone at approximately 12:00 p.m."

"How long will they need to make the adjustment?" asked Stilwell.

"They are fully briefed and will be ready to hit the ground running."

Stilwell raised his eyebrows. "Are you intending to put them both in at the same time?"

"It will make their adjustment to the live stage easier," said McHale.

*

"I'm telling you, Dillon. I almost fell on my ass. It was in New York at about midday, in a 7-eleven—I thought I was looking into a mirror."

"Did you manage to speak to the person?" asked O'Malley.

Jon Shepard frowned. "No. I was so surprised that it made me speechless for a few moments and when I finally came to my senses the guy had left. I ran outside but he disappeared amongst all the people on the sidewalk."

O'Malley chuckled. "So, you think you might have a twin your mother never told you about?"

"My parents definitely did not have twins. As you know I have one brother, two years my senior, and that's it."

"It's not uncommon for a person to have a double, though," said O'Malley.

"A close resemblance maybe, but not this close."

The two men sat next to each other at the bar counter and contemplated their drinks. Shepard drank beer and O'Malley, whiskey. It was getting late and both were tired.

"So, you're chugging it pretty late tonight. Trouble in paradise?"

O'Malley grinned. "Tam's working late. Besides she's not talking to me at the moment—thinks I'm having second thoughts about divorcing Janet."

"Are you?" asked Shepard.

"I don't want to rush things. It's hard to give-up on nineteen years of marriage."

"I feel your pain. It took me two years to get over my divorce," answered Shepard.

O'Malley glanced at the time and drained his glass. "I had better get going. She'll be home by now."

Shepard sighed and finished off his beer. "Me too. I still have to come up with a speech for the President's address at Harvard tomorrow. I guess I'll be burning the midnight oil."

"The White House getting you down?" asked O'-Malley.

"Naw. It's just the same old stuff. I can regurgitate it in my sleep."

The two men left the bar and parted company. O'Malley walked to the SUV, climbed in and pressed the starter. The powerful V8 motor fired up and he pulled out of the parking space into the traffic. The vehicle was one of the perks he enjoyed as an FBI special agent. He swerved around a slow-moving car and slammed his foot down on the gas pedal to catch the traffic light up ahead, coaxing every bit of power from the engine.

A twinge of guilt flitted across his mind as he careened through the intersection. He realized that three whiskeys should never be combined with driving and he eased off the throttle not wanting to draw the attention of the Police. Ten minutes later he pulled up outside his apartment block and parked the vehicle at the curb. The living room lights were on which meant Tam was waiting for him.

Similar past instances came to mind when a confrontation with his wife, Janet, loomed and she would wait up to offload the emotional deluge on her mind. O'Malley, however, knew he was the problem. The death of his daughter on her prom night haunted him constantly, like a stuck record. He had tried everything to move on with his life but to no avail. He had failed as a father and since Fallon's death, he had also failed as a husband. His only son, Steven, now seventeen, avoided contact with him and he blamed Janet for coaching the boy.

Things came to a head when he had met Tammy Clyde-Walker, a CIA operative, while on a case at the Groom Lake Base, situated at area 51. O'Malley's marriage, already in jeopardy took a step backward when he and Tam experienced a life and death experience together. Tam, divorced and vulnerable, latched onto the good-looking FBI agent which brought about a predictable reaction from O'Malley's wife, Janet. Janet filed divorce papers but O'Malley wouldn't sign them until he felt ready to do so. This reluctance on his behalf gave Tam the idea that he had second thoughts about the divorce.

With Janet living in Baltimore communication remained low-key and Tam pressed O'Malley to make up his mind, or she would move on.

O'Malley took the stairs to the landing, walked along the corridor to the apartment's entrance and let himself in. Tam, who had been watching TV stood to greet him and they embraced.

"Long day?" she asked. They sat down on the sofa and eyed each other.

"Yeah," he sighed. "Jon Shepard asked me to have a drink with him. How was your day?"

"Still working on the Brixton case, but let's not talk shop. Did you send off those papers today?"

O'Malley knew she would ask the question. Tam never beat around the bush and always tackled things head-on. She would never let sleeping dogs lie, a reason the CIA had recently promoted her to special agent status.

"No, I didn't have time."

She lowered her chin and stared directly into his eyes. "You didn't have time, or you didn't want to?"

"Perhaps a bit of both," he said. "We've been over this before."

"I need to know things are moving in the right direction for us, Dillon. You say that you love me, yet you continue to procrastinate over the very thing that divides us."

"Why does it have to divide us? We love each other—we sleep in the same bed every night. I don't see Janet at all—I don't feel this division you're talking about."

Tam grabbed his hand and shifted over on the sofa toward him. "A woman see's these things differently, my love. I can see you're having second thoughts. Is it because Steven won't talk to you?"

O'Malley considered the question. "Maybe—I don't want to lose my son. I need to know he'll get over the divorce and forgive me for being the cause of it."

"Are you sure he resents you for what's happened between you and his mother? Have you sat down and had a real heart to heart?"

"He refuses to see me. I don't really know what's on his heart. I need to give it more time."

Tam closed her eyes in frustration. "But you won't know until you take the step of confronting him directly. It seems as though you think he's just going to call you one day and say it's fine for you to get divorced from his mother."

"I know it sounds naive but I think the more time he has to think about it the more he will realize my marriage to Janet is over."

Tam felt a tinge of anger. "Do you believe your marriage is over?"

O'Malley looked down at their clasped hands and remained silent for a moment. He knew Tam's question probed at the indistinct feelings he had for Janet—feelings he couldn't quite quantify. The question raged in his mind: could he be in love with two people at the same time? Nineteen years of marriage created bonds that a man and a woman did not even realize until the union became threatened. He felt a confusion, closed his eyes and silently cursed his own ambivalence.

Tam released his hand and stood up. "I think your answer to my question is clear."

"Tam..." stammered O'Malley. "Wait. Don't jump to conclusions. I can explain...."

She turned and marched off to the bedroom. "I'm going to bed. You can sleep in the spare room tonight. When you're ready to be completely honest with me, we can talk."

He stared at her but made no attempt to follow. He heard the bedroom door close and lock. Sleep would be difficult under the circumstances but the bed in the spare room appeared to be the only remaining option. He shuffled off to the guest bathroom.

2

Three Days Later.

Jon Shepard waited outside the door to the Oval Office for Beverly Swales, the White House Chief of Staff. When Swales, an energetic woman in her late forties arrived, they stood and conferred for a brief moment.

"You ready?" asked Swales.

"Always ready," answered Shepard.

She knocked gently on the door and pushed it open.

"Good afternoon, Mr. President. I have brought Jon so you can explain what your thoughts are for the upcoming state of the union address."

President Chambers looked up from the monitor. "Yes, please take a seat."

He closed his laptop and joined them at the coffee table. Chambers, an aging man of a short stature with broad shoulders, steepled his fingers and stared at the speech writer. Jon Shepard had met with the president on at least a dozen occasions and found it odd that Chambers had not greeted him with the usual warmth and jocular style of previous meetings. The president seemed distant and preoccupied, an attitude, however, which caused Shepard little concern. After all, the job which faced the most powerful man in the world was bound to cause him a measure of mental conflict.

"At the end of the speech, when I have finished talking about the economy and the job establishment initiatives I want to cut to the chase with Congress," said the president. "The matter of North Korea and its quest for nuclear weapons must be seen in the correct perspective. I doubt whether they believe they could get away with a nuclear attack on the United States. I hope to take a softer stance with them in the hope that will ease off their nuclear program."

Beverley Swales looked shocked. "That is a sudden change in policy, Mr. President. Have you conferred with the Chinese?"

The president Lowered his chin. "I spoke to the chairman this morning. They are not too happy about us taking military action and that's another reason I want to look for a new way to handle the situation."

"What about the Russians?" asked Swales.

"The Russians are looking for super power status again and I don't want to provoke them unnecessarily either."

Jon Shepard leaned forward on his chair. "What do you want to say about the measures the United States should be taking, Mr. President?"

"Don't write in any details about the measures we are going to take. I don't want to alert them to any specific plan of action. Set out all the details of the DPRK's violations with regard to the UN charter on the development of nuclear weapons and then add that if the North Koreans do not stop testing their missiles the US will be forced to take counter measures."

Swales frowned. "I don't think the joint chiefs are going to like your approach, Sir."

"Frankly, I don't give a shit what the joint chiefs think," answered the president.

Shepard couldn't believe his ears. This wasn't the leader of the free world he had come to know. Only last week the president had ranted about North Korea's blatant disregard for the nuclear treaty and how the United States should confront them with the possibility of direct military intervention. He wanted to say something but bit his tongue instead. It was not that he disagreed with the president's sudden change of heart. The American people, however, would be critical of the flip-flop on a campaign promise to threaten military force when dealing with countries like the NDPK and Iran.

The president brought an end to the meeting. "Have the speech ready for my perusal by 2:30 p.m.tomorrow."

Swales and Shepard left the oval office and as they walked along the corridor he made a comment. "That's quite a turn about on policy isn't it?"

Swales pursed her lips. "Sometimes policy campaigns don't fit the future situations they're intended to resolve. It might seem like a potential flip-flop but I think the president is just rethinking his strategy. Do you think it's a flip-flop?"

"It's not what I think that counts—it's what the American people think," said Shepard.

"Screw the general populace. The majority don't have a clue what's going on, anyway," Swales returned.

Shepard raised an eyebrow but didn't comment.

"I'll have the speech ready by the appointed time," he said. They parted ways and Shepard headed for his office. He had an uncanny feeling something was wrong. Both the chief of staff and the president seemed strangely different. It wasn't that they looked different but rather they appeared to be acting differently. Swales had got him the job at the White House and he felt a loyalty toward her. She had never been afraid to tell the president when she thought he was making a mistake, however, that fierce independent thinking had appeared to have deserted her. The president also appeared more demure than before and almost cold. Shepard couldn't quite put his finger on it. He sat down at his desk and started on the speech.

*

Later that afternoon Shepard stopped in at the pub for a quick drink. The divorce from his wife, Amy, had afforded him a greater freedom than before and it was not incumbent on him to be home by any particular time. At the counter, he saw his old friend O'Malley gazing into space with a whiskey in hand. Shepard clapped a hand on O'Malley's shoulder and sat down next to him.

"This becoming your second home, Dillon?"

O'Malley eyed him laconically. "Not by choice," he answered.

"More trouble in paradise?"

"Tam's walked out on me—for the while, anyway."

"When?"

"The other night; after you and I had that drink together."

"Still about you having second thoughts?"

O'Malley took a sip of his drink and nodded. "How's your day been?"

Shepard ordered a Bud light from the bartender and pulled out his phone to check messages. "It was a strange day for me," he replied.

O'Malley turned to face his friend. "How so?"

Shepard proceeded to tell him about the strange behavior of the president and his boss. "I can't really say what we discussed because it's confidential but they both acted quite out of character."

"Maybe they both just had a bad day," said O'Malley.

"Maybe, but it appeared to be more than that to me. It was as if they were different people—I can't explain it."

"Just do the job and take the money. That's my thought on the matter," said O'Malley.

"I guess you're right. I can't be worrying about how they flip-flop on policies or conduct themselves. It's just been a weird week: first seeing my double the other day in that 7-eleven, and now this."

O'Malley chuckled. "Maybe there's someone out there cloning people. I think you're being paranoid, Jon."

Shepard finished his beer and motioned to the bartender for a second. "Maybe you're right. So what's with Tam?"

O'Malley sighed and straightened up on the barstool. "When I got home the other night she confronted me directly about my procrastination with the divorce papers. When I tried to explain why I thought it was better to wait she got angry and locked herself in the bedroom."

Shepard rolled his eyes. "Relegated to the dog house were you?"

"I slept in the spare room, for Christ's sake. The next morning when I awoke she had already left for work. I haven't seen her since and she won't answer her phone."

"What're you going to do?"

"I've left a message that I'm ready to talk and be honest with her. Tam's final words before locking herself in the bedroom that night were that she would talk to me when I was ready to come clean about my true feelings."

"What are your true feelings?"

"I love her but I need to speak to my son before going ahead with the divorce—I want to be sure he'll be okay with what's going to happen. My real feelings for Janet are a little obscure at the moment but I don't want to lose my son."

"What if Tam doesn't accept your sentiments?" asked Shepard.

"Then we'll have to part ways I guess."

"Life is never simple, is it?"

O'Malley shook his head and drained his glass. "I'd better get home."

He stood and placed a hand on Shepard's shoulder. The speechwriter raised a hand in salutation and O'Malley left the pub. He missed Tam's presence but the issue with his son bit deeper than her absence. Every father had a responsibility to teach his children the right way to do things but it seemed that the world conspired against his every effort to be a good parent. If he wanted to break the downward trend he needed to act more decisively and responsibly.

O'Malley stripped off his clothes and was about to head into the shower when his cell phone rang. He cursed the timing and returned to the bedroom to retrieve the phone. Janet's voice blared in his ear.

"Dillon? Is Steve with you?"

"I haven't seen him since we last spoke. Why do you ask?"

Janet sounded tearful. "He was supposed to meet me at the diner for lunch but he never showed up. I can't get hold of him on his phone and he isn't here at home."

"Didn't he go to school today?" asked O'Malley.

"He did but at 2:00 pm they had a scheduled game against another school and last week Steve was dropped from the team, so he was going to come home for the afternoon. I said I would treat him to a burger at the diner if he could meet me at 2:15 and he agreed."

"He was dropped from the team? Why?"

Janet paused for a moment. "He has been quite depressed lately and uncommunicative. I spoke to the trainer a week ago and apparently, Steve has become quite belligerent. The trainer said that although he's a good player he was purposely dropped from the team as punishment."

"Why didn't you tell me?" asked O'Malley.

"I'd hoped it was just a one-off thing and, as you know, he doesn't want to speak to you at the moment. I felt the need to cut him some slack so I didn't say anything."

O'Malley felt a sudden rush of anger but realized Janet was not the enemy. If anyone was to blame the finger should be pointed at him. He made an effort to calm his voice. "I'm coming over. I'll be there in an hour."

3

Replacement of White House Staff

Allan McHale frowned and fixed Elias Stilwell with a stony stare. "You say Jack saw his double?"

Elias squirmed a little but held McHale's glare. "He saw a man like himself in every detail. It happened in a 7-eleven in New York a few days ago. The man's name is Jon Shepard, a speechwriter for the White House."

"How is it that you missed this detail in the original planning?" asked McHale.

"It was missed because the detail sheet of the White House staff precedes Shepard's appointment. He is very new on the job."

McHale wrenched his stare from Stilwell's eyes and looked out across the Atlantic City industrial sector.

"Make sure Jack stay's out of sight for a while. You would think such a coincidence would be extremely rare. In a city of eight million people, the chances are nigh impossible but it's happened and there's not much we can do about it now."

"He is not likely to be seen again. Shepard lives in Washington DC and must have been in the Big Apple for a day. Nevertheless, Jack will make sure he doesn't do any business outside of the normal area."

McHale relaxed. "Our White House replacements are holding their own. Hastings is doing a marvelous job as president and Bowman equally as the chief of staff. They both say no one appears to have noticed any perceivable differences. I would have asked Bowman about Jon Shepard if I had known earlier. He must work with her."

Stilwell ran a hand through his hair. "When will the two targeted replacements be moved?"

"I've made arrangements with the captain to pick them up tonight at the dock. Jack will need to be there at about 8:00 pm tonight. Both Chambers and Swales have been kept in a drugged state and the captain's crew members will help Jack move them onto the Lady Gray."

"What will happen to Chambers and Swales when they reach the other side?" asked Stilwell.

"They'll be told the truth. There's no sense eliminating them or us trying to keep our secret. Given the circumstances, there's nothing they can do. They will become citizens and make the best of a bad situation."

"They will tell others."

"It's okay. No one will believe them," answered McHale.

Stilwell entertained a hint of a smile. "I still find it difficult to believe that the president of the United States and his chief of staff can so easily be replaced without someone noticing subtle changes."

"There is no way for anyone to know the truth of the matter. The general staff may detect small differences in demeanor or practice but let's face it, these things change over time with most people."

"It would be most noticeable with spouses, though. I can't imagine the president's wife not noticing something," said Stilwell.

"The president's exacting job will be blamed for any observable changes in traits or practice. Hastings and Bowman have been fully briefed on their particular target's personalities. Both are well prepared so I don't anticipate any problems."

Stilwell stood and turned to leave the office. "Are you happy with the timeliness of the replacements?"

"I've checked all the relevant information with regard to upcoming events and it all looks good," said McHale. "The ball is rolling and no one can stop it."

*

O'Malley knocked on the door of Janet's home. Despite the heavy traffic it had taken him only forty-five minutes to make the drive from DC to Baltimore.

Janet stepped aside and let him in. "Thanks for coming, Dillon."

"I'm as concerned as you are about Steve. Do you think he might be staying at a friend's place?"

"I've called all his friends and no one has seen him," answered Janet. They moved into the living room and sat down, each in a separate chair. O'-Malley had made sure Janet did not lack any of the comforts she had been used to when they had lived together.

"You said he'd become quite belligerent and un-communicative. In what way?"

Janet gave the question some thought. "He doesn't respond when I call him for meals or when I ask him to do chores around the house. He just wants to do his own thing and be left alone all the time."

"Sounds like a typical teenager to me," said O'Malley. "Remember how Fallon changed when she turned sixteen."

The mention of Fallon's name brought a sadness to Janet's heart and it showed in her demeanor.

"I understand that these changes will come but Steve seems to have a bitterness about him that isn't normal."

O'Malley knew Janet blamed Steven's mental condition on the marriage breakup and that he, O'Malley, carried a major share of the blame. She was right to think so.

"I've been meaning to take the bull by the horns and confront him about his attitude," said O'Malley.

"You can hardly blame him, Dillon. He feels that his family is giving no thought for his well-being."

"I know I'm the one to blame, Jan. Let's not go down that road again. I feel bad enough about the status quo as it is."

Janet brushed some offending strands of hair away from her one eye. "I see you haven't responded to the divorce papers yet. Is there a problem?"

O'Malley cleared his throat. "I must be honest with you. It's difficult for me to put nineteen years of marriage to death. I know I've been in self-destruct mode ever since Fallon died but things are becoming a little clearer to me now. You wanted me to move on and I always felt you were preventing me from fully grieving the event. I felt, in a way, you were the one reminding me of my inabilities and if we separated I could make a new start."

Janet raised her eyebrows but said nothing.

O'Malley continued. "I've discovered that it's not you. It's not your fault at all. No matter who I'm with—whether it's you, Tam or the kitchen maid, I am the one who must take the responsibility for not letting Fallon go. No one else can be blamed."

O'Malley closed his eyes. A sudden rush of emotion overcame him and he choked back any further explanation. Janet did not move. She had seen and heard it all before. Despite his brilliance in the field of law enforcement, her husband remained his own worst enemy. No one knew him or understood him better than she did. No one loved him as much as she did.

"Are you having second thoughts?" she asked.

"It's something I must work out for myself," he said.

"And what about the Clyde-Walker woman?"

O'Malley felt embarrassed but he needed to be truthful. "She's moved out because she thinks I'm having second thoughts."

"So, what are you saying, Dillon?"

"I don't know what I'm trying to say—just leave it at that. To answer your initial question, I'm not ready to act on the divorce yet."

Janet stared at the carpet. "Let's not forget the real reason why you came here—Steven."

O'Malley leaned back in his chair. He felt sick to the stomach that his personal life could be in such a mess. "I'm sure he'll come home when he want's to. I could ask my team to look for him but if he finds out it'll alienate him even further."

"He doesn't have to know the team is looking for him. They can just let us know where he's at," said Janet.

O'Malley stood. "I'll ask them to keep their eyes open. Let me know if he comes home."

Janet walked him to the door and leaned against the doorjamb as he turned to say goodbye. The sight of her brought back memories and he restrained an impulse to lean forward and kiss her. She looked as beautiful as she always did and her slim, shapely figure had not lost any of its allure.

"I had a very strange thing happen while I was in New York yesterday afternoon," she said.

O'Malley waited for her to elaborate.

"I was in Macy's when a woman came out of a change booth with a bunch of dresses in her arms. For a brief second our eyes met and I did a double take. I thought I was looking into my own face."

O'Malley stared at his wife in disbelief. Within a matter of days, two people now claimed they had seen their exact doubles. He didn't know what to make of it.

"You mean a strong resemblance?"

She shook her head. "The woman looked exactly like me. It was a brief encounter but I know what I saw. I see my face in my vanity's mirror every day and I tell you it was an exact replica of me. The hair color and style were identical and she also had a small beauty spot on her left cheek. I think I've been cloned."

Had it not been for Jon Shepard's experience O'-Malley would have thought the incident an amusing coincidence but something strange appeared to be taking place. His gut told him it had to be more than an omen. He made mental note to talk to Shepard again.

"That's really strange. You'll remember my friend at the White House, Jon Shepard? He had a similar experience while in Manhattan a few days ago."

Janet frowned. "The woman looked a bit spooked when she saw me. She dumped the dresses on the counter and walked off without looking back. I noticed how upright her posture was and her ass swayed a little as though she had had modeling lessons."

"Which you had before we were married. That's exactly how you look from behind," stated O'Malley.

Janet's spontaneous smile revealed the whiteness of her teeth. "You take care of yourself, Dillon. I'll call you if Steve comes home."

He nodded. "Thanks. I'll talk to the team in the mean time and see what they can come up with."

O'Malley tore his eyes from her, turned and walked to his car. He realized how much he missed Janet's temperate disposition. Tam, on the other hand, was more direct and in his face, not that this bothered him much. She had not yet contacted him with regard to his latest message. He felt conflicted and overwhelmed. O'Malley drove back along the 295 at a moderate pace toward DC and wondered what the incidents of Janet and Shepard, seeing their doubles, meant in the grander scheme of things.

On arrival at the apartment, he parked the SUV and climbed the steps to his floor. Back in the apartment, the light on the telephone answering service flashed its signal, He thought this to be strange as most phone calls he received came via his cell. He pushed the play button:

Dad. I need to talk to you. I'll be in Driscoes at 2:00 pm tomorrow if you can make it.

Steven's voice sounded like music to his ears. It was the first time in six months that his son had contacted him. Driscoes, a coffee shop in downtown DC, had served as a meeting place for O'Malley and his wife in the early years of their courtship. Steve appeared to be safe. He called Janet's cell to give her the good news.

4

Father and Son

O'Malley entered Driscoes and spotted his son sitting in a back-corner booth on his own. Steven took after his father in many ways. His grades at school were excellent and he played basket ball for the school's first team. He also had his dad's good looks, wiry physique, dark, bushy hair and blue eyes. Fallon had been the spitting image of her mother and both children had grown up well-adjusted until Fallon's death at the age of sixteen. When his parent's marriage began to fall apart Steven's world started to suffer and for a year or so his grades dipped until one of the teachers took him in hand. After that, he surfaced again and the most recent news of his son, being uncooperative and belligerent, deeply shocked O'Malley. He purchased a coffee and headed for the booth.

"Hi, Superman," said O'Malley. He always used the nickname he had given Steven as a little boy.

Steven gave a slight nod of the head. "Dad."

O'Malley sat down opposite his son. "How are you?"

Steven fixed his dad with a stony stare. "I'm good."

"Your mother is worried out of her skull about you," said O'Malley.

Steven dropped his chin and squinted at his coffee cup. "I know. I called her this morning to explain what happened and why I didn't meet her or come home last night."

"And why didn't you go home last night?"

"Something came up. I'll tell you about it but first I want to talk about our family," answered Steven.

"Go ahead," said O'Malley.

Steven composed himself for a moment before he spoke. "I know you and Mom have had trouble in your marriage since Fallon died. I think I understand a little about why the two of you are not getting along anymore—"

O'Malley couldn't believe his ears. His seventeen-year-old son was about to give him a lecture. He managed to subdue the hackles which started to rise at Steven's words. He realized this was not impudence but his boy's attempt at trying to make sense of a bad situation.

"I've begun to realize that you feel a lot of guilt about Fallon's death. The little I've read about the five stages of grief has given me some insight into the reason's why you and mom react the way you do with each other."

O'Malley clasped his hands and leaned forward in his seat as Steven continued.

"It's hard for me to understand everything the two of you are going through right now but I've thought a great deal about my own future. This is my last semester at school and I am looking at college for the next academic year. I know we had discussed that I stay in DC but I want to change that. I've been looking at a university in Alice, Texas."

O'Malley swallowed his disappointment. "I understand. I can't say I blame you for wanting to get away from the family feud. I'll support you in whatever decision you make. As much as I would rather see you stay here in DC I realize that you have become your own man and can work out, for yourself, what direction to take—after all, it is your life."

Steven looked pleased with his dad's answer. "I also want to say that you also have your own life and whatever you decide to do, between you and mom, is your business. I don't fully understand why the two of you can't get it together anymore but I'm going to focus on my own future."

O'Malley didn't know if this was good or bad news. "I hope you will still be in our lives in the future. You mother and I both love you very much. We don't want to lose you."

"I understand that but I don't want to be a party to your problems—I have enough of my own," answered Steven.

"Your mom and I will work things out between us. That's my promise to you. I'm not sure what the future holds but whatever direction it takes we want you to be a part of it."

Steven nodded and O'Malley took a sip of coffee. "So where were you last night? You said you would tell me about it."

"I spent the night at Gerry Swales's home."

"Swales? As in Beverly Swales, the White House Chief of Staff?"

"Gerry is in my class," said Steven.

"I knew he went to the same school but I didn't know the two of you were friends," answered O'-Malley.

"Well, we're not really. Not until yesterday, that is. Gerry spoke to me in confidence about his mom. He knows you are a special agent with the FBI and he was wondering if he could ask you a question."

O'Malley was taken aback. "Of course, what's it about?"

"I'll let him tell you himself."

Steven looked over toward the opposite corner of the room and nodded to a teen who sat alone in a booth. The lanky boy of about six foot got up and joined them. Steven introduced his friend to his dad. O'Malley shook hands with the youth and cut to the chase.

"So what's on your mind, Gerry?"

"It's a pleasure to meet you, Mr. O'Malley. I don't want to seem as one taking advantage of a school friend but I have a dilemma at home and I know you are involved with the FBI."

O'Malley put the boy at ease. "I will help you in whatever way I can, Gerry. Do you have trouble at home?"

Gerry relaxed. "I wouldn't call it trouble but it certainly is troubling. You know that my mom is the White House Chief of Staff and she is heavily vested in her job. Things, however, have taken a very strange turn."

"How is that?' asked O'Malley.

I don't believe the woman who comes home after work is really my mom."

O'Malley nearly fell out of his seat. "How do mean?"

"I know my mom, and this person is not my mom. She looks like my mother and to a degree acts like her but there is something different."

"Can you tell me what you find different?" asked O'Malley.

Gerry tensed up. "About a week ago she arrived home after work one day and I asked for my allowance. She responded by asking me how much it was that she gave me every week. A day later I saw her struggling with the alarm code setting. My mom knows that better than my sister and I do—and we know exactly how it works. She called our dog Turbo instead of Turbs, a shortening of the name which she has always used from the time he was a puppy. I have noticed a host of other differences and I'm telling you she's not my mom."

"Who do you think she might be?" asked O'Malley.

"I don't know, Mr. O'Malley. An imposter, perhaps. It worries me because of the high profile position she has."

"And what about your dad?"

"My mom and dad are divorced. She is totally wrapped up in her work and doesn't have time for dating."

"Has your mom been to the doctor lately. Maybe she's suffering a stressful type of amnesia or something?"

"Not to my knowledge but there are two more pieces of evidence which top everything else. Firstly, my real mom has a scar on the top of her head, the legacy of a horse riding accident when she was a child. She had not been wearing a helmet at the time. I know the scar was there because I saw it one day while she was bending down to pick something up and her hair parted just that little bit to expose it. The exact same scenario caused her to bow her head the day before yesterday—the scar was absent."

O'Malley's intrigue soared to new heights. "And the second piece of evidence?"

She has been communicating with someone on Skype at night and it's not a romantic exchange. She sits on her computer in her office and talks to this person for at least an hour. It's something she's never done before. One evening I crept to the door to listen to the conversation and it was like they were talking in a kind of code or something. I became suspicious and peeked at the screen which I could partially see through the open door. It sounded to me as though they were planning some sort of take over, of the government."

O'Malley couldn't believe his ears. "Are you sure?"

"I can't be sure, Mr. O'Malley but I know this woman is not my mom. She is an exact look alike and my meager knowledge of science would make me think she is some sort of clone or doppelgänger."

O'Malley would have chuckled under normal circumstances but he saw that Gerry meant every word of his hypothesis. The two incidents of doubles seen by Jon Shepard and Janet came to mind and made him take Gerry's testimony as truth. His gut told him these new circumstances represented something out of the ordinary. Gerry's comment about his mom's high profile position underscored the feeling in O'Malley's gut.

"What you say is very interesting indeed and I believe you're telling me the truth. I promise I will look into it. I want you to take my cell number and call me if anything else happens."

Gerry pulled out his phone and entered O'Malley's number in his contacts. "Thank's, Special Agent O'Malley—I appreciate it. My sister shares my concerns and has also noticed the difference."

"What did your mom say about Steven spending the night?" asked O'Malley.

Gerry and Steven looked at each other. "I didn't tell her. She came home a little later than usual and missed dinner. She never came into my room and we left after she had gone to work this morning."

O'Malley said goodbye to the boys after extracting a promise from his son that he would return to his mother and not mention anything about Gerry's dilemma. Steven also promised to make more contact with his dad which pleased O'Malley. He drove back to the J. Edgar Hoover building with mixed feelings.

The three members of O'Malley's team assembled in the briefing room at his request. MacDonald, a tall man with broad shoulders, slapped Martinez, the short tempered Hispanic, on the back.

"What you been up to Martinez? Finished your sock-knitting project yet? Are you ready for some real work?"

Martinez frowned deeply at the tall operative. "At least I do productive things with my time—I don't laze around smoking weed all day."

MacDonald laughed loudly and took a seat at the conference table. The third member, Gwen Farrell, an attractive brunette with a slim figure, eyed the two men and chuckled. "You two goofing off again?"

"Always," said MacDonald.

Martinez, not to be outdone, plus a keen eye for Farrell responded. "He not only goofs off but he does it brainlessly."

"Now, now—let's be nice to one another. We're supposed to be a team." Gwen was the new girl on the block. MacDonald and Martinez were seasoned operatives but this was her first experience of FBI work since graduation from the academy.

"Don't worry, little sister," said Martinez. "We're always complimenting each other. Mac's nothing but a large sack of rotten potatoes without a tiny brain."

MacDonald feigned a hurt look. "I'll take that as a compliment, Diego. Just remember next time your back's against the wall and you need someone to bail you out. I'll let the bad guys shoot you."

Farrell closed her eyes and shook her head in disgust. "I thought I had joined the FBI, not some sort of circus act."

O'Malley arrived and they quietened down. He frowned at MacDonald and Martinez. "You two trying to lead our newest member astray already?"

"Just showing her our better side," stated Mac-Donald.

O'Malley looked at Farrell. "Take no notice of these two girls. They would actually give their lives for one another."

"I'll bear that in mind," said Farrell.

O'Malley pulled out a list from his briefcase and set it down on the table.

"We need to look into a matter that may or may not be important. I've spoken to Ingram about it and he feels the circumstances are rather strange so I'm following my gut."

The team looked at him expectantly.

5

Prisoners

President Chambers opened his eyes and tried to focus on the object directly in his line of sight. Hampered by a blurry vision at first it took him a few moments to identify the outline as the shape of a human body. Sound and feeling returned to his numbed senses in slow but incremental stages until it dawned on him it was a woman. He knew this by the long blonde hair, prominent cheekbones, and lipstick. Continual focus on the woman's face brought a gradual recognition and he blinked several times before his vision cleared enough for him to be certain—Beverly Swales, his chief of staff.

Chambers tried to move but discovered his hands had been cuffed behind his back. The feeling began to return to the rest of his body and small movements brought painful reactions from his nervous system as he tried to position his head for a better view of the surroundings. A dull light in the ceiling cast shadows against the walls of the small room which appeared to be made of painted steel. The air reeked of oil and fumes. A vibration throbbed through the cold, steel floor and he surmised that they were in some sort of moving transportation, a road vehicle or a ship.

He glanced at Beverly Swales and made an effort to roll over toward her. Every muscle in his body hurt but he persisted until he managed to flop over onto his back and then over again, onto his side.

"Beverly?" Chambers called out several times but received no response and concluded that she was unconscious. He tried to recall his last wakeful moments before the lights went out in his brain and like a slow drifting mist, his memory returned. His appointed secret service detail, Mike Jennings, had entered the oval office to say that his chief of Staff was waiting outside on the back patio. He thought it odd that Swales had not entered the office to speak with him. He remembered walking out through the East door onto the patio that bordered the White House rose garden and then everything visual disappeared.

He recalled that Mike had opened the door for him, stepped aside to allow him passage and a moment later a sharp pain stabbed the back of his head. Someone had hit him from behind. Was it Mike? Who else would have the means and security clearance to abduct the president of the United States? Chambers had seen a figure step out before him as the world became strangely silent moments before he fell down onto the tiled floor of the patio.

He moved his legs and discovered they were not shackled. With one foot extended toward Swales's legs, he managed a light prod and she jerked her head back, to look up at the ceiling in confusion. He prodded her shin again and she turned to look in his direction, her eyes widened as she stared at his face.

"Are you okay?" asked Chambers.

She didn't answer immediately but swiveled her head in both directions to see if they were alone.

"Mr. President? What happened?"

"It looks as though we've been abducted," said Chambers.

"That's absurd," she said. Her voice sounded strained and full of emotion.

"I know, but it's true. Why else would we be in a cell on some sort of moving transportation?" he asked.

The truth sank in and Swales cursed. "What are we going to do?"

With a final effort, Chambers sat up and surveyed their prison. "I don't know. There doesn't appear to be much we can do for the moment. By the movement, smell, and sounds, I think we're on a ship."

"Any idea how long we've been unconscious?" she asked.

"It could be a few hours or a few days—I have no idea at all."

"This is ridiculous. Who would be able to get away with abducting the president of the United States? The whole world will be looking for us," retorted Swales.

"We are still alive so perhaps who ever is behind this must have some sort of a plan. Perhaps they are going to ask for a ransom."

Swales tried to sit up. After a few attempts, she managed to prop herself up against a wall. "These cuffs are hurting my wrists," she complained.

The president eyed her with raised eyebrows. As his chief of staff, Swales had always been cool and level-headed when faced with difficult situations. He wondered how she would hold up in these new and uncertain circumstances. Her background as a JAG lawyer, prior to the White House appointment, gave her a clear and concise approach to solving problems but this might be the first time she faced an imminent danger to her own life.

The hollow sound of footsteps in the confined area of the corridor signaled the arrival of someone.

They waited for the person to reach the barred gate of their cell's entrance and a moment later a large man with a ruddy complexion stood at the gate and looked down on them.

"Ah—I see you have finally woken up," said the man.

Chambers's anger flared. "Why have you taken us captive? Who the hell are you?"

"Let's just say we needed to replace you," said the man. He wore an old oilskin, seafarer's jacket and dark, blue jeans. A small U-boat-captain styled cap sat precariously on his head and round-framed spectacles balanced on the tip of a nose that looked as though it had been broken more than once.

"Replaced? How is that possible?" roared Chambers.

"We have ways and means," said the man. His voice remained calm as he pulled out a bunch of keys from his jacket pocket and proceeded to unlock the gate of the cell.

"I am Captain Vargas; master of the Lady Gray. Please turn over so that I can release your cuffs."

Chambers scowled but complied and a moment later he was set free. Captain Vargas then released Beverly Swales and the two prisoners rubbed their wrists vigorously to restore the blood circulation.

"What do you intend to do with us?" asked Swales.

"I am removing you to a far away place where your country's law enforcement will never be able to find you and don't worry—you will both be able to start new lives. We are not going to harm you."

"Who are you talking about? What is the name of your organization?"

"I will answer your questions in time, Mr. President but for now you'll have to exercise a little patience. We are not out of the danger zone yet. You will remain here in this cell and my men will take care of you. Someone will be down shortly to allow you each a bathroom break. I must go now."

Vargas turned, locked the cell gate and walked off. Chambers and Swales looked at each other in alarm. A small bench on an adjacent wall offered a place for them to sit once they had stretched their legs.

"Replaced? Have I been replaced? Who in heaven's name would be able to walk into the job of the president of the United States and just take over?"

They must have a look-a-like for each of us," said Swales.

"But to what purpose?"

"I don't know but perhaps the captain will eventually tell us. My two children would never be fooled by any stand-in."

"My wife might be. We see so little of each other these days," returned the president.

"I hope they don't intend to keep us in here too long. I want to pee," said Swales.

*

O'Malley passed out a separate list to each of the team and gave them a moment to glance through it.

"What're we looking at here, Dillon?" asked Mac-Donald.

"It's a list of everyone who works at the White House. Over the last forty-eight hours at least two people have expressed to me that they have encountered their doubles—exact lookalikes, in separate incidents and another has doubts about his own mother. One of those persons is my wife Janet and the other one works for the White House."

O'Malley proceeded to tell them about the strange circumstances which surrounded each observation and expressed his concern that something mysterious was afoot.

"It can't be circumstantial that three people in such a short space of time could experience these sightings. There has to be something sinister going on and I want to get a head start on finding out exactly what it is."

Martinez, an intuitive and detailed operative, posed a question. "According to these witnesses are their doubles just look-alike imposters?"

"Each witness declares emphatically that it was as if they were looking into a mirror, with the exception of young Gerry Swales, who shares the person he is living with is definitely not his mother," said O'Malley.

"Like a clone?" said Farrell.

"Since none of the witnesses have identical siblings I am assuming clones to be a possibility," said O'-Malley.

"Wouldn't that be something?" asked MacDonald. "White House personnel cloned for purposes unknown."

O'Malley gave the comment some thought. "Imagine if a foreign country wanted to gain control of our affairs. What better method than to replace the top politicians and military personnel with their own? Shepard also said that both the president and Swales seemed to be acting a little out of character."

Farrell raised her eyebrows. "It certainly seems strange. Is the cloning process a difficult one? How easy is it for someone to make a clone?"

"Assuming these doubles are clones my guess is that it wouldn't be very difficult for a country to secretively embark on such an ambitious program," said MacDonald.

Martinez frowned. "Maybe, but it would not be easy for them to get the material for their subjects. They have to obtain cells from each victim in order to clone them."

"Let's not get ahead of ourselves here," said O'Malley. "We don't know for sure that these doubles are clones and besides clones would take years to grow from infants into adults. They would have had to start years ago and how would they have known who would be politicians?"

"You have a point, boss," said MacDonald.

O'Malley scratched the back of an ear. "My wife's double does not work in politics so we have no idea, yet, of a plan or purpose. We do, however, have two people who work for the White House staff with possible doubles so we have to start with them. Jon Shepard is a senior speechwriter and has written material for President Chambers and the secretary of state. Beverly Swales is the chief of staff."

Martinez interrupted. "You said Swales's son Gerry is the one who has sworn to the fact that Swales is not his mother. Your wife said she saw her double and Shepard said he saw his double, which means that Janet and Shepard are both still the real Mc-

Coy. The finger of suspicion points at the Swales woman."

"My thinking exactly, Diego," said O'Malley. "We need to concentrate on Swales for a start. Unfortunately, I have no permission to look into any of the White House personnel's business so what we do must be clandestine."

"What about approaching the secret service?" asked Farrell.

"We could but if there is a conspiracy afoot members of the secret service might be the first to be supplanted by the perpetrators. I don't think there's anyone other than Shepard we can trust."

"How about we observe Swales's movements to start with," said MacDonald.

"You and Martinez can find out who her security detail is and make sure they don't spot you. I don't want to raise any suspicions," said O'Malley.

He looked at Gwen Farrell. "I have a contact in the NSA. I'll ask him to set up a surveillance on Swales computer interactions and phone calls. I will put you in touch with him and you can keep me abreast of Swales's cyber conversations. I'll speak to Jon Shepard again and see what he can come up with."

The team left the briefing room. O'Malley went back to his office, picked up the phone and called

Shepard. Jon's answering service picked up the call so O'Malley left a message.

6

The Lady Gray

Captain Vargas stared at the mist which hung like a curtain about six-hundred yards off the Lady Gray's port bow. He turned to the first mate. "We've arrived. Bring the prisoners up on deck."

The seaman nodded and disappeared below. The moonlight lit up the calm sea waters for several miles around the trawler and the slap-slap of wavelets beat a rhythmic tattoo against the boat's hull. Vargas moved out onto the back deck and awaited the arrival of their human cargo from the cell beneath. A few moments later the face of Beverly Swales appeared as she stepped out of the stairwell, followed by the taller Chambers. It was almost as bright as daylight and they appeared glum as they stepped out onto the deck. Both were cuffed and secured to each other by a three-foot-long chain tied at their waists.

"Are you going to drown us?" asked the president.

Vargas laughed. "If we were going to do that we would have done it a few days ago."

"You still haven't told us what you are going to do with us," said Swales. She had lost a lot of her composure and her body trembled with fear.

"We are sending you on a long journey which will only take a short time," said the captain.

"Where to?" asked Chambers.

"To Terra," said Vargas.

"Where are we now, exactly?" asked Chambers.

"You're in the Bermuda Triangle," answered the captain.

He turned to the first mate. "Load them up."

Chambers' eyes had adjusted to the moonlight and he noticed what appeared to be a compact vessel alongside the trawler. It looked like one of those special lifeboats used on large ships, more like a capsule than a boat and he looked around to see if they were being transferred to a larger vessel close by. All he could see, however, was a bank of mist sitting on the calm surface of the water. The two men maneuvered the captives toward the capsule and made them step up onto its landing where an open hatch awaited them. The shackles were removed and they stepped down into the interior.

The inside looked like an airliner's cockpit, with a myriad of dials and levers. Two rows of six seats took up most of the space and Chambers wondered what they were in for. The seats were of a special design and had straps to secure the occupants. In the back of each seat, folded neatly into a small box-like aperture was a rolled-up tube with a mouth piece. The first mate indicated for them to take their seats and then proceeded to strap them in. The deckhand brought two half-masks which they strapped to each passenger's face. The tube, which appeared to dispense oxygen, was connected to the lower end of the mask.

Swales looked across at Chambers and her eyes revealed the fear.

The president tried to console her with a nod of the head. She returned the nod and settled down in her seat. The first Mate and his helper exited through the entrance hatch and closed it. A motor started up and the vessel began to move through the waters toward an unknown destination.

*

Jon Shepard drove his Mustang to a destination in Atlantic City. The early morning caller had given specific instructions for him to follow. He was not to bring anyone with him and to speak to no one about the meeting. The caller, a woman, seemed pleasant but firm and would not give her name. She alluded to the person Jon had seen in the 7-Eleven a week before and said that if he wanted to find out more about the mystery he needed to believe her. The person referred to as his double would be present to speak with him.

Intrigued and curious Shepard took the bait. He had been tempted to call O'Malley as a precaution but decided against it. He rationalized that his FBI agent friend faced enough problems. The journey took just over an hour. At 5:45 pm he pulled up outside the address in Atlantic City and surveyed the premises. The business sign mounted on the fence, old and faded, could not be easily read but he assumed by the building's empty and rundown appearance it no longer served its original purpose. Shepard checked the notes he had made and stepped out onto the sidewalk and walked onto the premises. The only sounds came from the main road two blocks away and he strained his senses for any signs of danger.

Shepard approached a half-opened, roll up metal door with suspicion. At the entrance he called out:

"Hello? Anybody in there?"

His voice echoed off the inner walls of a large area which contained old, rusted machinery, long out of use. The late afternoon sun beamed through the high industrial-type windows, lighting up all the molecules of dust in the air to portray an atmosphere of neglect and decay. No answer came to his question so he decided to check the door at the far end of the work area which appeared to lead further into the building. The door opened with a loud, creaking sound.

A hallway led down to the building's far-end. The only light entered through empty office windows on each side as he crept nervously along in search of any signs of life. The hallway turned a corner and at last, he saw a dull electric light which shone from an office doorway. Eager to see if anyone was home he strode to the entrance and glanced into the office. A woman sat at a battered wooden desk typing on a laptop and looked up as Shepard peered in at her.

"I see you have arrived, Mr. Shepard. I thought you weren't going to come but now that you're here I want you to meet Jack."

She pointed to another desk in the corner and Shepard felt his world turn upside down. His double sat there with a grin on his face. Shepard couldn't believe his eyes. He looked back at the woman and stared at her.

"Janet? What on earth are you doing here?" He looked back at his double in astonishment.

The woman looked confused. "Janet? My name's not Janet—it's Vera."

Shepard's face turned pale. "You look like someone I know," he stammered.

Understanding dawned on Vera's face. "Who would this person be, Mr. Shepard?"

Shepard realized he should not divulge Janet's real identity or her marriage to O'Malley. "Someone I went to university with. She now lives in Houston Texas, I believe."

"You're lying Mr. Shepard. I know I have a double and she lives here, either in New York, Baltimore or DC. You are going to tell us where she lives."

Shepard regained his composure. "What's going on here? Who are you people and what do you want?"

"We are interested in the White House but that's not why you are here today, Jon."

Vera's sudden use of his first name had an ominous ring to it.

"You said I would learn more about the mystery of my double and what this all means. So, what are you up to?" asked Shepard.

Jack spoke for the first time. "We are involved in an operation called Terra Firma. It was an unfortunate meeting at the 7-Eleven the other day, between you and I, and should never have happened. For this, I apologize. We have to, unfortunately, take steps to remove you from the scene."

Shepard, who stood at the office door, felt a push from behind and he landed on his knees in front of Vera's desk. He turned over onto his backside and looked behind him to see another man with a revolver in hand.

"What are you going to do with me?"

Vera narrowed her eyelids. "Unfortunately we do not have a double to take your place. You were never marked for replacement so we have to take a drastic measure. Now, tell me where Janet lives?"

Shepard did not want to divulge the information. He felt a cold, icy hand grip his heart. "What do you mean by a drastic measure?"

"She ignored him and repeated her question. "Tell me where Janet lives?"

"You won't get away with this," screamed Shepard. He tried to get up onto his feet but the man with the gun pushed him down again, then sat on his chest and held both his arms.

"Tell me where she lives?" shouted Vera. All attempts at being polite had disappeared and her voice sounded hostile.

"I don't know where she lives," screamed Shepard.

Vera nodded at the gunman who pistol-whipped the speech writer across the face. Blood spattered from Shepard's nose and mouth.

"Where does she live, Jon?"

Shepard had never been a hero and the fear of further harm brought the answer Vera was looking for.

"Her name is Janet O'Malley and she lives with her son in Baltimore."

"We already know who she is. We just want to know where her new address because she no longer lives with her husband. Where does she work?"

"I don't know. She's a graphic designer. That's all I can tell you."

Vera turned to Jack. "You have got everything in hand?"

"I have everything planned. The drug will work its way out of his system in two hours and an autopsy will show death by heart attack. It's painless and quick."

"Good—I hate to inflict suffering," said Vera.

Jack came around his desk, in one hand he clasped a syringe and in the other a vial of fluid. Shepard's throat constricted and his heart thumped against his ribcage. Jack thrust the syringe into Shepard's arm and the speechwriter went out like a light. The gunman helped Jack carry him out of the back door to a carport where an old Chevy truck was parked. They loaded Shepard onto the back. Jack went through the unconscious man's pockets and found Shepard's car keys. He threw them to the gunman.

"Follow me," he said. The gunman ran off around the side of the old warehouse to the road where Shepard's Mustang was parked. The truck pulled out into the side road with Jack at the wheel and they drove at a fast pace toward the highway. Half an hour later, on the outskirts of DC, the truck turned onto a side road and drove toward a rise on a hill that overlooked a valley. Jack pulled over and waited for the gunman to arrive. The two men walked to the bend which overlooked the valley. A steep incline proceeded from where they both stood at the road's edge. Two hundred yards down the incline a cluster of boulders lined the end of the gradient.

"This is the steepest incline in the area on any of these roads. I thought it would make a good accident site," said Jack.

The gunman nodded. "Let's get him into the car and send it over the edge."

They walked back to the truck and moved Shepard's body to the Mustang. The gunman propped Shepard up in the driver's seat and strapped him in. He then turned the wheel to point the car toward the incline.

"It's a good thing there's no barrier here. The car will go over the edge and down the slope. Those rocks at the bottom will stop it."

Jack pulled an envelope out of his pocket and slid it into Shepard's inside jacket pocket. The gunman started the car and closed the car door. He leaned through the window, threw the gear lever into drive and the Mustang shot forward toward the slope. A moment later the two men watched as the car careened down the incline to crash into the rock boulders at the bottom. It flipped over onto its roof with all four wheels still spinning.

"Let's go," said Jack. They jumped into the truck and drove away from the scene.

✳

7

Bad News for O'Malley

The news took O'Malley by surprise and it came a day after he had tried to get Shepard on the phone. O'Malley's boss, James Ingram, the deputy head of the FBI, broke the news.

"They found his car at the bottom of an incline. From the autopsy report, it appears Shepard suffered a heart attack while driving. This is perhaps not out of the ordinary but what did come up as strange was the contents of his pockets. The investigating officer found a page of very sensitive information."

"What sort of information?" asked O'Malley.

"Classified stuff that was way above his personal pay grade. They think Shepard might have been leaking information on our operatives in Syria."

"Leaking it to whom?"

"We don't know that yet."

"It doesn't sound at all like the Jon Shepard I knew," said O'Malley.

"I wanted to ask you what you thought, knowing the two of you have been friends since your school days," said Ingram

"I'm pretty sure Jon was not the type," insisted O'Malley. "In fact, I could accept that he might have had a heart attack but to sell out his country, absolutely not."

"The doctor who performed the autopsy says Shepard's physical condition was good and he did not appear to have any pre-existing conditions. He looked for any other signs that would have brought on such a sudden condition but couldn't find anything," said Ingram.

"It seems suspicious to me. There are substances that can be used today to mimic heart attacks and leave no trace in the victim's system. It looks to me as though someone has gone out of their way to set him up as a criminal," added O'Malley.

Ingram looked out of the office window at the Pennsylvania Avenue traffic. "In light of what Shepard, your wife and the Chief of Staff's son have experienced I think you may have a point. Shepard worked for Beverly Swales. She has been contacted and told of Shepard's death. If young Gerry is correct in his assumptions then we might be facing some sort of effort to control business at the White House, however, I can't just sanction an interrogation of the president's chief of staff."

"What if some country is trying to replace the staff with lookalikes in order to gain control of the US military? The replacements might go further than the chief of staff," said O'Malley.

"I agree you should divert resources to investigate this but it will have to be top secret. Discretion will be of the utmost importance and we should decide on a special code to protect ourselves. If the entity is able to infiltrate the highest decision-making process in the land then no one in a leadership position is safe," said Ingram.

O'Malley gave the matter some thought. "What about the word, CHAOS. Remember the American domestic infiltration program of the early seventies?"

"Sounds good to me," said Ingram. "I can't inform the director about it as he is on vacation in the Bahamas but you had better let your team know."

"Do you think we should speak to the president and tell any other members of the law enforcement community?" asked O'Malley.

"We don't know how deep this operation is or if it is even a real threat. So, let's keep the matter between you, your team and me."

"We're already on it. I'll report in a few days," said O'Malley.

He walked back to his office and sat at his desk. The news of Shepard's death had shocked him and he allowed his mind to wander back through time to his school days and to their service in Iraq. For a moment he felt heart sore and then forced his psyche to focus on the strange circumstances of Shepard's demise. An hour later O'Malley stood at the brow of the hill where the accident had taken place. The wreckage of the Mustang still lay at the bottom of the incline and an FBI police officer, appointed to keep an eye on the scene, stood next to him. Due to the fact that Shepard had been a White House employee, the initial investigation would have been done by the secret service but with the absence of yellow barrier tape, the wreckage had not yet been established as a crime scene.

"Is the investigation complete?" asked O'Malley.

The FBI policeman nodded. "We're waiting for the wreckage to be collected. A recovery vehicle with a winch will be here any moment now."

O'Malley flashed his badge. "Mind if I take a look?"

"No problem—go ahead," answered the officer.

O'Malley picked his way down the loose stone embankment and approached the damaged vehicle. The secret service had removed Shepard's body and all the items they could find on the ground within reach of the cab. The headrests of the front and back seats propped the vehicle up with a minimum of clearance and the Mustang's soft top had collected in a tangled mess behind the backseat area and trunk. The shattered windshield lay flattened against the car's steering wheel.

The driver's door stood half open, wedged into the smaller stones beneath it and it wasn't until he kicked away some of the stones to free the movement of the door that he saw a glint of metal in the sunlight. He stooped down and dug away the stones with his hand. A cigarette lighter which had been previously hidden beneath the stones lay wedged in the ground. The secret service investigator had not tried to move the door and had missed it. O'Malley pulled the lighter out for scrutiny. He turned it over in his hand and saw an inscription: To David. Happy Birthday.

O'Malley hesitated. Shepard had not been a smoker. The lighter must have been inadvertently lost out of someone's pocket when they set Shepard's body up in the seat and belted it in. In appreciation of the Occam's Razor principle, this appeared to be the simplest explanation. O'Malley slipped the lighter into his pocket and trudged back up the embankment to the road. He thanked the policeman on duty and climbed into the SUV. It became clear to him that Shepard, having seen his double, became a target for elimination. His suspicions of an elaborate people's replacement operation now escalated into a real threat and a sudden fear coursed through his being: Janet had also seen her double.

O'Malley made the call from the vehicle's cell phone system but there appeared to be no reception. He looked at the dash clock: 12:00 noon. He knew Janet would be at work and beginning her lunch break so he put the pedal to the metal. It would take at least an hour to Baltimore but he had to warn her.

*

Janet finished off her latest project and called out to her assistant. "I'm going for lunch, Becky."

Becky, not ready to stop for the break, waved and continued on with her own work. Janet closed down her computer and picked up her purse.

She had been fortunate to get a job again at her age as almost eighteen years had passed since her first and only stint of employment as a graphic designer. When the marriage broke down she could have demanded that O'Malley pay for her keep until a settlement was reached but her pride and the need to keep busy derailed that idea. Being the cause of the separation O'Malley would have paid up whatever she demanded but earning her own way seemed to add another nail in the coffin of her husband's reasons to leave her. She had known O'Malley since their school days and first met at mutual friend's party, he in his final year and she in the eleventh grade.

She made her way down to a bakery shop not far from the office. A coffee, with croissant, was on special for the day so she made the purchase and looked for a table. The shop was half filled with people and she found one near a window that faced the street. She had an hour to eat her lunch and catch up on social media. Forty minutes later three people walked in and made their purchases at the counter. With coffees in hand, they walked down toward her table. It was not until they sat down opposite her that she noticed the only woman in the threesome. The woman looked directly at her and Janet's heart nearly stopped. It was her double. For a moment they stared at each other but the double did not show any surprise at the sudden meeting.

Janet looked down at her coffee not sure what to do. Her double stood, moved over to the table and sat down opposite, making herself comfortable.

"I thought I might find you here," said her double.

"Who are you?" asked Janet.

"My name is, Vera," said the woman. At that moment one of the men in the threesome vacated his seat and moved into the seat next to Janet's.

The woman leaned forward and whispered, "I want you to listen very carefully. My friend, sitting next to you has a gun with a silencer, pointed at your side. When he gets up you must follow and he will allow you to move out of your seat. He will then come up behind you and you will feel the gun's barrel in the small of your back. Do not panic but move slowly out of the store."

Janet's eyes opened wide and she took in a deep breath. "What do you people want with me?"

"We'll answer your questions in a little while but first let's get out of here," said Vera.

The man stood and Janet hesitated. All sorts of fearful thoughts raced through her mind but she decided to comply. She moved out into the walk-space between the tables and felt the barrel of the gun. At that moment Janet's cell phone rang.

"Don't answer it," whispered the man. She allowed it to ring and carried on walking until she stood at the bakery's entrance.

Across the road, a black SUV pulled up to the curb and her heart skipped a beat. It was O'Malley's vehicle. The passenger window rolled down and she could see her husband looking at her with a smile on his lips. She looked straight at him and then turned as the man behind her indicated a change of direction with his one hand while keeping the gun concealed, in the small of her back. O'Malley thought it strange. He knew that Janet had seen the vehicle and his face through the open window but she gave no sign of acknowledgment. It was only when the other two members of the three-some followed close behind that he realized why. Janet's double had found his wife and the very thing O'Malley feared was now taking place. He sized up the situation.

It would be easy for him to confront them but Janet might get shot in the process. O'Malley jumped from the SUV and followed on the opposite side of the road. The Glock in its shoulder holster brought him a measure of comfort. The group of four were making their way to a vehicle parked up the road. He dashed back to the SUV and jumped in, fired up the motor and waited. A moment later the group's vehicle, a white, double cab truck, pulled out into the road and took off. O'Malley followed at a safe distance. He knew how to tail a vehicle and had often been in similar circumstances before, the only difference this time being that the target held his wife captive. It would mean a great deal more caution from his side of things.

The truck drove onto the Turnpike and made off in the direction of New York. Two hours later the vehicle turned onto the Allentown Lakewood Road and headed into New Jersey, toward Atlantic City. O'Malley kept a good following distance and with the amount of traffic on the road felt certain his targets had not seen him. Forty minutes later the truck pulled off the main highway, on the outskirts of Atlantic City and headed into an industrial area. As the traffic thinned out O'Malley slowed and fell further back until he saw the truck stop outside a building.

He parked the SUV around the corner in a side street and locked the vehicle. The white truck had driven around the building, which appeared to be an old deserted warehouse, to the back area. He approached the front entrance with caution, the Glock held firmly in his hand

8

Strange Transportation

President Chambers could hear the gentle throb of the motor as the vessel moved forward in the tranquil sea. He tried to turn his head to look out of the small, round porthole at his left shoulder but found that a numbness had engulfed his body and restricted all movement. The interior of the cabin remained dark and supplemented only by the soft, green light emitted by the instruments. Beverly Swales, his chief of staff, sat strapped into the seat in front of him. He wondered how she was faring under the circumstances.

A sudden shuddering coursed through the craft's hull and increased in intensity until Chambers thought the vessel would break apart. Then as quickly as the phenomenon started it stopped, replaced by a high pitched noise. The instrument lights flickered and Chambers thought they were about to fail but after several moments the glow steadied up again. He closed his eyes and felt a sudden floating sensation. Weird images flashed before his vision in the form of past life issues which hung like holographic ghosts against a dark background in the theater of his mind.

*

Roland MacDonald and Diego Martinez watched the chief of Staff jog down the stairs of her home, onto the sidewalk and along 31st Street toward Montrose Park. Swales wore an orange track suit, white headband, and blue runners. MacDonald talked into a small handheld recorder and noted the time to be 6:30 am. Martinez waited for the security detail to pick up on the action and then pulled the SUV out onto the street. He kept the vehicle at a slow pace, well behind the secret service detail, who followed on behind. The two FBI agents had been waiting for an hour outside the Georgetown home and when the secret service agent stepped out of his parked vehicle they knew the chief of staff would appear. She never went anywhere without some form of protection.

The woman kept a good pace for her age. She did not look around but kept eyes to the front knowing that her body guard would take care of any security issues.

"Don't get too close, Diego," warned MacDonald.

"Listen, bone head. I've done this work longer than you have. Just keep your eyes on the woman," barked Martinez.

They turned the corner and the chief of staff crossed the road, still tailed by her security detail.

"I guess this is where we leave our vehicle," said MacDonald.

In preparation for the possibility, both men were dressed in tracksuits and runners, ready for a jog.

There were not many people around at that hour so they tried to be as inconspicuous as possible. The body guard turned his head and gave them a quick glance but they took no notice and dropped further back. A mile into the exercise she stopped at a bench where a man sat reading his newspaper. The security detail also stopped and joined her. They sat down next to the man. MacDonald and Martinez approached along the path and observed as the chief of staff made conversation with her the security detail. The man with the newspaper continued to read and took no notice of his surroundings.

As the two FBI agents passed by the bench the man with the newspaper gazed at them with disinterest. Martinez had a good look at the man's face as they came abreast and then ran on. Fifty yards further down the path MacDonald caught Martinez's eye.

"Did you manage to get a good look at that guy with the newspaper?"

Martinez, known for his near perfect memory, chuckled. "Etched into my brain, partner."

"It seems highly unusual that Swales would have stopped to have a friendly chat with her security detail and sit on the same bench as a strange guy reading a newspaper. I think something's up," said MacDonald.

"An arranged meeting of some sort. They could've been passing on information," concluded Martinez.

"Let's get back to the office. You need to chat with our sketch artist and get a portrait drawn of the man's face," said MacDonald.

*

The warehouse appeared to be run down and long out of use. O'Malley entered onto the property and crept along the outside wall toward the roll-up garage door which stood half open. He held the Glock with both hands and kept it at waist height until he reached the door. He knelt down at the entrance, raised the Glock to his eye level and sighted along the gun's barrel, as he moved into the gloomy interior. Old, rusted machinery greeted him without enthusiasm and a myriad of cobwebs confirmed the long-term neglect of a once productive enterprise.

A door at the end of the area encouraged further investigation. He crept along a corridor and made a brief stop to check each of the rooms. The passage turned ninety degrees to his right and as he rounded the corner the sound of a woman's voice floated through the air. O'Malley stopped and listened intently.

"I want to know all about you," said the voice. It sounded like Janet's voice but he assumed it was her double that was speaking. A short silence followed.

"Speak to me, bitch," said the voice. The anger was tenable.

Silence followed for a brief moment and then came the sound of a slap.

"Where is your home? Why are you no longer living with your husband?"

O'Malley had heard enough. He crept forward to the doorway of the office in the building and stepped into the room with the Glock at the ready. Two men and Janet's double, surprised by the sudden interruption, turned to face him. Janet on her knees and with her hands tied behind her back ogled him in shock. Consternation showed on all the faces and one of the men reached for a weapon which had been tucked into his belt. The second man charged the FBI agent. He needed to cover a distance of about three yards to where O'Malley stood in the doorway but it turned out badly for him. The Glock bucked twice in quick succession and both men collapsed onto the floor.

O'Malley sighted on Janet's double but as he lined her up he froze. The woman stood behind Janet and held a knife to Janet's throat. O'Malley felt tempted to take a shot but he knew it was too close.

"Let her go or I'll shoot." O'Malley's voice remained calm.

"Do your best. I'll cut her throat in the blink of an eye. Go ahead and shoot."

O'Malley kept the visible part of her head lined up and remained stationary. He raised the Glock in the hope of sending a menacing gesture to Janet's assailant but the woman would not back down.

"Move further into the office, away from the entrance," she said.

O'Malley did not move.

"Do as I say or I'll kill her." The voice indicated to O'Malley that the woman meant business. The woman tightened her grip on the knife and O'Malley saw a few drops of blood appear on the white skin of Janet's throat. He decided to comply with her request but in order to move into the room he needed to step over the body of the man who had attempted to rush him. He did not take his eyes of Janet's double and kept the Glock aimed steadily at her head while stepping over the inert body. The man on the floor caught O'Malley's one foot in his hand, swiveled and tried to throw the agent off balance. He shouted an instruction to the woman.

"Run, Vera."

O'Malley couldn't maintain his balance and fell down heavily to one side as the man reached over to grab the agent's wrist. The two men wrestled around on the floor for a brief moment until O'-Malley overpower his assailant and freed himself. By that time Vera had let go of Janet, sprinted to the door and slammed it shut. O'Malley heard the click of the door lock.

He rushed to Janet's side and cradled her in his arms. The sound of movement behind him caused him to turn his head and out of peripheral vision saw the man reach for his dead partners gun. O'-Malley let go of his wife, raised the Glock and fired. The man toppled over and slumped onto his stomach. Blood began to pool on the floor from a neat hole in his forehead.

Janet stared with vacant eyes at the prone figure on the floor. O'Malley returned to hold her tightly.

"It's okay, babe. He can't harm us now."

After a minute she found her voice. "In all the years we've been married I've never witnessed you shoot anyone."

O'Malley sighed. "It never get's easier, believe me."

"I saw you outside the bakery and I knew you would do something but it was so scary. For a moment I thought they were going to kill me," said Janet.

"I realized that you might be in danger after the police found Jon Shepard's body in a car crash late yesterday. He had also seen his double in a 7-Eleven about a week ago."

"Jon's dead?"

"The accident was a setup and I believe he was murdered. You and Jon had both recently seen your doubles so I put two-and-two together. It's becoming apparent that something's going down and whoever is involved is trying to tie up loose ends."

Janet lifted her head and looked into O'Malley's eyes. "That woman, Vera, escaped which puts me in danger. What am I going to do, Dillon?"

"I will ask Ingram to appoint you a guard for the time-being. I think these people, knowing we are onto them, will keep a low profile. You could possibly take a vacation but I think it would be better if we carried on our lives as normally as possible."

"What about Steve?" Janet asked.

"Don't tell him anything about your abduction. It will affect him adversely if he thinks you are in any danger. My team and I are on the investigation and hopefully, it won't take us long to discover what's going on."

"What about these two men?" She pointed to the bodies.

"I need to call MacDonald. The team will take care of this." He pulled out his cell phone and placed the call. A moment later MacDonald answered and O'Malley explained their situation.

"They'll be here in about an hour. I need to check these two for identification," said O'Malley.

He helped Janet up and sat her in a chair. A quick search of both bodies produced no identity of any sort.

"We may be able to come up with something by using their fingerprints. I have a hunch, however, they will both be doubles of someone local."

Sometime later a soft knock on the door followed by MacDonald's voice shook O'Malley and his wife out of their reverie.

"Dillon? Are you in there?"

"Go ahead, Roland. Break the door in," said O'Malley.

MacDonald chuckled. "There's no need to do that."

O'Malley heard the sound of the key turn in the lock and the door opened to reveal the smiling faces of the other three team members.

Martinez looked at the dead bodies and gave a low whistle. "Jeeze, I see you've been busy, boss."

O'Malley turned to Gwen Farrell. "You need to arrange for the coroner to pick up these two bodies and tell them I want fingerprint identification on both men. I saw Janet's double with my own eyes and I'm almost sure we'll find that these two are doubles as well."

✳

9

Vera and McHale

Vera sat opposite the desk from Alan McHale in their operation's headquarters. She twisted a handkerchief nervously in her fingers. The boss was not pleased.

"How in heaven's name did this guy get the drop on three of you?"

"He had the element of surprise. I guess he followed us from the bakery where we abducted the O'Malley woman."

"What did he look like?"

Vera looked up at the ceiling for a few brief seconds. "He was athletic, about six foot tall with dark bushy hair and piercing blue eyes—quite a good-looker. I'll never forget the fierce look in his eyes."

V contemplated her answer. "If he was carrying a gun he has to be a cop or an agent. At a guess, I would say it was her husband, Special Agent O'-Malley, the FBI's top agent. He is slated for replacement at a later date."

Vera leaned back in her chair. "He definitely knew the woman. Why else would he follow us?"

"We're looking into the O'Malley woman's details as we speak. We'll know soon enough. You say that Simmons tried to shoot your attacker and Baker rushed him, but also got shot?"

"When I saw Simmons go down I took evasive action. Fortunately, my knife lay on the desk and I managed to hold the O'Malley woman hostage. Baker, although wounded, grabbed Simmons's gun. I ran for the door, locked them in the office and heard a shot but was too scared to go back."

McHale relaxed. "There's nothing in that office to incriminate us or compromise our operation but we will need to abandon the warehouse as a meeting place—you need to lie low for a while. Corporate planning failed us."

"What do you mean?" asked Vera.

"We didn't take enough care to find out who, other than the targeted officials, had doubles in the area. It's too late now."

Another woman entered the office. "We have a positive identification on the person who entered the warehouse and shot our men."

She handed a piece of paper to McHale. He glanced at the photograph and gave a sigh. "As I thought—it's Dillon O'Malley of the FBI. We had only planned to substitute him in about two months, following the abduction of his boss,

James Ingram. In a way, it's a pity he is down for switching—I would have looked forward to rubbing out the person who took out two of my best men."

Vera frowned. "Why not take the bastard out anyway?"

"The Council won't allow it. If a person is down for replacement they are to be sent back to the homeland. That's the rule and I don't want to jeopardize my position by disobeying it."

*

President Chambers regained consciousness but lucidity took a little longer. When sound returned he realized he had not dreamed up Captain Vargas's ship and their consequent transfer to a capsule-like vessel. The soft green glow of the instruments, now replaced by a brighter overhead light, made him wonder what the shaking and the high-pitched noise was all about.

They felt a slight bump as their capsule nudged up against a solid object and several moments later the sound of voices could be heard.

The hatch opened, allowing bright sunlight to filter into the cabin and two men climbed through the opening. They removed the half-masks and loosened the straps.

Chambers spoke to one of the men. "Who are you and where are we?"

"Captain Penn will brief you shortly. Please stand up." The answer was short and curt.

Chambers felt weak but managed to stand with a little help from the man.

"Please move out onto the deck."

He pushed passed the man and pulled himself along toward the exit. Outside the sun almost blinded him and he raised a hand to shield his eyes. Another helper grabbed his arm.

"Please move toward the gangway and watch your step."

He could make out a much larger vessel anchored alongside and moved obediently onto a steep walkway which led onto the adjacent vessel's deck. A short man with a dark beard stood in a doorway and beckoned to him. "Step over this way. You don't want to linger in those rays—they'll burn the shit out of you."

Chambers could feel a burning sensation on the back of his neck and wondered where the capsule-like vessel had carried them. The men on the deck wore heavily, lined clothing, gloves, and large brimmed hats.

"Who are you and why have you brought us here," demanded Chambers.

The man did not stick out his hand in greeting but motioned to one of the deckhands who cuffed the president's hands.

"To answer your question I am Captain Penn. I will be transporting you to the mainland. Welcome to Terra."

Swales joined them. The deckhand cuffed her as well and the party moved into the ship's interior and along a corridor. Steel steps led to the ship's bridge where they were able to look out through the large windows and across the tranquil sea.

"I've never heard of a place called Terra," said Chambers.

The captain chuckled. "I'm not surprised, Mr. President. You won't have heard of it because it's not in your world."

"What do you mean?"

"You are no longer in your universe but in one which lies parallel to it."

Chambers looked at Swales and she, in turn, stared at the captain. They were both stunned by the answer. Chambers had many questions.

"But how is that even possible. Parallel universes are just a theory."

"Apparently the theory is true. We have found a link which enables us to move freely between your universe and our own."

"But why are you doing this? Why have we been abducted?"

"Despite the premise of parallel universe theory not all things in our universe conform exactly to yours. Our world is dying and we need to take over yours to survive."

*

James Ingram, deputy head of the FBI, looked thoughtfully at O'Malley.

"You actually saw your wife's double?"

"Even her voice sounded exactly like Janet's. It was uncanny."

"So you think a group of people is involved in some sort of replacement program?"

"I'm not sure what it's all about yet but we'll get to the bottom of it. Shepard's death was not an accident and I found this item at the scene. It must have fallen from the car when it flipped over." O'-Malley produced the cigarette lighter found at the scene. "Shepard was not a smoker."

"Is there any report back on the two men you shot?"

"They had no identification on them and I suspect we won't find them in the databases," said O'Malley.

Ingram looked puzzled. "I'm not sure I can get my head around any real purpose here. Why replace Shepard and Janet? It doesn't make sense."

"They may just have been collateral damage, however, I'm thinking of young Gerry Swales's story about the sudden change in his mother, Beverly Swales. If Swales is an imposter it's as close to the president as you can get."

"You are proposing that Shepard, Janet, and Swales are victims of a switch-out program?"

O'Malley handed over a piece of paper. "I'm not sure who is targeted for the replacement but my team followed Swales yesterday. She went on one of her jogs in Montrose Park and they believe she might have met with a stranger. Martinez took a snapshot with that amazing memory of his and the artist came up with this sketch."

Ingram took the sketch and studied it. "Is there anything in our data bases on this person?"

"No, but that doesn't mean he isn't a person of interest. Swales's security detail, Miles Grabner, appears to be in on what ever took place. We have sent the sketch out to all of our operatives, plus the CIA. Maybe something will come of it."

"The idea of switching our top politicians for imposters could change the decision-making process of our country and that scares me," said Ingram.

O'Malley took back the sketch. "It would mean that even the president might be in danger."

Ingram looked at his watch. "I have a meeting. In light of this, we should use that password you thought of whenever we meet—we both want to make sure we aren't speaking to clones." He raised his eyebrows and stared at O'Malley who chuckled.

"Chaos?"

Ingram smiled. "We can't take any chances. Make sure your team uses it."

Ingram stood to indicate the end of the meeting. "Keep me informed."

O'Malley nodded and left the deputy director's office. After completing some computer work he glanced at the timepiece on the wall: 6:30 pm. He had an important meeting with his wife and son, the first of such meetings in six months, for which he did not want to be late. His cell phone rang and revealed a familiar number on the call display.

"Hi, honey." Tammy's voice echoed in his ear.

O'Malley, taken a bit by surprise hesitated for a second. "Hi, yourself, stranger," he answered.

Her tone sounded calm and friendly. "I believe you're ready to talk?" she asked.

Again, O'Malley hesitated. So much water had run under the bridge since they last spoke to each other and his entire world dissolved into a sudden confusion.

"I didn't think I would hear from you again. I left that message almost ten days ago," he said.

It was her turn for a moment of silence. "I know but I thought I would give you some more time to think about our relationship. I love you, Dillon and I want to spend the rest of my life with you, however, you can't live in two worlds. I won't be a part of it until I know you are wholly invested in this relationship."

"I understand, and I love you too. Unfortunately, I'm on a classified case at the moment which is taking all my time and energy. Can we get together and talk in a few days?"

"Of course, whenever you're ready." Her tone changed from eager expectancy to disappointment.

O'Malley picked up on the inflection. "I'll call as soon as I can."

"Promise?"

"Promise," he answered.

The call ended and he felt a hollow feeling in the pit of his stomach. The happiness he felt after Janet's rescue seemed to evaporate into a tangle of doubts and he realized that Tam's sudden call reflected on the real state of his mind. It took a concerted effort to shake off the feeling and restore the excitement of the evening's impending family dinner. O'Malley roared out of the FBI's parking and into the street. His thoughts returned to the conversation with Tam. He wanted to see her again and he wanted to be with her but nineteen years of marriage stood in his way.

An hour and fifteen minutes later he pulled up into Janet's driveway. Steve, with his elbows on the railing, stood out on the front balcony and waited for his father. The sight warmed O'Malley's heart and he looked forward to the evening. All three, for the first time in their family history, had a common interest; the case of the clones. If it took this to draw them together as a family again then the experience would be worth it. Janet had not told their son about her abduction.

Janet opened the door and leaned against the jamb. She looked stunning. Her usual long, blonde hair had been cut and she wore a pretty, floral patterned dress. His heart gave a jump when he saw her and it seemed like old times. O'Malley stepped up onto the balcony and embraced his son. He turned and pecked at Janet's cheek but she stood with her arms open as an invitation for him to embrace her. This was how things used to be, he thought. This is how he hoped it would continue but one obstacle stood in his way—his relationship with Tam. Which of the two did he want more?

He embraced his wife and they held each other for several moments while Steve looked on with a broad smile. When he released Janet his son gave him a playful punch on the shoulder.

"I have something of interest to tell you, Dad."

10

General Mumford

A man dressed in a general's uniform walked through the back entrance door of the Pentagon's elite officer's facility in Washington DC. Behind him, pushing a large mobile laundry basket, followed another man dressed in a blue dust coat. Many miles away Allan McHale and Elias Stilwell watched a live stream on a large, wall-mounted screen in the operations room of their office suite. The two men were watching Operation Terra Firma's third targeted replacement undertaking.

The video revealed a frontal view of an entrance area. McHale spoke into the system's mic. "Where are you?"

"I'm entering the back entrance of the officer's club facility. General Mumford should be in the sauna area. So far no one has taken any notice of us."

"Good," said McHale. "Tilt your cap down a little so that the camera view is not so elevated."

"Sorry, Allan—I'm used to wearing my cap where it is now but I'll make the adjustment."

McHale grunted as the camera lens took a sudden dip. The man on the ground, a veteran officer in the Terra Firma military, looked left and right in quick succession which brought a quick reprimand from McHale.

"Don't look about so much. Keep the general view straight ahead, if possible."

"Copy that," said the man in uniform.

"Is your helper ready?" asked McHale.

"He is, and if I may say, he certainly looks the part of a laundry collection worker."

"I hope you're right. We can't afford any more setbacks. This has to be done right or we could jeopardize the whole operation."

"Don't worry about a thing. I've got this. Two years of research and practice has made me a direct replica of General Mumford in every way."

McHale and Stilwell watched as the man in uniform entered the sauna's locker room. At the back of the room, he could see a line of single sauna's, each with a club member's name on it. The highest ranked officers in the club never used the communal saunas but preferred their own private cubicles. The two men walked toward one of the sauna doors and McHale could see the name inscribed on it: General John. D. Mumford.

"This is it," said the man in uniform. No body else appeared to be in the locker room at the time; a near perfect scenario for the operation.

He yanked the door of the sauna open and through the steam the saw a surprised face look directly at him.

Hands reached out to grab General Mumford by the throat and he was pulled out of the cubicle onto the floor. Another hand clapped over the general's mouth as he tried to scream and a hypodermic syringe was plunged into his neck.

McHale and Stilwell could hear the sounds of the struggle but it did not last long. General Mumford exhaled a long breath as his body relaxed under the drug. The two abductors dumped him into the mobile laundry basket and covered the body over with towels. The man in uniform moved to the lockers and found the right one. He removed general Mumford's suite and dumped it into the basket on top of the unconscious victim.

"Target successfully captured." said the abductor.

McHale turned to Stilwell. "So far, so good."

Stilwell nodded his head. "That went better than expected. In half an hour our replacement will return to the Pentagon as General Mumford."

McHale picked up his cell phone and made a call.

"Jack? They are leaving the building. I'll call Vargas and let him know you will deliver the package this evening."

*

O'Malley smelled the familiar aromas of his wife's cooking, one aspect of their marriage he missed dearly. Tam, because of her busy schedule as a CIA agent never had much time to perform the normal domesticated rituals he had become accustomed to with Janet. He detected his favorite dish in the making: rock salt encrusted prime rib with vegetables.

"Dinner will be ready in about half an hour. Steve, please pour your dad a whiskey."

She disappeared into the kitchen while Steven opened the liquor cabinet.

"So, what is this matter of interest you alluded to?" asked O'Malley.

Steve poured the drink and brought it to his dad. "It's about Gerry's mother. She is definitely, according to Gerry, an imposter. Apart from the scar on the head which is missing, their mom also appears to be missing her cesarean scar from the birth of her kids. Gerry's sister, Kate, saw their mom change out clothes while getting ready for a formal function. Kate had seen her real mother do this on countless occasions and always noticed the scar."

"Interesting," said O'Malley.

"If you remember, Gerry overheard his mom talking to someone on Skype one evening. It happened again the other night and Gerry decided to barge in under the pretense he was looking for a missing book on fly fishing. She became very upset, reprimanded him severely and tried to shut down the picture on her monitor, but he saw the man's face in the brief second it was exposed."

"Does Gerry think he would recognize that face if he saw it again?" asked O'Malley.

"He believes he would. He also heard a phrase uttered by his mother directly before he entered: They were talking about an operation called Terra Firma."

O'Malley considered the options. "If I send a picture to Gerry's phone would you ask him to let me know if it's the same man his mom was talking to?"

"You bet." Steve pulled out his phone and sent a message. He gave O'Malley the phone number for the picture to be sent and they waited for the reply. He had taken a photo of the sketch supplied by Martinez and the original had been filed away. The answer came back with immediate effect.

One and the same.

"Tell Gerry to keep up the act and not to let the woman know she has been discovered. My team and I will take it from here."

Steve sent the message. "I can't believe I'm cooperating on a case," he said.

"You're a chip off the old block, son. The acorn never falls far from the tree, as they say."

Janet called from the kitchen. "Please take your seats at the table, dinner is about to be served."

After a sumptuous meal, the family moved back into the living room and Steve excused himself. O'Malley glanced out the window.

"Your security detail is at his post, I see."

"There are two of them—a man and a woman. I feel quite safe now. Do you have any idea yet what this is all about?"

"I suspect a conspiracy to infiltrate our government and change things."

"But who? Do you think it's the Russians?"

"I really don't know yet. We're working on it but in the mean time Ingram and I have come up with a code word to verify our real identities."

"You mean in case one of us gets switched for an imposter?" asked Janet.

"Exactly—the word to use is, chaos."

"I'll remember that for the next time we meet. I'll tell Steve."

An awkward silence followed as they stared at each other. After several moments O'Malley spoke.

"I really enjoyed the dinner."

"Steve and I enjoyed having you, Dillon. We miss you."

"I know," he said. "It's not by chance that I've delayed the divorce proceedings. I need time to think everything through."

"I thought a divorce is what you wanted?"

O'Malley went on the defensive. "Divorce is very final. We should both be sure before we go through with it."

"Is the Clyde-Walker woman still staying in the apartment with you?"

"No, she's not. She has her own apartment."

"But she did move in with you?"

O'Malley sensed the beginnings of an interrogation. "Yes, she did move in but because I wouldn't rush the divorce she moved out."

Janet looked down at her hands and O'Malley could see the muscles around her mouth tighten. She didn't say anything.

"I just need time to process all that's happened over the last year. I'm thinking of taking some time off when this present problem is resolved," said O'Malley.

Janet lifted her chin and stared at him. "This present problem?"

"This double, or clone mystery, we're confronted with."

"I won't try to force your hand to sign the papers, Dillon but I'm sure you want to move on with your life. If it's over between us then it's over."

O'Malley leaned forward and held Janet's eye. "Do you think it's over?"

A moment's silence followed his question before Janet answered. "You took steps to end our relationship when you took off with that woman. I assumed you had found what you wanted."

O'Malley felt the beginnings of a slippery slope. "I know I acted inappropriately but I have found that nineteen years of marriage cannot easily be dispensed with."

"Shouldn't you have thought of that before you decided to jump into bed with someone else?"

"It's complicated," said O'Malley. Guilt, with regard to his infidelity, overtook him.

"To answer your question more clearly—I don't think it will ever be over from my side of things. As you say, nineteen years of marriage is a difficult experience to dispense with, and there's Steve to think about," said Janet.

"I don't want to fight about it. Let's just enjoy the evening and allow time do what ever needs to be done We should not be getting at each other's throats," cautioned O'Malley.

Janet was not finished. "Do you love her?"

O'Malley hesitated. "I don't know. She filled a gap in my life when I needed it."

"A gap I couldn't fill." Janet lowered her head and looked at the carpet.

"It's not your fault, Jan. It's all mine. One good thing has come out of our conversation this evening—"

Janet lifted her head and stared at him. "What good thing?"

"I haven't thought about Fallon once all the time we've talked. It's not something that could have happened before."

"What are you saying, Dillon?"

"I'm saying that something is changing in my psyche about the very thing that has been a trigger for me."

They stared at each other for interminable seconds. A cough brought them both down to earth and they looked up at the living room entrance. Steven stood there with a smile on his face.

"I'm going to make coffee. Any takers?"

O'Malley grinned and leaned back in his chair. "That sounds like a great idea to me, Superman."

The evening progressed until O'Malley looked at the time. "I should be going."

"Will you keep me abreast of how things are going with the case?" asked Steve. The excitement of being involved was palpable.

"Whatever isn't classified," said O'Malley.

He stood to leave. Janet opened the front entrance door for him and offered her cheek as he passed her. "I would like to keep in touch," he said.

"Do that. There's no need to be a stranger." A hint of a smile played on her lips s she spoke.

The drive home allowed O'Malley time to reflect on the evening's conversation. He attempted to sum up his thoughts in light of Janet's question with regard to his feeling for Tam. He felt torn between his newfound love and the nineteen years of marriage to his wife. The street lights whizzed by and, in a state of preoccupation, he saw the red traffic lights at the intersection ahead change to green. An instinctive reaction caused him to floor the SUV and he raced the light to get through. The headlights of a vehicle which approached the same intersection from his right at a high rate of speed did not register until the last second when he realized the other vehicle was about to run the red.

A split second later O'Malley felt the impact of the crash as the vehicle plowed into the SUV and sent it spinning across the intersection. He felt a floating sensation as it rolled over twice before smashing into a tree on the edge of a corner property. His final thoughts were of Janet and Steven before the light faded from his eyes and darkness engulfed him. A cloud of smoke wafted upwards as the vehicle threatened to catch on fire. The other vehicle, a large truck with a heavy bull-bar attached to its front-end, skidded to a stop and two men jumped out. They ran to the overturned SUV and pried open the driver's door. One of the men released the safety belt and the other man produced a knife, slit the airbag and together they pulled the inert body out of the vehicle.

Moments later the truck sped away. People came running out of the surrounding houses along the street to see what the commotion was about. At the same time, the SUV started to burn and one of the bye-standers called 911.

11

11

Arrival on Terra

"I can't believe this," said President Chambers. "You mean that life raft thing we arrived here in is some sort of dimension jumping, time machine?"

"You could call it that, I guess," said Captain Penn. "We find that the vehicle doesn't have to be of a special design—just strong enough to withstand a lot of shaking and rattling. The real science is hard to explain but apparently, right at a certain point in your Bermuda Triangle a link between our two universes exists where a sort of wormhole allows passage through from one side to the other."

Beverley Swales interrupted. "What are you going to do with us?"

Captain Penn stared out across the waters. "You will be placed in a detention zone for a while. After that, I don't know. The Council decides everyone's fate."

"The Council?" asked Chambers.

"It is a group of intellectuals who run Terra. Unlike your democracies which do not work, this group handles all our affairs. They decide who trades with who and how business is done between countries. War is practically a thing of the past although certain groups do cause trouble from time to time."

"You mentioned that your world is dying. What has transpired?"

Captain Penn turned his head and looked directly at Chambers. "Our magnetic field started to reverse about ten years ago but the outcome has been far worst than expected. The sun's rays are burning everything on our arable lands, turning our lakes into steaming pockets of dryness. Our seas are evaporating, leaving large congealed deposits of sun-caked salt on every shore. Humanity is being forced to erect domes over cities and in some cases to go underground."

Swales frowned. "So, when you discovered this link you decided that our world would become your new home?"

"The Council decided it would be expedient for us to save a part of our humanity. An elite group will be chosen to be transferred from Terra to your Earth but it was decided that before that could happen we needed to bring your present society into a new era."

The truth dawned on president Chambers. "You're using doppelgängers to impersonate our leaders."

"You've got it, Mr. President. We have a sophisticated plan to lead your world society into a greater truth by taking over your strongest military presence and using it to bring any opposition into compliance. The US military is the most powerful, conventional force in your world."

"You are saying that I have been replaced by an imposter?" asked Chambers.

"Both you and Mrs. Swales have been switched and no one is any the wiser. We plan to infiltrate the Pentagon as well and some of your law enforcement positions," said Penn.

"You'll never get away with it. My kids will know the difference between me and an imposter. It will never work," shouted Swales.

"Calm down Mrs. Swales. There is nothing you can do about it. I agree that we won't be able to fool everyone but if we can get away with it for even a short while and cause enough deception we will be able to grab power. Eventually, even the genuine leaders who remain will be suspected as imposters."

Captain Penn turned to one of his men. "Take these two down to their cabins and lock them in—remove their cuffs."

The man stepped forward and pushed the two victims toward the exit. Captain Penn had a final word: "It will take us about twenty-four hours to reach Liberty City. You will recognize it as your own New York when you see it. In the mean time make yourselves at home in your cabins and enjoy the ride. You will find the Lady Anne a comfortable ship."

*

Twenty-four hours later the ship sailed into port and Chambers heard a key turn in the cabin's door lock. Apart from receiving meals from one of the galley's staff neither Swales nor he had spoken to anyone. The door opened and the same man who had brought them to the cabins beckoned them. Chambers knew the drill. He turned and allowed the man to cuff his hands. They moved to a cabin further down the corridor and the procedure was repeated with Swales. They eyed each other.

"You okay?" asked Chambers.

Swales nodded and their custodian motioned for them to move through an open, steel door and onto the deck of the ship. Another man waited outside, draped thick, lined cloaks over their shoulders and set wide brimmed hats on their heads. He also provided a pair of dark glasses for each prisoner and they marched toward a gangway which led down onto the dock. They could see the dock area for the first time and as Chambers turned he could see a replica of the statue of Liberty in the distance. The dock had been extended further into the sea due to the evaporation of the oceans. They were marched to a waiting car and transported out of the area into a street which Chambers vaguely recognized. After ten minutes he knew they were on Pennsylvania Avenue, or what he thought to be Pennsylvania Avenue until he saw the name on the first floor soffit of a building: Constantia Avenue, the sign read. Chambers shook his head.

Further along the avenue he recognized the FBI building but was astonished to see the corporate logo and institution's name. Instead of the standard Department Of Justice seal, an entirely different logo was represented. He turned to Swales.

"Did you see that logo and name? It's not the "Federal Bureau of Investigation" but the "The Legal Institute of Universal Investigation". Everything looks the same but the names don't match up."

"I guess no one knew what the 'many worlds' in the theory would really look like. This is all so strange," said Swales.

The car drove into the underground parking and they were escorted via an elevator to a floor near the top of the building. A man with a shiny, bald head awaited them in a large office. He stood behind a large wooden desk as they entered.

"Greetings, President Chambers and Mrs. Swales. Welcome to Terra—please be seated." He motioned the guard to remove their cuffs. "I must say you both look exactly like your counterparts."

The two prisoners sat and stared at the man. He walked around to the front of the desk and sat in an adjacent chair.

"I can't say we're excited to be here Mr.—"

"Denzil Roshē," said the man. I am the director of the Institute. I understand this is a shock for the two of you but the sooner you accept your fate the easier it will be."

"What is our fate, Mr. Roshē?"

"You will spend some time in a detention zone. It will help you to accept that neither of you will ever see your Earth again. In the zone, you will retrain into new careers and eventually be allowed to enter the mainstream of our society."

Swales dropped her chin and struggled to keep the tears back. "What about my children?" she murmured.

"You could say they have become casualties of circumstance," said Roshē.

Swales buried her face in her hands. It had all become too much for her. Chambers jumped up and stood by her side. He placed his hands on her shoulders. "Don't give up, Beverley. We'll find a way out of this, somehow. I promise."

He turned to Roshē. "How many people on Earth do you propose to replace?"

"Not a great a number. We've planned this for five years. Our key members will effect the desired steps toward change on Earth before Terran citizens, chosen for transfer to your universe, are sent through the link."

"If only a certain number of your people have been chosen for transfer what will the rest of your humanity do?" asked Chambers.

"They will make the best of this dying world. We, on the other side, will help by sending through resources from your world to help sustain them. Any new children born here, during the time of our takeover, will be transferred to Earth. Their parents will remain here and eventually pass away. In a hundred years Terra will be completely barren and deserted."

"Why did you not dispose of us?" asked Chambers.

"It is the rule of Council. We may be desperate but we are not monsters."

"It is a plan hatched by a bunch of monsters if you ask me," returned Chambers.

"We tried every other conceivable plan but in the end, nothing would suffice. Our efforts at space travel are not even as advanced as yours on Earth and although we do have plans to colonize space in the future we do not have the time. When the dimensional link to your universe was discovered our Council conceived the plan of a take-over."

"Is there not a different approach that we can take?" asked Chambers. "We could help you find a solution—put our heads together and come up with a way to overcome this."

"Cooperation with your people was discussed by the Council but they decided your societies are still too predisposed to war and this would need to change first before any collusion could take place."

"Would I be allowed to address your Council?"

"Under no circumstance would we permit you an audience, Mr. Chambers. You will be confined to the detention zone for a period of one year before you and Mrs. Swales will be allowed into our society. This is the best we can do for you."

Roshē glanced over at the man who had escorted them to the office. "Please take Mr. Chambers and Mrs. Swales to the clinic."

The man stepped forward and motioned for the two prisoners to leave the room. Roshē made a final comment. "The clinic's doctor will prepare you for your stay in the detention zone. Eventually, you will be joined by the others whom we have targeted for replacement and life will not be so lonely. Make the best of it."

President Chambers glared at Roshē. "You will never get away with this preposterous plan. We will somehow find a way to defeat you and your council."

Roshē waved them away and returned to sit behind his desk. Chambers and Swales were herded out of the office to the elevator which took them down to the building's basement. They were met by a short, gray-haired man with bushy eyebrows as they entered the clinic.

"Please take one of the cubicles on your left and remove your clothing. You may leave under-garments on. I will be in to examine your medical condition and then you will receive a chip in our forearms."

"A chip?" exclaimed Chambers. "Why?"

"It will contain all your information and become your new means of identification."

"But..." stammered Chambers.

"No questions. When I have done the preliminaries you will both sit down at separate computers and answer the questions posed."

Half an hour later they left the clinic. A band-aid covered the incision in their forearms where a small microchip had been inserted. They both felt traumatized and void of any hope that they would ever see their planet again. Beverly Swales broke down and could not stop crying. President Chambers wondered about the detention zone as an aircraft transported them to a place far from the city.

12

O'Malley's Transition

O'Malley regained consciousness to find himself strapped into a reclined leather seat. The putt-putt sound of a small motor, the type fishing vessels used for trolling, filtered through to his ears. He appeared to be in the cabin of a small craft with rows of seats on each side of the walkway. A soft, green glow from a bank of instruments set into a console up front, provided the only illumination. A mask covered the lower half of his face and he appeared to be receiving oxygen through a tube.

His memory tried to retrace the last moments of consciousness. He remembered a bright light and a loud bang on the right-side of the SUV, followed by a floating sensation before the outside world spun out-of-control. The evening with Janet and his son Steven seemed distant and unreal in light of the present circumstance. A question of his present surroundings vacillated between a hospital and the afterlife. He realized his SUV had been tee-boned by another vehicle and he may have been killed in the accident. But why the sound of a motor, the special inclined seat and the oxygen?

He couldn't make head or tail of the situation. Without warning a sudden shuddering and vibration swept through the vessel, accompanied by a high-pitched noise which seemed to be all around him. It lasted for many minutes and the instrument glow became intermittent for a short time. Then the vibration disappeared and the lights returned to normal. The high-pitched sound quietened down to a low hum and in sudden concert, memories of the past intermingled with strange monster-like creatures which flashed across his vision. Their eyes bulged and tongues flailed which caused him to cringe back into his seat in fear. I'm hallucinating, he thought.

Then it all passed and an overhead light came on. All motion ceased and he heard the sounds of activity outside and water lapping against the vessel's hull which confirmed his transportation to be a small boat. A few moments later the hatch opened and the smell of sea air invaded the cabin. A figure appeared next to his seat and began to undo the straps which held him. A young man helped him stand up, then motioned for him to move out onto the deck of the vessel. Outside, the sun which seemed unnaturally bright blinded his vision. Another man clamped cuffs around his wrists and a heavy, lined cloak was draped over his shoulders.

"Put these sunglasses on, Sir. You don't want to damage your eyes."

His vision cleared and with the aid of the sunglasses, he could see a larger vessel berthed alongside. O'Malley became conscious of a second person behind him who received the same treatment as he did and wondered if it was the driver of the vehicle which had slammed into him. They formed a procession with one of the deckhands leading the way and climbed a set of steel stairs to the ship's bridge. Waiting for them was a man in navy uniform.

"Greetings, General Mumford and Special Agent O'Malley. My name is Captain Penn."

*

President Chambers and Beverley Swales donned their wide-brimmed hats, stepped out of the aircraft and made their way carefully down the stairs onto the tarmac. The midday sun blazed down on them and they could feel its heat through the heavily lined cloaks which they wore draped over their shoulders. Their special Polaroid sunglasses filtered out the harmful rays but cast the entire surroundings in a surreal and almost pure white color. The terrain, bleached over years of exposure to excessive amounts of radiation, caused a glare that would blind the unprotected eye.

The sand dunes, naked under a clear, azure sky, posed a silent presence of desert austerity and spread out endlessly before them.

"I guess we won't be able to trek out of this place with any ease," said Chambers.

Swales, recovered from her meltdown, looked out across the expanse. "Trek? Where would we trek to? There's only one way out of this mess and that's via the dimensional link through which we arrived."

Chambers rubbed his chin. "I'm not giving up. By the sounds of things more of our kind will be arriving and once we have more numbers we will come up with new ideas."

"I heard that bald shit say we would be in the detention zone for one year before they allow us to enter the main stream of their society. We can't do anything until then," lamented Swales.

"It gives us time to plan an escape. I am willing to bet that many of their people have no idea what's going on—that their council has made a way out of this dying world, but only for themselves. If we can convince people to help us we may be able to turn the tide."

"I see why you became president," said Swales. "You're such an optimist."

They walked toward a sun-bleached building which served as an airport terminal and tried to assimilate what they had seen so far. Their cuffs had been removed and the door to the cockpit had remained locked during the flight. They had spoken to no one since leaving the clinic. Nobody came to greet them and they assumed they would be alone. Chambers thought of his family. His wife, Claire, might pick up a sudden change in her husband's personality but she would put it down to the pressure of the job. They had not been intimate for some years due to their advanced age so she would not detect any change unless his replacement was still sexually active.

He rarely saw his children who now lived in other parts of the country following successful careers. Their grandchildren, part of a generation hijacked from real living by technology, also didn't feature very high on their visitation agenda. He gathered that the likelihood of someone discovering that his replacement was an imposter seemed very slim. It would be the same with Swales. She had not even dated since her husband left her for a younger woman five years prior. Her children, however, might see the difference.

They entered the terminal, removed the cloaks, hats, and glasses, then looked around. It appeared to be empty until a voice called out to them. "Over here—in the office."

The voice came from a small room at the back of the main area and belonged to a matronly woman in military uniform. She sat at a desk behind a computer and continued to work as they approached. As they entered the office she looked up from the computer screen and smiled.

"Welcome to Camp Logan. My name is Hilda and I'm the camp administrator."

They thought they might have been left to their own devices but the notion quickly dispelled. Chambers found his tongue. "How many people live here?"

"The numbers of inmates vary from twenty-five to fifty on an annual basis. We have a staff of ten."

"What exactly do you do here?" asked Swales.

"It's essentially a political reconditioning camp. We retrain the politically polarized. People who have caused the Council problems with alternate, or harmful political attitudes in conflict with our general persuasion."

"Do you know who we are?" asked Chambers.

"Of course I know who you are, President Chambers. You and Mrs. Swales will find our programs very compelling. You will see how the Terrans managed to reach a stage of near utopia and by the time you leave here you will have gained a greater appreciating of our society."

"But we will never be able to live it out in your world, which I believe is dying," said Swales.

"We still have a few years left, Mrs. Swales. You'll be able to apply what we teach you within the timespan left to us. I fully understand your apprehension regarding this sudden change in your lives but your sacrifice will save the lives of others. Let me show you to your accommodation."

Hilda left her desk and walked out of the office. When Chambers and Swales didn't move she stopped and beckoned to them.

"Come on. There's plenty of time for you to ask questions. We'll make you as comfortable as possible."

They followed her with reluctance. "Please never forget to wear your cloaks and hats. They are lined with radiation protection and will save your lives when out in the daylight. Every roof of every building is lined with protection so while you are inside you will be safe."

She opened a door to the outside, walked quickly along a stone-lined pathway and across a quadrangle to another group of buildings. There were no gardens, grass lawns or trees anywhere, only sand. They entered another building which appeared to be a dormitory and walked along a corridor with numbered doors on each side.

"I have only single quarters available but they are well equipped with television, small kitchenette, and a bathroom facility," said Hilda.

She stopped outside a room numbered, 100. "This will be your room, Mr. Chambers. On the back of each room's door is a map of the camp's layout. Meals are served in the canteen three times a day and the times are subsequently posted. The camp has a clinic with a nurse in attendance for your medical needs. You will report promptly for work at 9:00 am every morning and the day ends at 5:00 pm which includes an hour for lunch."

Chambers raided his eyebrows. "Work? What can you possibly be doing way out here in this desert?"

Hilda gave a low chuckle. "No one lives for free Mr. Chambers. There is a large oil deposit below the surface in this area. We operate a large, very automated refinery that extracts the oil and processes it for the entire west coast of Americania."

"Americania? I guess that corresponds to our continent of America. I haven't done any manual work for at least thirty years. I'm a politician, not an equipment operator or laborer," exclaimed Swales.

"It will all be explained to you tomorrow when you attend the induction process. The plant is very automated and robots do the hard labor so you will more than likely end up with a monitoring job."

"How many others are incarcerated in this place," asked Chambers.

"We have thirty-four, excluding the two of you, Mr. Chambers. Everyone, other than the security detail and management staff are being politically rehabilitated. Your room is next door, Mrs. Swales—number 102. Your places have been set at the dinner table and you both must be very hungry. At 8:30 am tomorrow morning we meet behind the airport terminal building for transfer to the plant."

"What happens if we refuse to cooperate?" asked Chambers.

"Our security staff will deal with that problem should it arise. There have been a few objectors over the years but they soon comply. The security detail is staffed with rough men who don't care for dissenters and you are welcome to try their resolve. I will leave you both now as I must get back to my office."

Hilda turned and strode off down the corridor to the exit without saying another word.

Chambers and Swales looked at each other in dismay.

*

13

All is the Same yet Different

The deckhand pulled the cloak off O'Malley's shoulders and hung it on a hook behind one of the doors which led off the bridge. He did the same for General Mumford. Captain Penn stared at the two men for a brief second and then smiled.

"You can remove the glasses now. Our bridge windows are specially darkened for glare. I suspect you are surprised to find yourselves here and are wondering what this is all about."

The two prisoners looked each other over first, then stared at Penn. The general found his voice before O'Malley.

"What in God's name do you think you are doing? Do you know who I am?"

Penn answered in a calm voice. "Of course I know who you are, General. You are chairman of the joint chiefs at the Pentagon." He looked over at O'Malley. "—and you are an FBI special agent—I believe the top operative of the year for the past two years?"

The two men continued to stare at the captain until the general spoke again. "What are we doing here?"

Captain Penn gave them the same story he would give all the others and after the briefing, the two prisoners were confined to separate cabins, until the ship docked in the Liberty City harbor. O'Malley had by this time gained a greater perspective on the conspiracy which he had suspected since seeing Janet's double in the warehouse outside Atlantic City. He found it difficult to believe, however, that they were in a different universe, until the docking. Confronted by familiar scenes, such as the statue of liberty and the general layout of the streets as they were driven to the brief orientation with Director Roshē, in what he thought should be Washington DC, convinced O'Malley that they were indeed in a different world. It was New York but many aspects were different. The deadly heat of the star's rays also served to convince him that this was a different climate to the one he had been used to.

A greater shock came when they drove into the parking lot of what looked exactly like the J. Edgar Hoover Building, home of the FBI. The logo and Institutional name, "Legal Institute of Universal

Investigation" were completely different. He stared out of the car window at his surroundings in disbelief.

General Mumford in tandem with O'Malley, could not believe his eyes. The two men had barely spoken to one another and now for the first time, O'Malley addressed his fellow prisoner. "Can you believe what you're seeing?"

The general shook his head and ogled the building. "Everything's the same, but very different. Were you aware that anything like this was taking place?"

"We were just starting an investigation into certain people having suddenly seen their doubles for the first time. I thought there had to be a foreign clone operation going on but I never suspected an alternative universe," said O'Malley.

The general concurred. "I thought I'd lost my mind when my sauna door suddenly burst open and I saw my double for the first time. I was pulled out of the sauna and then everything went black. I woke up in the cabin of that dimension hopper, thing."

"This magnetic field problem appears quite far advanced. I can understand their need to find an alternative but invading our universe is not the correct one," said O'Malley. He shared his own story of the accident and how he too, woke up in the strange vessel's cabin.

Their escort ushered them out of the vehicle and up to Director Roshē's office. After the director had told them what would happen they were taken to the clinic to receive a chip each. O'Malley felt like a prisoner of war being prepared for a lifetime of incarceration. He managed to extricate some information from the doctor which neither Captain Penn or the director had told them. Camp Logan, the detention zone, was in a desert called, "Thousand Dunes". The camp, a detention center for the politically disobedient, was accessed mainly by air. There were tracks which led from some of the small, surrounding villages but the journey normally proved too difficult for standard vehicles. Back at home the desert's geographical location corresponded to the Great Basin Desert, close to the Sierra Nevada Range. O'Malley knew the area well. It lay between the Nevada Mountain range and the Rocky Mountains. The Great Basin desert, normally cold and often in snowy conditions, lay on a high elevation between three and six thousand feet above sea level.

The flight to Camp Logan lasted six hours. The two prisoners took the opportunity to get to know one another and chatted about their backgrounds, hopes, and fears. At the journey's end, the aircraft landed in the desert terrain and O'Malley observed quite a different climate to the one he would have thought. Then it dawned that the climate had been radically altered in this universe and that snow was no longer a reality. Before their disembarkation, an automated voice reminded them to don the protective gear before leaving the aircraft. They put on the cloaks and wide brimmed hats for the short walk to the terminal building at the edge of the airfield's perimeter.

"Welcome to the edge of beyond," exclaimed the general.

O'Malley gave a grunt of despair. "It's hard to believe that this is what life has come to."

The general turned to him. "The last thing we must do is give up, O'Malley. We have to find a way to return to our domain and stop this madness."

"I hear you, General," said O'Malley. "It just looks so barren and austere. I'm still trying to come to terms with everything that's happened. It all seems like a bad dream."

"I know it does but we must face reality. I wonder if we are the first replacements they have made?" said Mumford.

O'Malley pulled the brim of his hat lower over his eyes. He could feel the heat seeping through the cloak's protection.

"I have a feeling we will find the Chief of Staff, Beverley Swales, here already. If you remember I mentioned that her children observed a radical change in their mother's demeanor, plus her missing scars."

Mumford recalled their conversation during the flight from Liberty City and nodded his head. "I think we might be surprised as to who they are choosing to switch—maybe even the president of the United States. I should think him a prime candidate."

They reached the terminal building and O'Malley spotted the office at the backend of the reception area. "I think there is someone waiting to greet us." They strolled through the building to the office and spotted Hilda behind the desk.

"General Mumford and Special Agent O'Malley—welcome to Camp Logan. Did you have a good flight?"

O'Malley eyed her skeptically. "I guess it was as good as it could be under the circumstances."

"My name is Hilda and I am the administrator of the camp. Although it's a detention zone you will find that living here will not be so bad. I will show you to your accommodation."

She beckoned them to follow. Mumford, a man always in control of his destiny and used to giving orders, gave vent to his feelings.

"We're not going anywhere until you tell us what the hell is going on here in this forlorn corner of your world."

Hilda turned and the smile left her lips. "You must realize that your circumstances have changed, General. Whether you like it or not you are here for a period of one year and if you are going to be belligerent about it I will simply call security to put you in your place. Now follow me. I will explain as we walk."

"Camp Logan is a camp for the politically incorrect. It is The Council's wish that the people from Earth are reprogrammed politically so that you can fit into our society."

"You want us to fit into a society that is going to die when your magnetic field disappears completely? It doesn't make sense," said O'Malley.

"Everyone dies, Mr. O'Malley. We are busy trying to save a part of our humanity. Not everyone will be saved but The Council wants to make sure that a certain amount of us do survive. In order for that to happen some people will have to give up their right to live."

"There is still time to find an alternative. We should be helping your people to do this rather than you trying to steal what is rightfully ours," said Mumford.

"Spare me the moral lecture, General. Your society is different to ours. You people take resources that don't belong to you and go to war for any little thing. You discriminate against people who are less fortunate than yourselves and there hasn't been a moment's peace on your planet since the birth of Earth's human race."

Mumford followed on behind Hilda, his face a picture of hostility. O'Malley stayed out of the verbal exchange. He knew they held a bad hand but he hoped it would change as soon as he could find out what made Camp Logan tick.

"Please remember to wear your cloaks, hats, and glasses whenever you venture outside. There are two of your colleagues here that I'm sure you will be happy to meet."

The threesome crossed the quadrangle and entered the dormitory building. O'Malley noticed the numbered rooms on each side as they progressed down the long corridor of the dormitory. They stopped outside number 100. Hilda pointed to rooms 106 and 108 and knocked on the door of 100. A moment later it opened and a man looked out at them. Both General Mumford and O'Malley recognized him immediately.

"I have brought you some friends Mr. Chambers. You can share the details of the orientation which will be held for them tomorrow." She gave the general an insolent glance and walked off.

"Welcome to hell, General Mumford," said President Chambers. He looked at O'Malley and cocked his head. "I recognize you but I can't remember your name."

O'Malley stuck out his hand. "Special Agent Dillon O'Malley, FBI, Sir."

President Chambers' eyes lit up."Of course—the FBI's top agent—my apologies, O'Malley. I guess the shock of finding myself in these circumstances must have dulled my memory."

"No need to apologize, Mr. President. I think we all are in shock. Where is Mrs. Swales?"

The president gave O'Malley a surprised look. "How did you know about my chief of staff?"

O'Malley shared how he had come to suspect the switch of Swales for an imposter.

"I'm extremely glad you and the general are with us, O'Malley. We can begin to form some sort of plan. I don't know about you but I, for one, do not want to live out my life on Terra."

The door to room 102 opened and Beverley Swales appeared. She stared at O'Malley and Mumford in surprise. "I heard the voices. What's going on?"

President Chambers explained who they were and Swales let out a loud sigh of relief.

"Don't get me wrong, gentlemen. I'm not glad that you have been brought to this place but I am glad that the President and I are not alone."

They crowded into President Chamber's room and sat wherever they found a vacant space. The first subject for discussion was brought by President Chambers.

"Does anyone here know anything about the parallel universe as a theory?"

General Mumford jumped in. "I'm not an expert on the subject but it's part of the 'many worlds theory', first theorized by Hugh Everett, an American physicist. He believed that quantum mechanics, which deals with the very smallest of particles, produces a situation of probability when in the wave or superposition form. To cut a long story short, it appears that theoretically, the probability of infinite and complete universes exactly like ours could exist parallel to this one.

Beverley Swales frowned. "Are these universes identical to ours? I mean with landmass, geography, people, animals, birds, etc?"

Mumford considered the question. "I guess they might be identical in every way."

"But although the continents appear identical the names of places are all different," said Chambers.

"But the people are all identical," said O'Malley.

"I guess free will is not duplicated," said Mumford. "Evolution appears to have operated exactly the same as in our universe. Human progress also appears to have kept exact pace in both places and yet their magnetic field is failing. There do appear to be some differences. I doubt whether the theory is that well understood."

"Isn't it also akin to the multiverse theory?" asked Chambers.

"It is probably one and the same thing, Mr. President. If I remember, the multiverse theory is where bubble universes form within universes but it isn't clear whether they are identical replicas of each other. The consensus is that in a multiverse you can have different laws which may not be the same in all of them. As I said before I'm not an expert, I've just read up a little on the hypotheses."

O'Malley decided to change the subject. "Irrespective of what the theories say we find ourselves in a different place and what I have seen so far compels me to believe we are in another universe."

He pointed to the overhead light and gestured to the others for everyone to leave the room.

Outside, in the corridor, O'Malley spoke again. "We have to be careful of listening devices. Okay—now listen to me very carefully. We have to find a way to get back to the point where the dimensional link operates. If we can't do that we will remain here forever."

"Do you have a plan?" asked Swales.

14

The Presidential Clone

Norman Hastings read through the preliminary report on NATO's involvement off the coast of North Korea. He felt pleased with the previous evening's performance, an engagement at the University of Wisconsin, which required him to deliver a difficult speech. His task in Operation Terra Firma, as the replacement for the President of the United States, appeared to be taking on the desired illusion he had hoped it would create.

Mrs. Chambers, the first lady, seemed none the wiser and this might be due to the fact that Chambers and his wife led separate lives. One would think that after thirty-five years of marriage they would know each other intimately but it appeared to be exactly the opposite. The years of public service in the political arena had taken its toll. Jenny Chambers did notice a slight change in her husband's social habits but put it down to the pressure of the job. Chambers had won the race for the White House as an independent, leaving both Republicans and Democrats wondering how he had hijacked the top job.

Hastings was not new to the political arena. He had spent several years serving in a minority government on Terra as the country's president before the political system changed. It happened after the citizens of Americania nearly tore themselves apart when a non-political oriented president had been elected to "Premier House", the country's main seat of political government. The media consumed each other and eventually, civil unrest broke out. The president was eventually impeached, not because he did anything wrong but because the people just couldn't tolerate him. Loyalists fought back and civil unrest turned into civil war. The military stepped in and took over in a coup that saw the imposition of a council to run the affairs of the country.

Hastings's experience as a past president set him up for the job as Chambers replacement in Operation Terra Firma. He had studied all the available data on Earth's political endeavors since the discovery of the dimensional link. The operation's operatives, Alan McHale and Vera Day, had done a sterling job of extracting the details on those who would need to be replaced. A huge step forward came with the replacement of the White House chief of staff and now the more recent replacement of General Mumford, chairman of the joint chiefs, would start the process of government and political subjugation in earnest.

"Are things coming together?" Francis Bowman asked.

He glanced up at her. "I'm reading the report on my speech last night at the university. Never underestimate the minds of young students. They have since voiced their opinions on my foreign policy and the press picked up on it."

"What do the students think?"

"They think my line of approach will save the world from going to war over rogue nations like North Korea. Their mantra is that American aggression has caused the destabilization of countries like Iraq, Afghanistan, and Libya. The consensus amongst the student body is that American intervention in another sovereign country's affairs is a criminal act—that the U.S. should be promoting peace and trade rather than trying to promote democracy everywhere in the world. Opposition to the White House's softer line approach will grow, however, as our military begins to inflate the dangers of my foreign policy in the face of rogue nations and use of nuclear weapons. When one of these rogue nations finally attacks America and the White House refuses to retaliate in the interests of world peace, the tide of opinion will turn against the government. The people will demand retaliation and military action to protect American interests."

The doppelgänging chief of staff steepled her fingers. "So you're setting up the illusion that North Korea is on the point of using its arsenal against the USA?"

"It won't be an illusion. The countries of the world will see North Korea launch a missile at us from a remote area of its northern region. It will be from a place close to the Chinese border."

Bowman chuckled. "When you refuse to retaliate in the interests of world peace people will think America has become soft and that we fear retaliatory action from China or Russia should we blast the DPRK into oblivion."

Hastings smiled. "It's unfortunate that an intercontinental missile will hit American soil but we need a real incident for the American people to rise up in arms and reject their leadership," said Hastings.

Bowman's eyes lit up. "They will be calling for your head. America will have sustained a catastrophic blow and all the world markets will go into a tailspin. With Congress in a dither, the people will be screaming for responsible leadership."

Hastings nodded. "A crisis will exist—the military will be forced to stage a coup and depose me as president. This will be backed by the Joint Chiefs and they, in turn, will facilitate the eventual election of a council which will rule the country and ultimately the whole of Earth."

Bowman stood and made to leave. "I look forward to the day when the Terrans will rule the planet."

"It's a long way off. We have much to accomplish before that can take place. But if we can subjugate the military we will have the power to make the rest of the world cower."

*

Later in the day Damian Hall, dressed in a four-star general's uniform, walked into the oval office. No one even vaguely suspected he was not General Mumford.

"Norman—what a pleasure it is to see you again. I bring you greetings from the mother planet."

Hastings came around the desk to greet him. "I was glad to hear that your project went off smoothly. The real Mumford is languishing in the detention zone by now. Sit down, Damian. We have a few things to discuss."

Before we start did McHale brief you on the latest situation with North Korea?"

"He told me you had made contact with a mercenary group who have unwittingly offered their services."

"Money can buy anything theses days. I will leave the negotiating to you but cover your tracks. Nothing which might bite us in the ass must be left undone."

"I promise I'll be discreet. The mercenaries will have to be eliminated afterward but no one will miss them. Tell me about the target," asked Hall.

The president settled into the couch and cleared his throat.

"It's a missile base situated near the Chinese border, stocked with two inter-continental ballistic missiles that can reach American soil. The North Koreans have been using it as an intimidation factor. We have obtained all the codes required for a launch."

"Sounds good. Thanks to the research McHale and Day have done on the general Mumford's life and behavior no one suspects me as an imposter and being a widower makes it easier, although he does have two sons who live in Wyoming and Washington State, respectively."

Hastings returned to his desk and opened one of the drawers. He extracted a red folder, and a cell phone. "Here are the details of your contact. They won't come cheap but do your best. When the cash is required contact McHale and he will see that the money is transferred."

"I'll offer them fifty percent as a deposit and fifty when the job is done. How trustworthy do think they are?"

Hastings rubbed his chin. "The leader came highly recommended but you never know. I think they will go through with it—no one likes the DPRK."

The two men shook hands and Hall left.

Back at the Pentagon Damian Hall sat at his desk and perused the file's details. Satisfied he placed a call on his burner to Alan McHale.

"Tell me what the leader of this mercenary group is like."

Settled into his office chair with his feet on the desk McHale stretched a hand to the keyboard of a laptop and pulled up a file.

"He calls himself Kurtis Banks. He fought against ISIS in the Syrian debacle and led a group of commandoes on a series of daring raids which the record shows were successful in crushing the enemy and leading to a victory. The highest rank he held was that of captain but due to an altercation with a general, he was discharged from the military. He formed a small band of loyal combatants and started mercenary operations around the world."

Hall gave the resume some thought. "Do you have a ballpark figure of what they might expect?"

McHale considered the question for a moment. "Probably about five million tops. I wouldn't pay more than that."

"Do we have that much money?" asked Hall.

"We actually have a lot more than that but we don't want to waste our resources."

"It sounds like a dangerous mission—I"m sure that silo has stringent security."

"That will be Banks's problem. He sounded optimistic when I broached the subject."

"Thanks, Alan. I'll give him a call."

*

Hall keyed the contact number for Banks into the phone.

It rang twice and a gruff voice answered.

Hall spoke with confidence after verifying that it was Banks.

"I believe my colleague has contacted you regarding a certain mission in North Korea. I am a general at the Pentagon and will be handling the negotiations on our side."

Banks did not ask for a name. "I'll come straight to the point, general. We want ten million for the job. Five million now, and five when the job is done."

Hall smiled. "If you have no reservations about your success I'm sure we can meet your terms, Mr. Banks. If you give me the account number I'll transfer the money." He picked up a pen and scribbled the number down on a notepad.

Banks seemed elated. "I will get my team ready, General. You have the missile's activation codes and coordinates for the target?"

"Give me a moment." Hall opened the red folder and sighted down a row of figures. He called them out and Banks wrote the numbers down.

"Do you have a specific day you would like to see this happen?" asked Banks.

"Plan it for Sunday, the 25th. That gives you three weeks."

A silence followed as the mercenary leader ran the coordinates through his mind. Conversant with coordinates he did a rough extrapolation in his mind.

"This is a drastic move, General. These are thermonuclear warheads we are talking about."

"This is why we are willing to pay you top dollar, Mr. Banks. The target is not something you should be concerned with or discussing with your men. You are a mercenary and you need to treat this mission as such. There also has to be absolute secrecy. Are you up to it?"

Banks considered his position. This would be the most dangerous mission he would ever undertake. He thought of the collateral damage and for a moment wondered if he could go through with it. He would pay his men one million each and that meant he would receive seven million for his efforts.

"I believe I'm up to the task, General. I do not want to know the reasons."

They discussed the logistics of the trip to North Korea and Hall shared his plans for their transportation. The mercenary commander made notes.

"When the deposit is transferred I will begin our preparations. The second payment will be expected within an hour of the missile striking American soil," said Banks.

Hall smiled. The conversation ended and the general sat in deep contemplation of the impact the event would make on the world.

After a few minutes, he made a return call to McHale.

"The negotiation is done. Transfer the five million at your earliest convenience."

McHale sounded dubious. "You giving them the full amount off the bat?"

Hall laughed. "They asked for ten million but will never receive the second payment. I will have a surprise for the team when they return from the DPRK."

※

15

Janet O'Malley

Janet O'Malley sat slumped in one of her living room chairs. Opposite her sat James Ingram the deputy director of the FBI. She nervously twirled a tissue between thumb and forefinger of one hand. Both cheeks glistened with tears and her mascara had smudged a little.

"I'm so sorry to be the bearer of this bad news, Janet. I thought it would be better if I delivered it in person. Dillon and I have known each other for a long time."

Janet dabbed at her eyes with the tissue. "But what do you think has happened to him?"

"We honestly don't know. First responders at the scene of the accident put the fire out but when they searched the wreckage they did not find any human remains. All the bystanders who arrived, mostly within five minutes, say they didn't see anything. No one appears to have witnessed the accident. One of the home owners said she heard the skid of tires and then a terrible crash. When she came out of her house all she could see was smoke and then the fire started. She called 911."

"You said someone heard a vehicle pull away. It had to have been the other vehicle involved."

Ingram shifted in his seat. "That is all the information we have. For any vehicle to have survived the cash and drive away means it had to have been a large truck, perhaps with heavy bull-bars fitted to the front. It could have been a deliberate act."

"Dillon would not have left the scene without reporting it," said Janet.

"Which makes it all the more mysterious," answered Ingram. "I'm sorry but I have to ask—did he have anything to drink while visiting with you and Steven?"

"He only had one whiskey all evening and he was definitely sober when he left here."

"The police will ask once they find out he visited with you," said Ingram.

Janet blew her nose into the tissue and then reached for another. "I think that someone targeted him after he rescued me. You know much more about what's going on, James. Don't you think it has something to do with the appearance of all the clones? I know about Beverley Swales and Jon Shepard and there was my abduction by my double who one of my assailants called Vera. This is all a part of the same equation, isn't it?—a possible conspiracy."

Ingram narrowed his eyelids. "I'm sure it's all connected. Did Dillon discuss the password with you?"

"Yes,—he said we should be able to identify each other."

Ingram pulled out his phone. Just so we can be sure of each other, type the password on your notepad and I will do the same. We can then show each other simultaneously."

Janet picked up her phone and typed in the word, as did Ingram.

"Ready?" he asked.

"Ready," she answered. They both placed their phones, screens up, on the coffee table and checked each other's passwords.

"Good," said Ingram. At least you know I'm the genuine Ingram and I know you are the genuine Janet."

Janet managed a weak smile. "It doesn't tell us what happened to Dillon, though."

The deputy director sighed and stood. "I have to get back to the office. I can only pray that he is okay. There was no sign of a body, which is a good thing."

Janet stood and walked to the door. "I don't know what I'm going to tell Steve."

"Perhaps you should delay saying anything until we know more," said Ingram. He leaned forward and kissed her cheek. "Keep your chin up. I'll be in touch." He walked down the porch steps to his car and left.

*

Gerry Swales still had some restrictions on his driver's license but with it being a weekend he would be allowed to drive until 11:59 pm. His mother, Beverley Swales had been very strict on his adherence to these restrictions but lately, it would seem the woman who claimed to be his mom didn't care.

Gerry and Steven sat in Gerry's Mustang which he had parked near the entrance of the Primrose park and waited for Swales. Both boys had their baseball caps pulled low over their eyes as they watched from a distance. Swales came at a jog, entered the park and ran a little way up the path to a bench where she sat down next to a man who appeared to be busy reading the morning newspaper. The security detail who followed on behind Swales stopped and also sat down. The man with the newspaper appeared to take no notice of them and after a few minutes Swales stood and continued on with her run. Gerry, with a pair of binoculars glued to his eyes, grinned.

"It's the same guy I saw her speaking to on Skype the other night. I notice that he didn't turn to face her but his lips were moving. We'll wait for him to leave and see where he goes."

Five minutes later the man stood, folded the paper and walked back toward the park entrance. They watched as he climbed into a vehicle parked on the verge nearby and pulled out into the traffic. Gerry started his car and followed on behind. He made sure to keep a good following distance so as not to raise any suspicions.

Four hours later they entered the outskirts of Atlantic City, New Jersey. The man pulled into the parking lot adjacent to a two-story building, in the industrial area, left his vehicle and enter the building through a set of double-glassed doors. Steven had wanted to contact his dad but Gerry felt the FBI agent would refuse them permission to follow up and spoil their chances of making a significant discovery. They parked close by and waited while Steven watched the office entrance through the binoculars.

"What do we do now?" asked Gerry.

"We wait until we see someone exit the building. I want to see who else is involved. It looks like he might be involved in a business. The sign above the doors reads Event Planning Ltd."

Gerry made a face. "I hope we don't have to wait for long, I'm hungry."

An hour later the boys grew tired of the vigil. "We'll come back again later in the afternoon," said Steven.

Gerry started the car, pulled away from the curb and headed out of Atlantic City and back toward Philadelphia.

Later in the afternoon they returned to Atlantic City and parked in the same spot. Steven planted his elbows on the dash to steady the binoculars and kept a general eye on the entrance to the office block. After an hour their patience paid off as a group of people exited the building and walked toward two vehicles parked in the front of the premises.

"Here we go," exclaimed Steven. "I count seven people in all—two women and five men."

After the two vehicles left the office block Gerry followed at a distance until the vehicles entered downtown Atlantic City and pulled into the parking lot of a local pub.

Gerry parked at the far end of the parking lot and the two boys walked to the pub's entrance. The bar was age restricted so they didn't enter but waited outside, beyond the corner of the building, under the extended branches of a gray alder tree. Gerry pulled out a pack of cigarettes and offered Steven one but the boy refused. They decided to wait.

*

Alan McHale and Elias Stilwell raised their glasses for a toast. They didn't often leave their Atlantic City office facility but for the sake of not contracting cabin fever, it had been decided to celebrate at a local pub. Vera, Jack and the three assistants raised their glasses in accompaniment. McHale had asked for a small private room so that they would not be observed by anyone.

"To operation Terra Firma," said McHale.

The others echoed him and they all clinked their glasses together. Voices were kept low-key and McHale had given strict instructions that no one was to get drunk. The process of switching White House and military personnel had been successfully concluded that afternoon. Elias, Jack and the other three assistants were due to return to Terra in a few weeks which would leave McHale and Vera Day to orchestrate the conspiracy through the imposter personnel.

"To you and the others, and to a job well done," toasted McHale.

The others grinned and chugged back their drinks. A second round was ordered and everyone chatted about the finer details of their accomplishment until Stilwell stood to his feet to make an announcement.

"This is more than just a celebration of our work. I also want to congratulate Alan and Vera on their engagement."

This did not come as a surprise to Jack and the others. They had seen the signs of a burgeoning romance between the couple. They all stood and clapped. Stilwell raised his glass once more. "To Alan and Vera."

They echoed the toast and sat down. An hour later McHale called an end to the celebration. "We must get back to the office. I have one more detail to take care of before everything is in place for the great manipulation."

They all drained their glasses. McHale and Vera made their way out of the room and the rest followed on behind. On the way out of the building the procession of Terran's, all in conversation with one another, failed to notice the two young men in the dark shadows under the tree. When the group entered the main road to head back to the office block a car pulled out and followed.

One of the men in the second vehicle became suspicious of the old 64 Mustang, with its familiar racing-stripe down the middle of the hood, in procession behind them. He pulled out his phone and called McHale who sat in the rear seat of the car in front.

"We have attracted some unwanted interest. I believe someone is following us."

McHale's voice remained calm. "Just keep your cool and let them follow. We'll make a little detour to the abandoned warehouse."

The other man countered. "Aren't the FBI onto that venue?"

"I doubt whether they'll expect us to return there. It's been several days since Vera's escape. We'll do a slow drive by and if there's no one around we'll pull in and see what happens."

The two vehicles diverted from the normal route and drove to the abandoned warehouse where O'-Malley had encountered Vera and her two assistants. The building appeared deserted.

"Okay, there's no one here; We'll pull in and drive around to the back. Follow us."

The man in the second vehicle acknowledged the instruction and the two vehicles drove around to the back of the building.

*

Gerry pulled his car off the road and onto the verge when he saw the vehicles pull into the warehouse.

"Looks like an old warehouse. I wonder what they use it for?"

Steven strained his vision to see the details of the building. "We need to be careful. This could be a trap."

The lights of another car approached from behind and the two boys ducked down. The car continued on past the warehouse and turned into an adjacent road. The boys breathed a sigh of relief and returned their attention to the warehouse.

"It's no use sitting here. We should investigate," said Gerry. Steven gave his friend's observation some consideration.

"Let me try my dad one more time."

He made the call but received only the answering service. "He's probably busy on the case. Let's take a quick look but we need to be ready to run if there's the slightest sign of trouble."

They undid their seat belts and stepped out of the car. The nearest streetlight provided limited illumination of the building's frontal and the boys walked up to the open gate where they stopped to have a look around. No threat presented itself so they proceeded on toward an open, roll-up door at the end of the building. Steven took the lead and peeked into the open space beyond. He waited for his eyes to adjust to the interior's darkness before stepping inside. Gerry followed and they crept past all the old machinery toward an open door at one end of the large space. Through the door, they could see a dim light and further down a passageway, distant voices could be heard in conversation.

Steven touched Gerry's arm and motioned with his head toward the passageway.

"Let's see if we can get close enough to hear what they're talking about."

They moved into the passageway with the least noise possible and crept toward the dim light and the sound of the voices.

With sudden brilliance, the overhead light in the passageway turned on and neither Steven nor Gerry could see anything until they recovered their vision. Ahead in the passageway stood a man with a gun. They turned to flee but stopped in their tracks when another man appeared in the passage behind them.

The man with the gun sneered. "Now, what do we have here?"

16

A Plan of Escape

O'Malley leaned against the wall of the corridor. The other three prisoners gathered around him and stood with their arms folded.

"I don't have a plan of escape as yet but it will come when we know more about our present surroundings. I want to share some of my observations with you. There is a camera at each end of this corridor so we need to make sure when we talk together we keep our voices down. We can be sure they will be monitoring us most of the time. The camp has its own source of power. It's a generator room which has two reasonable size electrical generators. I saw the building as we entered the dormitory—it's to the left of the terminal's exit door and has two visible four-inch flues poking through the one side wall.

Also, there is one way in and out of the camp. A road leaves the perimeter and judging by the position of the sun heads due east. I think that would lead to the facility you told me about."

President Chambers interrupted. "Do you see a possibility of us getting out of here?"

"I'm formulating a plan but need to know more about the security, the meal times and when supplies are delivered."

"We have only been here one more day than you have," said Swales. "All I can say is that security appears to be at a minimum and they don't expect their charges to run away. The few people that are here wouldn't talk to us at the meal times. You will see the plant tomorrow after your orientation with the supervisor. We were herded like cattle from the terminal and taken to the plant which is approximately ten miles away. It's extremely desolate terrain."

Not to be left out General Mumford jumped into the conversation. "What is the work facility like?"

"Like any other oil refinery on Earth. They extract the oil from below the ground and put it through a process of refining to produce the different grades. Beverley and I, however, have only been to the orientation so, we haven't been into the plant yet," said Chambers.

"Did you see how they transport the oil from the facility to any outside source," asked O'Malley.

Chambers closed his eyes and tried to recall the memories of his first day.

"I didn't notice any big pipes leading out so if there are they may be underground. There are dozens of storage tanks but I didn't see anything else."

"No doubt once we start work we can get a better look at possible escape routes but getting out of the desert may not be our greatest challenge. Finding and gaining access to the dimensional link which serves our universe might be far more difficult," said O'Malley.

The door opened at the far end of the corridor and a security guard shouted at them. "No social gatherings are allowed in the hallways or rooms. Dinner is ready in the canteen."

He carried an assault rifle strapped over one shoulder. The group looked at each other in surprise and decided they were all hungry.

"Follow us," said Chambers as he and Swales made for the door at the opposite end of the corridor. "The canteen is at the end of this building so you won't need your cloaks and hats."

They entered the dining facility through a set of double doors which opened into a large area with tables and chairs. A serving counter with trays of steaming food lined the entire wall on one side. About fifty percent of the tables and chairs were occupied by people, all dressed in coveralls. The inmates looked up to observe the newcomers as they entered. Chambers made his way to the service counter and picked up a plate. The others followed and then found a table with four chairs.

"Not the greatest spread I've seen but they are making an effort to keep us alive," said Swales. Everyone else in the room resumed their conversations and continued to eat their dinner.

O'Malley looked around at the people. "Have you met anyone yet, Sir?" he asked Chambers.

"Not yet—I guess Beverley and I will meet some of them tomorrow when we start work in the plant."

After dinner, they walked back to their dorm. President Chambers opened the door to his room and turned to O'Malley. "There's an alarm, preset for 6:00 am, on the dresser next to your bed. We'll see you in the canteen for breakfast. After that, they will take us out to the plant."

O'Malley entered his room and looked around. A window high up in the wall possessed a single opening frame which stood ajar to allow the cool night air in. The rooms appeared to have no air conditioning and he could feel the day's heat dissipating. A single closet contained four coveralls, laid out neatly on the shelves, along with a supply of underwear and socks, plus a pair of heavy, leather boots and a construction hard-hat. He assumed they had taken the size from his existing clothing at the clinic when he underwent the medical examination.

O'Malley stripped off his clothes and stepped into the shower. The sight of the small scar on his forearm where the doctor had implanted the chip caught his attention and he knew at some point he would have to remove or neutralize it. As the lukewarm water flowed over his shoulders thoughts of his home planet and loved ones filled his mind. Things were bad but they could have been far worse. The mattress was firm and the sheets clean. As he lay on the bed his mind turned to thinking about a means of escape.

*

The alarm woke O'Malley out of a deep sleep and he realized how tired he had been the night before. He dressed in the coveralls provided, pulled on the boots which seemed a good fit and made his way to the canteen where found the general and President Chambers already eating their breakfast.

"It's a type of cooked oats. Looks a bit sloppy but tastes okay," said President Chambers.

O'Malley poured the oats into a bowl, grabbed a spoon and sat down with the two men. Beverley Swales arrived and took a mug of coffee. She sat down next to the president and glanced at each one in turn.

"Everyone sleep okay?" she asked. They all nodded and the general looked around the room. "I can't believe this is happening. If we don't get out of this place I'm going to go crazy."

166

"We must keep our hopes up," said O'Malley. "Once I've had a good look at the facility we will begin to formulate a plan, but for now we need to gather as much intelligence and knowledge about this place. We must try to find out how things work."

"Perhaps we should try to make some friends amongst the other inmates. There's bound to be some very disgruntled people," said Chambers.

"That's a good idea but we need to make sure not to give our intentions away. It may be in our interests to join forces with anyone who intends to escape but I would think it would be a low priority for any of the Terrans. They know they are only here for one year and then they will get to go back home. We don't get to go home unless we can escape," said the general.

A buzzer sounded and President Chambers swallowed the last of his coffee. "We need to get our protective gear. The buses will be leaving in fifteen minutes from behind the terminal."

They all completed their breakfasts and left for their rooms. Ten minutes later everyone assembled behind the terminal. O'Malley looked around at all the other people dressed in their cloaks and wide brimmed hats. He couldn't suppress a chuckle. "Looks like something out of science fiction movie."

Two guards with assault rifles strapped behind them motioned everyone toward a waiting bus. One of the guards, a large man with broad shoulders and small waist seemed to be in charge.

"Everyone get on board. We're running late so move your asses," he shouted.

The other guard gave those in the rear of the group a shove to hasten them on their way. One who received a shove from behind was O'Malley. He turned and looked at the guard in defiance.

"Move!" shouted the guard who reached for the rifle on his back and brandished the weapon, butt first, to threaten O'Malley.

President Chambers cautioned the agent to relax. "Don't put up a fight. It won't do us any good."

O'Malley turned, moved forward and stepped up onto the bus. He sat next to the general and the bus moved off toward the perimeter of the airfield onto a service road which headed out into the desert.

"That idiot of a guard had better watch his step," said O'Malley.

The general made a face. "A typical roughneck but Chambers was right. It won't pay us to get into skirmishes with them. It's what they would like."

The bus continued along the road and there was nothing but sand in every direction. A while later the steel towers of the oil refinery appear on the horizon.

"We are here," said Chambers. The bus pulled up outside a concrete structure and stopped. Everyone rose out of their seats and filed off the bus onto the concrete apron which skirted the structure.

"This is the control room for the entire plant. It's the only habitable building above ground; all the offices, meeting rooms and washrooms are below ground for obvious reasons," said Chambers.

The star's rays beat down on them with a merciless heat and they were thankful for the protective gear which shielded them from its harmful radiation. Two of the guards who had accompanied them jumped off the bus and ushered the group toward an entrance portal which led underground. O'Malley looked around at what he could see of the plant. Dozens of steel pipes ran in horizontal rows, supported on columns and girders. Fractionators, pressure vessels, and storage tanks were dotted all over the place, each joined by pipes carrying fuel or steam. Heat exchangers, compressors, and pumps moved the product in all directions forming a familiar picture for O'Malley who had at one time worked in an oil refinery between semesters at the university.

"The large storage tanks contain tons of refined product," said Swales. "The president and I have to meet with the shift foreman who is going to show us what we will be doing. You and the general will meet the plant trainer in the projection room. We'll see you at the end of the shift."

O'Malley and General Mumford walked off down a long corridor lit by neon lights while Chambers and Swales made their way to the control room.

The projection room, so called because management showed a lot of training videos, was air conditioned and the men could feel the difference as they entered the facility. Rows of chairs faced a screen at the far end where a man waited for them.

"Welcome to the Thousand Dunes Refinery, gentlemen. My name is Kieth Harbor and I will be the one who trains you for the work to be performed in the plant. Please do not bother me with your plight as an inmate at Camp Logan, or ask why it is you are here. I don't care. I will see to your work-related needs as best I can."

"You have a plant identity number programmed into the chip in your arm—present it to the scanner whenever you record anything. Lunch will be at 1:00 pm in the canteen and then you will both return here to complete your orientation. Take a seat and the video will start shortly."

O'Malley and the general each took a seat while the trainer went into the projection room. Minutes later the video came on to instruct them on all the main details of the plant and its layout. It was followed by a video on plant safety and what to do in the event of an emergency. At 11:00 am the trainer appeared and handed them each a book. "You will find several multi-choice tests in the book. You can sit at the back of the room at the tables provided and complete them. Pens are provided. You need to finish by 11:45 am so we can have time for questions. Please begin."

Both O'Malley and General Mumford felt as though they had been cast back in time to their school days. They looked at each other and grinned. "Bet I beat you in the final score," said the general.

"You're on," said O'Malley.

Forty-five minutes later they handed their tests in. Kieth Harbor took the books. "Time for questions."

O'Malley asked first. "How is it that you can trust prisoners to work in a plant that is as potentially dangerous as this?"

"That's easy to answer, Mr, O'Malley. Our prisoners are merely political dissidents. They are not hardcore criminals who want to sabotage things. They know they are only here for twelve months and all want to get back home again. We are far from any towns or cities and it would not make sense for them to escape. No one would make it through the desert in the heat, anyway. Also, to sabotage any of the equipment is to sign one's own death warrant."

"How is the final product delivered and to where?" asked the general.

The trainer turned to a white board and picked up a dry marker pen. He made a circle to indicate the plant and then in the top corner of the board he made another circle to indicate the end-point of delivery.

"This is the plant's storage facility and here is the end stage of delivery." He pointed to each of the circles. We have a five-foot diameter pipe running between the main storage tank and the end stage. It's a distance of three-hundred and fifty miles."

Knowing a little about refineries O'Malley made a comment. "Where we come from our refineries have a special process of inspection along the line. It's called a pig and it's also used to deliver non-fuel goods to the final destination and stuff needed at the source."

Harbor nodded. "We have exactly the same thing."

A plan began to form in O'Malley's mind.✳

17

Seventeen

Kurtis Banks checked off the items on the list. The other three mercenaries stood by hoping their accumulation of weapons, ordnance and provisions met with the leader's approval. Banks came across as a hard task master but a fair one. His men respected his judgment.

"We seem to be missing a case of ammo. I asked for four cases—I see only three."

The tallest of the three combatants gave the explanation. "One case is in the emergency pack, Commander."

Banks turned to a large backpack which stood upright against the wall and opened the flap.

"What else is in this pack?"

"Eight extra grenades and four M16 cleaning kits, Sir."

Banks gave the man a look that would wither a lion and moved on to the four M16A4 assault rifles which also leaned against the wall. He picked one up, turned it over in his hands and sighted down the barrel. "What about the MB40?"

"It's ready to go, Sir."

The tall mercenary soldier lifted the cover off the machine gun and several belts of ammunition which lay on the floor. He stooped down, lifted the weapon and handed it to Banks for scrutiny.

"What about the rations?"

One of the other men a short, squat man with huge biceps answered.

"We have enough food and water for five days, Commander."

"Good—everything seems to be in order," said Banks. "Let's talk tactics."

He moved over to the opposite wall and cleaned off some writing on the white board. An adjacent notice-board contained a range of aerial photographs of the target. Banks drew a circle in the center of the whiteboard and a perimeter around it. "This is the silo. Our approach is from the Yellow sea and up along the Yalu River. We will pass through Dandong, on the Chinese side, and then further up we will pass through Chongsu. A wide bank of sand in the river will serve as our landing point, where we will leave our vessel. It is a matter of one day's hike to the silo from the river. The silo is situated in between the Sea of Japan and the Chinese border. It is the extreme north end of DPRK land."

The tall man raised a hand. Banks lifted his chin and narrowed his eyelids. "I'll take questions when I'm through talking, Ian."

The man looked at the ground and gave a sheepish grin.

"Finding this amusing, Ian?"

The man gave him a wounded look. "No, Sir."

Banks continued. "Our vessel is an old fishing boat which I've hired from one of the local Chinese. They make regular trips up and down the Yalu River and he says we should have no trouble getting into North Korea from our drop-off point. As I said, one day's hike will get us closer to the perimeter of the silo."

Banks pointed to a photograph on the notice-board. "This group of trees will make good cover and a place to rest before we attack our target."

He pointed to the tall mercenary. "You and the Brat will do a recce of the silo area and verify the guard's positions. Any questions?"

The tall man jumped in. "Our mission is to blow the silo?"

"That's correct. We are getting good money for this mission and our client doesn't want any questions asked. I am the only one who knows the details. You guys will deal with the guards and the security system. You will set the explosives. Is this clear enough for you?"

"Yes, Sir," said the tall man. None of the men dared cross their commander.

The short man with the muscular biceps, known as the Brat, raised his hand. "How are we traveling?"

"I have plane tickets for Seoul in South Korea where our client has arranged passage with our ordnance and supplies, to a spot off the Chinese coast. We will then use a zodiac to slip onto a remote beach at night. It will be a short hike to the fishing village on the Yalu River where my Chinese contact will take us in his fishing boat to the drop-off point."

"When do we leave," asked the third man. He had been quiet up to this point.

"In two weeks—so, make sure you're one hundred and ten percent ready when the time comes. We will meet here and drive to the airport."

*

The four mercenary soldiers arrived at the airport on time to catch the plane to Seoul. They were all in high spirits. There would be time for ruminating on the possible outcome but for the next few hours they would drink and be merry. Commander Banks delivered the ordnance to a specific address as agreed with the general and he trusted that the supplies and arms would find safe ferry with the military jet which would fly everything to the base in Seoul.

On their arrival in Seoul, they cleared customs and made their way via taxi to the American base situated near the border with North Korea. Once at the base Banks spoke to a contact given by the general and they were driven to the South Korean Navy harbor where a frigate awaited them. The men were all confined to a cabin below deck on the captain's orders and all they could do was wait. At two am the next morning a knock came on their cabin's door and they knew the dangerous part of their journey had begun.

A Zodiac, on deck at the back of the frigate, would serve as their transport to the Chinese mainland and the men climbed in. A bundle of goods had been crammed into the bow and Banks checked to see that it contained all the supplies and ordnance for the job. Moments later the zodiac hit the water. Ian started the outboard and the others hung on for dear life. The Zodiac's bow raised high in the water and they sped off toward the distant coastline. Two hours later the breaking of waves ahead revealed that they had arrived. It took another hour before the Zodiac landed safely and was pulled up the beach to a cluster of bushes where it would remain hidden until their return. The three mercenary soldiers offloaded the ordinance and supplies while Banks checked for the one item he had not included, but which the general promised to supply—a satellite phone.

Each man took his share of supplies, all in backpacks and laden down, they made their way along the beach to a point where Banks found the path to the village.

"Can't believe we're in China," said the Brat.

"Chinky, chinky, chink," said Ian. You had better pull your eyes into slits with your fingers if we come across anyone."

"You speak Chinese don't you, boss?" asked the third man.

Banks reprimanded them. "Shut your traps. We're in enemy territory and sound carries in the cold air."

They marched on in silence. All four men, fit and strong, were in the prime of their lives. The military had taught them to be violent and tough. Each carried a M16A4 assault rifle and the Brat, who boasted to be the strongest amongst them, carried the machine-gun, as well. Three hours later they detected the breaking of dawn on the horizon and Banks stopped to check his compass. Satisfied that they were headed in the right direction he gave the order to carry on. Ten minutes after that they saw the light of a fire and the outlines of several rural huts.

"Wait here," said Banks. "I'll go ahead and see if I can find my contact."

The sun began to rise and the men could see they had reached the banks of a wide river.

"It must be the Yalu," said Ian.

"I'm hungry," said the Brat.

"You're always hungry," said the third man.

Banks appeared with a wizened little man wrapped in a blanket.

"Meet Jong Shoo," said Banks.

The little man bowed and spoke in broken English.

"Welcome in China, gentlemen."

'Do you have coffee in your hut?" asked the Brat.

"Me have black tea and goat's milk," said Jong Shoo.

"I'll drink oil if I have to," said the third soldier.

"Let's go. We'll have to spend the day out of sight in Jong Shoo's hut. He will be leaving to sail up the river tonight, so you will at least be able to get some sleep."

The men followed on, crossed the village perimeter and entered a mud-brick, yurt-type abode which Jong Shoo proudly proclaimed as his home. They settled in while Jong Shoo made the tea. He dished up a bowl of rice for each of them and heated up some goat's meat on a small wood-burning stove. There were no beds or chairs so the men spread out sleeping bags, ate the meal and slept for the rest of the day.

Later that afternoon Banks woke them and they made ready to leave when darkness fell. Their guide assured them it would take several hours to get to the place of disembarkation and to be on the safe side they were to remain in the single cabin below deck. Around two am in the morning Jong Shoo poked his head through the open floor hatch.

"We here," he said.

Most of the width of the Yalu River was considered to be Chinese territory but tradition gave both North Korea and Chinese fishermen equal fishing rights. According to Jong Shoo, there had never been any incidents. Banks came up on deck and scanned the opposite bank. The moon shone brightly, unhindered by the skimpy cloud cover and he could see the sandy beach clearly. A low whistle brought the other three mercenaries up onto the deck, each with backpack and rifle. The Brat handed Banks his gear and with nods to Jong Shoo, they slid into the bank in midstream. A short distance remained between the midstream bank and the river bank. A short swim in the cold water brought the mercenaries to the river bank where they regrouped and crept into the bushes like ghosts.

Their coveralls, made of special water resistant material, dried quickly as they made their way deeper into the bush. Banks consulted his compass to get his bearings and they struck out toward the silo. Each man felt the emotional rush of adrenaline as they crept along, their senses honed for any sound or sighting which might spell danger. Everything appeared to be running like clockwork but Banks, a fifteen year veteran of special force operations, would be taking no chances.

An hour later Banks held up a closed fist and the men all stopped in their tracks. He listened intently and then gave the signal for them to move off the path and fall flat in the high grass. The reason for the command became evident moments later when a group of DPRK soldiers, came jogging along toward their position. The mercenaries lay silent in the grass and waited. The leader of the group came to a sudden stop and looked around. He turned and babbled a few curt sentences in Korean to his men. They responded with grunts of obedience and went down on their haunches. The section of the path meandered through the open ground with only a scattered bush here and there. Banks cursed their luck that this band of soldiers had chosen the exact spot where he and his men lay hidden in the grass to stop for a break.

The grass extended to knee-height which gave the mercenaries very little depth to hide in. Each man lay as still as he could and listened. Their eyes were turned toward the position in which they last saw their leader. If he gave the order they would come up on their knees firing but each knew it was too early for any confrontations. The best course of action would be to wait it out. The Korean soldiers would move on as soon as their leader felt they had taken sufficient rest.

As the minutes ticked by Banks realized that the soldiers had not detected their presence and he continued to wait. Moments later the leader stood up and gave an order. The soldiers all rose to their feet with one accord and continued on their journey. When they were out of earshot the mercenaries stood to their feet and breathed heavy sighs of relief.

Banks gave an order. "Come on ladies—you're not on a shopping trip. Let's move."

"They were so close I could smell their stinking breath," said the Brat. The other two soldiers laughed, but Banks tore into them.

"Shut your traps and concentrate. Neither of you fagots heard them coming because your egos were caught up in the moment. We still have an hour to go before we arrive at the silo."

For the next fifty minutes, the men all jogged along in silence until Banks held up the closed fist again and they all stopped.

"We're here," he said.

✳

17

Gerry and Steve in Trouble

Gerry and Steve, caught in the sudden glare of the overhead light, froze at the sight of the man who blocked their escape. He stood over six feet tall with broad shoulders and huge biceps in both arms. His bald head gleamed and his eyes held theirs with malevolent intent. The man behind them made a suggestion.

"Why don't we step into the office and talk?"

The two boys, terrified out of their wits, recognized him as the person in the park. He turned and motioned for them to follow. Moments later they all stepped into an office and the man indicated for them to sit on the floor against one of the walls.

Gerry found his tongue. "What do you want with us?"

"That depends," said the man. "Why did you follow us and what are you doing here?"

"We weren't following you," said Steven.

"Then why are you here?" asked the man.

Steven tried to think of a good reason other than the real one.

"We thought it might be a good place to smoke some pot."

Their captor chuckled. "Oh, come now, young man. You honestly don't expect me to believe that?"

"It's true," echoed Gerry.

The man turned to one of his accomplices. "Search their pockets."

The accomplice complied and came up with nothing but a packet of cigarettes, however, Steve's wallet contained his driver's license.

"I see your name is Steven O'Malley." Said the man.

Steven stared at him but said nothing.

The man continued. "An ordinary pack of smokes is not pot. Why are you lying?"

The boys did not know how to answer so they remained silent. At that moment Vera stepped into the room which caused Steven to gasp in surprise. For a second he thought it was his mother but then realized it could not be her. He did not know anything about Janet O'Malley's abduction and consequent rescue by his father but he remembered she had seen her double a few days previously. In a quick act of deduction, he knew this woman had to be an imposter. It stunned him to see how closely she resembled his mother.

"You are the FBI agent's son, aren't you?" Vera asked.

Steven gulped and remained silent.

"You did not follow us by mere chance," said the man. "This is not a coincidence, is it?"

Neither of the boys could speak. Both felt an overwhelming sense of foreboding. These people were criminals and they knew Steven's dad was an FBI agent.

Gerry's nerve broke. "Please don't harm us. We saw you speaking to my mom in the park this morning and just wondered who you were."

"Bullshit," said the man. "You have obviously realized the woman, who has recently entered your home, is not your mother. My guess is that you and your young friend here tipped the FBI off and decided to follow her this morning to see who she was meeting with. You must have also followed me back here to Atlantic City."

Both boys stared at him with fear in their eyes.

The man scowled and he turned to Vera. "We have to eliminate them. I cannot sanction their transfer to Terra as they were not targeted for replacement—the Council will not allow it."

"They're so young, Alan. We can't just eliminate them," answered Vera.

"I know it seems harsh but it's the only way."

He motioned to the bald-headed, muscle man. "You know what must be done—eliminate them. We have to get back to the office and remove any evidence of the operation. I must conclude that our main office has been compromised."

*

Gwen Farrell watched young Steven O'Malley exit his home in Baltimore and climb into Gerry Swales's Mustang. Her assignment from O'Malley had been to keep an eye on his son's movements. In light of Janet O'Malley's recent abduction, it had been felt that the family might be in some danger. Several agents had been charged with the job of keeping an eye on Steven and his mother. It meant a boring period where each agent would have to endure hours of vigilance.

All the detailed security took it seriously. ever, It had fallen to Gwen to keep an eye on Steven. The agents used their own private vehicles so as not to raise any suspicions from the neighbors and parked as inconspicuously as possible outside the O'Malley home. Janet, watched by one of Gwen's colleagues, dropped her son off at school each morning. Once Gwen knew he was safe she would go back to her other assignments and return to the school at the close of the day. Since Janet's abduction and consequent rescue, there had been no suggestion of any danger and Gwen was beginning to think the assignment a waste of time.

The situation had, however, become more omi-nous with the sudden disappearance of O'Malley. Deputy Director James Ingram felt confident that Janet's abductors and O'Malley's sudden disap-pearance were linked to the same people. All the agents had become accustomed to precede their personal greetings with the password, each time they met.

It was Saturday and Gwen had started her day's vigil outside the O'Malley's home at 5:30 am. Ger-ry Swales arrived at 6:15 am to pick Steven up and they took off. She witnessed most of what took place that morning. At midday, the boys left the office block for downtown Atlantic City where they enjoyed a meal of burgers and fries and then sub-sequently window-shopped for clothes before heading out to the industrial area again.

Gwen continued to tail them. After an hour's wait at the office block, she saw a group of seven people exit the building, climb into two vehicles and drive off toward the downtown area. The boys took off after them and ended up outside a local pub where they hung around and waited beneath the canopy of a tree. Two hours later the group of seven exited the pub and drove to a warehouse in the light in-dustrial section of the city.

The Mustang pulled off the road and parked on the verge while the group entered the warehouse premises and drove around to the back. Gwen recognized the building to be the warehouse facility in which O'Malley had shot and killed the two men. She drove on down the road, turned right at the next intersection, parked the vehicle and made a quick call to Roland MacDonald. He answered immediately.

"Where are you?" she asked.

He told her that he was following up a lead in Philadelphia and suggested she wait for him to arrive. Gwen considered his comment but anticipated the danger the two young boys were in.

"You're at least an hour away, Roland. I will need to take some action if the boys get into any trouble."

MacDonald conceded and made a further suggestion. "Keep as low a profile as possible—use your own discretion, but be careful."

It took Gwen a minute to walk to the intersection. She peered through the gloom toward the warehouse, illuminated by the dull, yellow glow of the streetlight.

She waited. A few moments later the two boys left the Mustang, crept along the fence toward the warehouse and entered the building via a roll-up door. Moments later Gwen followed them into the dark interior.

A light in an adjoining corridor came on with a sudden flash of brilliant intensity and Gwen's heart skipped a beat. She pulled her pistol from its holster and crept along the corridor with caution. Somewhere in the building, she could hear voices. The corridor took a right-angled turn where she stopped to listen and heard a man's voice give a clear instruction to someone else:

"Eliminate them."

Gwen quickly concluded that the instruction referred to the two boys. She cursed the fact that MacDonald was so far away. Her heart beat like a solo drum in consideration of the options which remained to her. It would have been better if MacDonald was present to take the lead. The thought of waiting for reinforcements crossed her mind but two young lives were at stake.

One of the youngsters cried out in fear and Gwen knew something would have to be done. A moment later a man exited from an office and headed for a door which appeared to lead outside. Two woman and two men followed in his footsteps. Gwen remembered the original number of the group to be seven people and a quick calculation revealed that two men were still in the office with the boys.

She waited until the outside door had closed before making a move. Fear coursed through her body like a wave as she tried to remember her training. She hesitated for a moment and then stepped into the office and sighted along the barrel of the pistol.

The two men who stood in the center of the office whirled around to face the young agent. The boys, crouched down at the back wall, stared in surprise at her sudden entrance. One of the men went for his gun.

18

Putting the Plan into Action

The canteen in the refinery provided meals, mostly comprising of sandwiches and salads. O'Malley and General Mumford sat at a table in a corner, far from the service counter and chatted. There were no windows as the facility had been built below ground. Most of the habitable work spaces were sub-surface in order to shield from the star's harmful radiation. The air-conditioning worked effectively and the overhead lights provided good illumination. Several other workers sat at the tables eating their lunches and no one took any notice of O'Malley or Mumford.

O'Malley swallowed a bite of his sandwich and eyed the general. "I have a plan. I'm sure you noticed that the destination of the refined oil, via the pipeline, is on the West Coast of the continent. It would correspond to California in the USA."

General Mumford nodded. "This refinery seems to be part of a grid which supplies their entire west coast. What do you propose?"

"If we can find our way to the maintenance station where the pigs are deployed into the main pipeline I might be able to smuggle myself on board one of them."

"How do these things work," asked Mumford.

"A pig is simply a capsule that fits snuggly in the pipeline and acts as a division between different grades of refined oil. It prevents the different products from mixing with each other. The pig also cleans the line and has a chamber which provides a means of sending certain articles, documents, and parts to the end destination."

"You mean the pig returns to the refinery? How does it do that?" asked Mumford.

"The pig is returned by compressed air after each batch of product has reached the destination. This is where the line is cleaned and excess oil is pushed back to be pumped into the refinery's slop tank for reprocessing."

"Is there breathable air in the chamber?" asked Mumford.

"It's hard to say but the area of the chamber is about 125 cubic feet and will probably contain enough breathable air for about six hours before a dangerous amount of carbon-dioxide from exhaled breath accumulates."

Mumford narrowed his eyelids. "We'll need to find out a few more details. I remember Harbor said that the end destination was three-hundred and fifty miles away. We need to know how fast this pig thing travels."

"I will get these details from our trainer. I wonder what job he's going to give us?" ventured O'Malley.

"What happens at the destination? When the pig arrives you will be discovered when they open the chamber."

O'Malley rubbed his chin. "If it operates the same way ours do then the pig will be removed from the line and the chamber will automatically be opened by the master control computer. The contents will be deposited onto a platform and transported by a conveyor to the parcels receiving area. I will be able to step off the platform when the boxes are deposited onto the conveyor."

"Aren't you assuming a bunch of things?" asked Mumford.

"Perhaps, but we have to take a few risks if we ever want to see home again," answered O'Malley.

With lunch over the two men headed back to the training center. Kieth Harbor handed them each a manual.

"The procedures for the jobs you will be perform-ing are in these books. It's not rocket science and men of your education level will find it easy, maybe even boring. As the months go by, however, I'm sure we'll find you both more interesting things to do."

"What job do you have for me?" asked O'Malley.

"Since you appear to have some experience of refineries and the transfer of oil I have allocated you a job in the batch deliveries department. You'll pick it up very quickly. It entails tracking the product batches delivered to our distribution depot on the West coast. You will report to the department manager, James Iverson and he will get you started."

Not to be left out General Mumford interrupted. "What do you have for me?"

Harbor smiled. "You will be working with production, planning, and control. The job entails the ongoing planning of production in accordance with the projected consumption figures for our part of the country."

The general raised his eyebrows but held his peace. Kieth Harbor motioned the two men to take a seat at the tables in the rear of the center to begin their studies. "You can spend the rest of the afternoon going through the manuals—tomorrow, I will introduce you to your departmental managers."

He returned to his desk and left the men to peruse their respective manuals. After three hours a klaxon sounded and they made their way back to the change rooms to retrieve their protective clothing.

*

That night after their return from the refinery to the camp O'Malley and Mumford conferred with President Chambers and his chief of staff, Beverley Swales, as they all sat around a table eating dinner.

"In what part of the refinery are you working, Mr. President?" asked O'Malley.

"In the maintenance planning department. I have to work out the labor and materials for all the scheduled plant maintenance."

"What about you, ma'am?"

"I'm working in the canteen making lunches. I saw you and the general at lunchtime but couldn't leave the task I had been given," answered Swales.

O'Malley shared the work details he and the general had been allocated.

"I couldn't have hoped for a better assignment. I have a little experience of how refineries work and saw an opportunity to escape. I planted a seed in the trainer's mind and it worked."

He shared the plan with them. The president frowned deeply.

"This will be extremely dangerous, O'Malley. You run the risk of suffocating in the pig's chamber plus being caught when the operator opens the chamber at the destination."

O'Malley chuckled. "No pain, no gain, Sir. Believe me, I've been in worst situations than this. If I can get away, return to the dimensional link and get back to our universe, we may have a chance of turning the tide. I am the best equipped to make this escape attempt."

"No contest, O'Malley. I'm sure if anyone can do it, you will be that person. But say you are able to get back to our universe, what will you do?" asked the president.

"I'll find out who else has been compromised and expose the imposters. Once we have the decision-making process back under control special forces will return to Terra. The three of you will be rescued along with any others who might have been replaced."

Swales saw problems. "How will you find your way back to the dimensional link?—it's on the other side of the continent."

"I don't know, but I will find a way. Once I'm in a big city it will be easier for me to work my way across the country to Terra's replica of New York."

Mumford chipped in. "If my memory serves me correctly Captain Penn called it Liberty City."

Hilda, the camp administrator entered the canteen and headed straight for their table. She stopped next to O'Malley.

"How was your first day at the refinery, Agent O'-Malley?" she asked.

"It was very interesting. It will certainly help me pass the time," he answered.

Hilda placed her hands on the table and stared into O'Malley's eyes. "We are well aware of your abilities, Mr. O'Malley. You're probably thinking of escaping from this place but forget it. If we find that any of you are planning something you will be isolated from each other. That chip in your fore-arm will tell us exactly where you are at all times."

"Thank's for the heads up, Hilda. We'll bear that in mind," said O'Malley.

She looked around at each one with a smirk on her face. "We have a political orientation class in fif-teen minutes. This is where you get to learn how things operate here on Terra. Make sure you are in the main hall." She straightened up, turned on her heel and headed out of the canteen.

Mumford glanced at O'Malley. "I forgot about the chip. That makes things a little more difficult for you."

O'Malley nodded. "We will have to think of a way to circumvent that. Maybe I can remove the chip when the time comes. I think we'll need to plan this escape very carefully and make sure all the bases are covered."

"You should leave it for a while. Let them think you're settling down," said President Chambers.

"That is a good idea, Sir. I suggest we all give it some thought and I will look at the refinery's product delivery schedule to see when would be a good time for me to make a move."

They finished their meals and returned to the main meeting hall. About forty people sat in the chairs waiting for the commencement of the indoctrination.

"This should be interesting," remarked Swales.

"Maybe we'll actually learn something from their system of government," said Mumford.

A tall, bearded man arrived and took the podium. He introduced himself as Doctor Victor Sands and gave an impressive list of his qualifications before launching into his lesson.

"You are all here at the pleasure of The Council—"

*

MacDonald drove furiously along the highway toward New Jersey. Martinez's hands cradled his revolver and his eyes, void of expression, stared at the road as they raced toward the warehouse.

"We shouldn't have left her on her own," growled MacDonald.

"She'll be fine," answered Martinez.

"It's her first time, for Christ's sake. She might panic and get herself killed."

"She's well trained, Roland. Sometimes the first experience brings out the best in a new agent."

"I hope you're right. I just wish we had all stuck together."

"You know only too well that we couldn't cover all the bases if we had done that," said Martinez.

Macdonald glanced at the dash clock. "I hope we're not too late."

They approached the warehouse and MacDonald slowed down. All looked tranquil in the yellow light of the street lamp and the first thing they noticed was Gerry Swales mustang parked on the verge.

"I don't see her car."

"She may have parked around the corner up ahead, so as not to be seen," answered Martinez. They parked behind the mustang and slipped out of the SUV both with weapons in hand and crept quietly up to the front entrance of the warehouse. MacDonald tried the door but found it locked.

"There's a roll-up door down at the end of the building. It's half open," said Martinez.

The two agents left the front entrance and walked quickly along the wall to the half-open door. Mac-Donald pulled a flashlight from his jacket's pocket and shone it into the interior. The light revealed the old machinery and equipment on the floor. A distant internal light in the corridor which led from the factory area beckoned them and they crept passed the machinery to investigate further. The corridor took a ninety-degree turn and as they approached the next office they heard a groan.

MacDonald rushed forward with his gun at the ready and Martinez followed closely on behind. They stepped into the office.

19

Gwen Slips up

Gwen took in the man's movements with an eye trained to anticipate consequences. She saw the flash of light on the hammer of his revolver as he tried to beat the projectile he knew would come his way. Fractions of a second later the bullet from Gwen's gun knocked him off balance and he crumpled to the floor, dropping his weapon. The other man froze with one hand hovering over his own revolver which had been shoved into the top of his pants. The look on his face portrayed his surprise at Gwen's sudden appearance.

"Don't even think about it," she said in a calm, clear voice. He did think about it but Gwen held the ace in her hand, pointed directly at him. She moved forward as he stood in front of her.

"Lift your hands above your head." Her voice remained steady as she reached forward to remove his gun. The moment she touched the revolver she realized it was a mistake. The man took advantage of the split second she had torn her eyes from his, to glance down at the gun. It happened quicker than she could react. His right hand moved like lightning and knocked her gun hand downward while his left fist jabbed straight at her face. In the brief second, she had to contemplate the maneuver he caught her on the side of the jaw. The blow was not enough to knock her down but sufficient to divert the shot instinctively fired from the gun she held.

He pulled his own weapon, pointed it and at point-blank range pulled the trigger. It all played out in an act of slow motion in Gwen's mind. She cursed herself for breaking one of the golden rules of her training—taking her eyes off her quarry. The bullet from the man's gun ripped into her midriff and blasted her over backward. When the gun smoke cleared she lay on her back and stared up at the ceiling with wide open eyes. Darkness closed in and only a buzzing in the ears remained until that too, disappeared.

The two boys continued to stare in horror at the scene. Their salvation seemed so close until the tables had turned in favor of their captors. The first man whom Gwen had shot groaned and tried to sit up. The other man checked the agent over and decided she would not give them any more trouble. He turned to his wounded comrade and saw that Gwen's bullet had hit him in the shoulder. He pulled out his cell phone and made a hasty call.

"You need to return immediately. We've had an event and Bruce is injured."

Alan McHale's voice grated in his ear. "What sort of an event? Have you dealt with the two boys?"

The man explained what had happened and waited for his instructions.

"Wait there. I'm turning around and we will be there in ten minutes."

"What about the two boys?" the man asked.

"Hold them. Don't do anything—I have an idea."

A short time later McHale, Vera, and the others re-entered the building and made their way to the office. They all helped to remove the fallen man and carted him back outside to the waiting vehicle.

The two boys, still bound, were herded into the back of the minivan. Three members of the group returned to the white truck which had been parked at the back of the building. Vera took the wheel and ten minutes later, out on the highway, the departing vehicles passed a black SUV traveling in the opposite direction at a high rate of speed.

McHale turned to Vera. "It looks like we managed to dodge the reinforcements."

Vera chuckled. "They're in for a surprise."

"I need to make a quick call," said McHale. He reached into the glove compartment and pulled out a burner.

*

McDonald and Martinez found Gwen sitting up and rubbing her midriff. She gave them a baleful look. "I know, don't say it. I blew it. My first confrontation and I broke the golden rule."

Martinez helped her to her feet. "Lucky you were wearing a vest."

"It still knocked me out and it hurts like hell," she complained.

"You could have been killed. Why didn't you wait for us?" asked MacDonald.

"I heard one of the boys cry out and I concluded that these people were going to hurt the youngsters." She shared what had taken place.

"Put it down to a first experience. You won't make that mistake again," said Martinez.

MacDonald looked around the office. "They must have taken the two boys with them. We need to return to that office block in Atlantic City. My guess, however, is that they will realize it has been compromised. We need to check it out, anyway."

They filed out of the building and back to the SUV. By this time Gwen had recovered from her ordeal and suffered only painful abs. The worst negative for her lay in the mistake she had made. They drove off in the direction of the office block. Half an hour later they parked and crept up to the building. No sign of anyone remained and Mac-Donald looked at his watch.

"It's 10:00 pm and there doesn't appear to be anyone home."

Martinez looked at the sign. "An event planning business. It makes a good front for their real occupation."

MacDonald tried the front door. "It's open. I think the birds have flown the coup."

They searched the open area on the ground floor and then made their way up the stairs. Three offices and a meeting room revealed nothing of importance until Martinez discovered a box with some effects. "Looks like they forgot to take this with them."

Gwen piped up from the meeting room. "There's three cups of half-finished coffee here. I think they left in a hurry."

Martinez poked around in the box and pulled out a cell phone. "Look at this. It's FBI issue and I'm sure it belonged to Dillon."

The others crowded around him to have a look at the phone Martinez held in his hand. "That's his phone," said MacDonald. "I don't know if this is a good or a bad sign. All it tells us is that they removed him from the vehicle accident."

"If he had been killed we would have found him by now," said Gwen.

"Do you think they have him holed up somewhere?" ventured Martinez.

"It seems probable. We have to find out where they've gone."

"That'll be like trying to find a needle in a haystack," said Martinez.

"We need to get back to the office. I'll call up the sketch artist and you will need to give him an idea of what these two guys looked like," said MacDonald.

Gwen nodded. "I had a good look at the guy who shot me but the first fellow went down when I pulled the trigger and I don't remember much about him."

The three agents returned to their respective vehicles and headed back to Washington DC.

MacDonald knew he had one difficult call to make. Janet O'Malley would be wondering why her son never returned home and thought anxiously about how much he should share with her. Back at the office, the sketch artist waited for Gwen to finish her cup of coffee and the two of them got to work. MacDonald reluctantly placed the call to Janet

O'Malley. She answered on the first ring and he took a deep breath.

"Janet, I have bad news for you."

Her silence told its own story and he continued. "Steven and Gerry have got themselves into a bit of trouble."

He told her the story up to the time they found Gwen in the old warehouse outside Atlantic City. Janet began to cry and give vent to her fears. "It has to be the same group who abducted me. What are we going to do, Roland? First Dillon goes missing and now Steve. I can't lose both of them."

MacDonald steeled himself to answer. "We are doing everything we can to locate Steve and Dillon. Just sit tight and I hope to have more news by the morning."

He was not sure why he said that but he realized they did not have any answers and wanted to end the conversation as quickly as possible.

*

After McHale had spoken to Francis Bowman, the woman who had replaced Beverley Swales as chief of staff, they drove to a private home in Atlantic City, New Jersey. The home, an investment made by Swales many years prior, would serve as their new office. Bowman, now impersonating Swales, had given the tenant notice in order to keep the premises as a backup in case their headquarter offices were compromised.

On arrival, McHale gave two of the men orders to lock the boys up in a steel cargo container, situated in the backyard of the two-story home while the rest trooped up the stairs. The container could not be seen from the street.

"What are we going to do with the boys?" asked Vera.

McHale sat down at a desk and opened up a laptop. "Just in case the FBI gets onto us I'm going to keep them as an insurance."

"That's not a bad idea—that way we will not have to eliminate them. When the time comes for us to make our escape we can release them," said Vera.

"I'm afraid we will not be able to release them. They have seen our faces and by now they know something about our operation. We can't take any chances."

Vera looked a little crestfallen. "I understand."

McHale closed the computer, stood to his feet and took Vera in his arms. "The only other person who might know what we're up to is Special Agent O'-Malley and he is on his way to Terra."

"What about his wife, Janet?" Vera asked.

"I doubt she knows anything. The only person she has seen is her own double, which is you."

They kissed passionately for a few moments until Vera pulled her head back and looked into McHale's eyes. "When do we get to go back home?"

"Three doppelgängers will arrive in ten days, or so. Once they are in place and I have monitored their progress for a few weeks, we can think about returning for a rest."

She smiled. "I'm looking forward to tying up the loose ends back on Terra but I guess it will be sometime before we can return to Earth."

McHale concurred. "At least eighteen months, my sweet. Our people have much to accomplish and time is, unfortunately, a commodity we don't have on our side."

20

O'Malley and The Pig

One detail of O'Malley's plan remained to be resolved before he could execute an effective escape. The security at Camp Logan ran a daily monitoring program to ensure that all of the inmates were present on the camp property or at the refinery. An alarm would be raised should there be a cessation of any chip signals.

The only viable option he possessed was to remove the chip and keep it responding to the satellite while it remained hidden in someone else's pocket. Even with the correct equipment, it would be a painful extraction and a pain-killing drug would be needed to help him function as normally as possible in the immediate aftermath of the extraction. O'Malley, under the pretense he had a migraine headache, visited the small clinic where he managed to secure a scalpel and a box of painkillers, while Beverley Swales distracted the camp's nurse. That night General Mumford performed the small operation while O'Malley stoically bared the pain of the chip's removal. He kept it in the pocket of his coverall for a few days to make sure the extraction had not been picked up by the security.

A week later the product delivery schedule revealed that several boxes of documents were due to be delivered to the central distribution plant on the west coast. All the details with regard to runtimes and speed of transfer satisfied O'Malley that there would be sufficient oxygen in the chamber for the duration of his journey. That morning General Mumford slipped away from his office to shut the special agent into the pig's service chamber along with the documents for transfer. Under normal circumstances, it would be O'Malley's job to load the boxes and seal the chamber before sending the pig on its way.

The night before the planned escape Chambers, Swales and Mumford whispered their farewells to an excited O'Malley as they sat at the dinner table in the camp's canteen. The three alien inmates knew the FBI agent held the only hope of ever seeing Earth and their loved ones again. On the following morning, the journey to the refinery seemed to take forever and O'Malley could not wait to get on with it. He explained the delivery procedure to the general once the boxes were packed inside, and then climbed into the chamber. All Mumford had to do was push one key on the computer's keypad and the system would take care of the rest.

"I'll see you when I see you," said O'Malley.

The general placed a hand on O'Malley's shoulder."The journey to the final stage for distribution should take four-and-half hours. You will only be missed at the end of the day when they take roll call, before the journey back to camp."

"I should have arrived at the end destination by then," answered O'Malley.

General Mumford stepped back to close the chamber's hatch. "Fare thee well, my friend," he said.

O'Malley had one final suggestion to make. "They will not know what happened to me provided my escape is not detected at the other end. Don't forget to keep my chip with you during the day and leave it in my room overnight. Should you fall into any danger of being interrogated over my disappearance then get rid of the chip immediately."

"I will—may God go with you," said Mumford.

"Thanks, General. I could certainly do with a miracle. Look after the president and his chief of staff. I make you a promise I will return for you," said O'Malley.

Mumford handed him a parcel. "Your protective clothing. You will need them."

The general closed the chamber's hatch. The station's system would insert the pig into the main pipeline when the batch viscosities changed and O'Malley would find himself propelled along at close to eighty miles per hour until the pig reached the final delivery destination.

Mumford stepped up to the controlling computer's keyboard and pushed a key. The system started up and synchronized with the waiting oil product which started its flow into the line from one of the storage tanks. He watched for several minutes until the pig took off from the station to meet up with the main delivery line and provide the buffer between the two different products.

O'Malley closed his eyes as the chamber vibrated and hurtled into the main duct. The pig came in at the tail end of one product and he felt a distinct lurch as the second product, of a different viscosity, slammed into the back of the pig. He felt a minor sensation of movement and settled himself down to wait. Compliments of FBI standard training he slipped into a controlled breathing procedure to ensure the least amount of air consumption. It would ensure that only a necessary amount to sustain his mental faculties would be consumed.

An hour and a half into the journey O'Malley sensed a sudden slowdown in the rate of transfer. He did not panic but waited. The only possible cause of the slowdown would be either some unforeseen problem at the receiving end or a computer glitch. Neither of these had been experienced during his short tenure of supervision but he remembered reading about them in the operations manual. The slowdown continued until the flow of oil in the pipe stopped altogether.

O'Malley began to perspire as his natural body heat began to warm up the chamber. He prayed that whatever caused the stoppage would be rectified by the system's diagnostic program and the pig sent on its way again. After ten minutes he experienced a mild panic attack. Had his escape been discovered? The minutes ticked by and the chamber began to warm up considerably. He calmed himself and tried to further regulate his breathing. The perspiration began to pop out in tiny bubbles on his forehead.

O'Malley knew the time presented a critical factor to his survival. The darkness of the chamber seemed all consuming and he felt the slow erosion of his self-confidence. For several seconds he blacked out, only to be brought back to consciousness by the sudden jerk of the chamber. He breathed a sigh of relief as the pig started moving at a slow rate and picked up to a normal pace again. At least twenty minutes had been consumed by the delay. It would be touch and go by the time the pig reached the terminal and he tried not to think of the consequences which awaited him if the air in the chamber ran out before its arrival. He would be spilled out of the chamber by the system and left to lie unconscious on the platform until he came too, or someone discovered him. Worse still he could be moved onto the conveyor together with the boxes, to end up in the receiving department.

The process was monitored by closed circuit TV and the chances of discovery would increase if someone happened to be watching the screen when the cargo was dumped onto the platform. He knew there would normally be only one person handling the receiving end of things and hoped that it might be a busy morning for that operator. It would take him only a few seconds after being deposited onto the platform, to find a place to hide. Pictures in the manual confirmed that the receiving platform had low barriers to prevent deposited articles from falling onto the ground and it was angled toward the conveyor, which allowed the cargo to slide onto the moving belt.

Two hours later the rate of oil flow remained constant but the air in the chamber had diminished to a life-threatening degree. O'Malley struggled to keep his mind alert and dosed off on several occasions. When the pig arrived at the terminal the system stopped it while the product in front was diverted to a storage tank. When the transfer ended the pig was diverted off the main line to its receiving station and the oil behind it directed to another storage tank. When it came to a standstill in the station O'Malley lay slumped and unconscious against the chamber's inner wall. The air had run out.

The processing program sprung the chamber's hatch and the pig tilted to offload its cargo. O'Malley's body rolled out with the boxes and lay spreadeagled on the platform. The boxes slid down onto the conveyor but he, being much heavier, remained stationary. At that moment the receiving operator, Charley Minx walked past the screen and stopped dead in his tracks. He stared at the screen and his mouth dropped open. He reached over to press the alarm button but changed his mind and made for the door of his office, which led out into the receiving area. Charley could see the inert body lying on the platform as he jogged the short distance alongside the conveyor track and wondered what it all meant. There could be only one answer. Someone had made a deliberate attempt to escape from the thousand dunes refinery. He knew this for a fact as he, ten years prior, had been a prisoner in the very same place.

Charley jumped up onto the platform and knelt beside the unconscious form. The chamber's hatch closed and the pig made its way to the main line for transfer back to the refinery's s storage facility.

O'Malley lay on his stomach and did not move. Charley turned the body over and noticed the swollen forearm and cut where the chip had been removed. He looked down at the pale, expression-less face. Trained in first aid he recognized that the unconscious man, whose skin had turned a tinge of blue, needed urgent resuscitation. He got to work and a moment later his efforts were reward-ed as the man coughed, jerked awake and attempt-ed to focus his eyes.

"Take it easy, my friend. I guess the chamber must have run out of air," he murmured.

It took O"Malley about ten seconds before he real-ized where he was. He looked up into Charley Minx's green eyes and gave a weak smile.

"I guess this must seem odd to you," mumbled O'Malley. His voice sounded weak and strained.

Charley grinned. "Don't worry, my friend. I know exactly what you've been up to. It's a chance I also thought of taking once but never had the guts to go through with. You were obviously a prisoner at Camp Logan."

O'Malley sat up and looked around. Apart from the operator they were alone. He still felt weak from his ordeal and would not be able to overpower his captor so he chose to keep up a dialogue until he was strong enough.

Charley saw the look in O'Malley's eye and smiled. "Don't worry, I'm not going to turn you in. I know exactly what you are going through because I spent a year at the refinery. I have a question, though."

O'Malley shot him an enquiring glance. "Go ahead."

"Why not just sit out the time at Camp Logan? All you have to do is accept their indoctrination process and you will be set free when your time is up."

"My situation is different from yours. I have to get back to where I came from."

Charley looked doubtful. "What do you mean different? You're a political dissident, aren't you?"

At that moment the phone in Charley's office started to ring. He looked up and shook his head. "The bossman is checking up on me. I'd better get back to my post. Can you walk?"

O'Malley nodded and Charley helped him to stand. The tilted platform made it difficult for him to maintain his balance but managed to step over the low barrier onto the floor. Charley gave support until O'Malley could walk on his own and they proceeded along the walkway toward the office.

"I will help you get out of here but you'll need protection from the elements."

O'Malley remembered the bundle. "I think you'll find my cloak and hat already at the receiving point. It was in the chamber with me."

Outside the office lay the three boxes for delivery and the bundle, deposited by the conveyor for pickup.

"Come in and sit down. No one will bother us here for the rest of my shift. I'm keen to hear your story."

O'Malley decided to conceal his real identity. He made up a story about a job he had in Liberty City where he had first met the director, Roshē. He told Charley that he had been in the employ of the Institute of Universal Investigation when they discovered he possessed plans for resisting the government process.

Charley took it all in. He related his own experience and then talked about Camp Logan. The phone rang again and he lifted the receiver. A short conversation followed and when the call ended Charley turned to him.

"You will have to hide. My boss will be arriving in a few minutes."

✳

21

Aftermath of the Escape

General Mumford returned to his office after activating the product delivery system on O'Malley's behalf and settled down at his desk. His thoughts remained centered on their mission to escape the camp and the thousand dunes refinery. There were many things which could prevent the agent's success and destroy their collective hopes but he did not want to entertain any of them.

Sometime later he heard a buzzer go off in the deliveries section. The sound almost brought his heart to a standstill and he knew something had gone wrong with the flow of oil from the refinery to the distant terminal. The close proximity of his office to O'Malley's pig-loading station meant that he could hear most sounds that emanated from the delivery area. He wasn't sure what to do. He did not know enough about the delivery system to rectify any problems and he knew that an early discovery of O'Malley's disappearance was at hand.

The manager of the section came running past Mumford's office and close on his heels ran Kieth Harbor, the trainer. A moment later the buzzer stopped as one of them canceled the alarm. He could hear the conversation but did not understand the questions that they were shouting at each other, all but one: "Where is operator O'Malley?"

Fifteen minutes passed before the two men returned and the first place they stopped in was Mumford's office.

"Have you seen your comrade?" asked the section manager.

Mumford gave him a puzzled look. "He walked with me from the bus station earlier this morning and, to the best of my knowledge, entered his office. I haven't seen him since," said the general.

Harbor fixed Mumford with a hostile stare. "Are you sure you guys haven't cooked up some sort of sabotage or escape?"

Mumford remained calm. "Not at all—where would we go and why? We are from an alternate universe, remember?"

"It doesn't mean you won't try something. I thought I could trust O'Malley," said the section manager.

"Maybe he had a medical emergency or something," said Mumford.

"I'll check the washroom," said Harbor.

The general sat down and continued with his work but a few moments later Harbor returned with the manager in tow. "He's not in any of the washrooms."

"Then, I don't know where he's got to," said the general.

Harbor turned to the section manager. "We need to ask the camp security if O'Malley's chip is still providing a signal. If it is still responding to the program he must still be here somewhere. If he's not on refinery property then he might have tried to escape in the pig. I'll call the terminal and alert them."

"I doubt that anyone would be crazy enough to try that," said the manager.

Harbor stepped passed Mumford and picked up the phone. He dialed a number and waited. After a minute Mumford heard the unmistakable voice of an automated answer emanating from the earpiece.

"Damn," shouted Harbor. "The lines are experiencing an overload of electromagnetic interference. It might take me a while to get through to the terminal."

"Keep trying and in the mean time I'll try to get hold of the camp security," said the section manager.

Harbor turned to Mumford. "You haven't heard the end of this, general. I'll be back with questions if we determine that O'Malley is no longer on the premises."

Mumford narrowed his eyelids. "You do that. I assure you I have no idea where he is."

Harbor gave him a prolonged stare and then walked out. Mumford breathed a sigh of relief and hoped that the telephone communication system remained down for as long as possible. He returned to his production planning.

*

Charley Minx pointed to a door which led from his office. "It's a store room. No one will look in there."

"What's happened?" asked O"Malley.

"My boss received a call from someone at the refinery. He says one of the operators have gone missing and wanted to know if anyone had seen him arrive in the pig."

"That was quick. I wasn't expecting to be missed until the end of the shift which is still an hour away," said O'Malley.

"Fortunately for you, there has been a lot of electromagnetic interference from the sun and they couldn't get through until five minutes ago. The camp security has also just responded to say that the chip is still responding to the program and shows that you are still somewhere in the refinery. You had better hide. My boss will be here in a few minutes."

O'Malley left the office and entered the storeroom. The walls were lined with shelves which contained various items and documents and in one corner he spotted a canvas tarp draped over some boxes, a good place to hide. He crawled under the tarp's one corner and lay between several crates. After a pensive wait, the door opened and he heard Charley's voice.

"You can come out now, he's gone."

"What did he say?" asked O'Malley.

"He asked me if I had seen anyone exit the pig which arrived around 1:00 pm today. I laughed and said no one in their right mind would try such an escape. They have searched the refinery premises and couldn't find you anywhere so they're guessing you used the pig. Other than attempting to walk out, through the desert, it would be the only other way out."

O'Malley breathed a sigh of relief. "I'm really thankful that you didn't turn me in."

"Don't mention it. It's a way for me to strike back at the Council without getting into trouble. The authorities just mustn't catch you anywhere on the west coast."

"I'll do my best. Is there any way you can help me? I need to find a good way of making the journey back to Liberty City without being seen."

Charley raised his eyebrows. "You want to go back to the place where they caught you?"

"I have friends there who will be able to create a new identity for me," said O'Malley.

He didn't feel it a good thing to tell Charley why he really needed to get back to Liberty City. Charley gave his request some thought.

It's going to be difficult to remain invisible while you make your way across the country. The Institute of Investigation will be looking for you. You will need a disguise of some sort. Do you have any money?"

O'Malley shook his head. "As you know they don't pay us at camp Logan."

Charley laughed. "Of course they don't. Will you be able to access any of your bank accounts?"

"They will have frozen all that by now."

"Right. Don't worry. I will loan you some. You can pay me back whenever you get settled with a new identity and a job."

"I would be most grateful," said O'Malley. He couldn't believe his good fortune. Of all the people at the terminal-receiving depot, he could have got a hostile operator, who would have turned him in.

"I keep a small stash of dollars in my drawer which will help you buy some food but you will need to find your own transport," said Charley.

"Is there a railyard anywhere near the oil depot?" asked O'Malley.

"There's a large terminal on the outskirts of West Langauria. There are shunting yards there with trains which go to every point of the continent. Have you never been in this part of the world before?"

"I've spent all my life on the East Coast. This is the first time I've ever been to the West," said O'Malley. He knew his ignorance regarding the geography might trip him up and he didn't want to jeopardize this new-found relationship. He returned to the question of the rail yard.

"Is there a way I can get there other than walking?"

Charley laughed. "Its too far for anyone to walk, Dillon, but I have an idea. There's a load of lubrication oils that leaves every day by road from the terminal and stops in at a distribution point in West Langauria, not far from the rail yards."

"How will I get onto the delivery vehicle?" asked O'Malley.

"Not a problem. One of my friends drives the truck. He is also an ex-camp Logan dissident."

"What about the terminal's security?"

"It's not very tight on the lube oil side. He will be able to get you through, I'm sure."

Charley opened the drawer of his desk and took out a small tin box. He opened the lid and removed a small roll of dollar notes. He counted off five hundred dollars and laid them on the desk for O'Malley, who for the first time since his arrival on Terra, saw the local currency. He marveled at how similar the notes appeared to American dollars.

"I really feel bad about taking money from you but I am at a bit if a loss. I'm extremely grateful and I will pay you back as soon as I'm able," said O'Malley.

"It's not a problem at all. I hope you will be able to get things sorted out for yourself," answered Charley. He tore off some paper from a desk pad and drew a diagram.

"This is my office. There's a door leading off this corridor. You will need your protective gear, which is a good thing because everyone here who moves outside wears the same garb. I'm sure it's the same on the East Coast."

"How far to the lube oil terminal?" asked O'Malley.

"You will need to walk about a quarter of a mile along this road." He drew two straight lines to indicate a road and its general direction. "I will call my friend Eric and ask him to pick you up outside a storage tank numbered T26. There's a shelter there where you can wait."

"How much daylight is left," asked O'Malley.

Charley glanced at his watch. "About two hours. I'll call Eric now to see if he'll do this for you."

A short conversation followed before Charley ended the call. He looked at O'Malley with a smile. "He's willing to do it. When he heard you had escaped camp Logan he had nothing but admiration for your courage. You will need to find your way to tank 26 as quickly as possible because he needs to leave within the hour."

Charley went to a clothes locker and pulled out a pair of clean coveralls. "You won't get far in that refinery garb—wear these. People will think you're an employee."

O'Malley removed his refinery clothes and pulled on the coveralls. He picked up the bundle which comprised his protective gear and unraveled the cloak. With the hat perched at an angle on his head, he donned the dark glasses and the two men shook hands. Charley surprised O'Malley by wrapping his arms around his shoulders in a strong bear hug.

"Look after yourself, Dillon and when you're settled come back for a visit—don't forget you still owe me five hundred big ones."

O'Malley embraced Charley for several seconds. "I don't know how I will ever be about to thank you. I owe you a lot more than the five hundred dollars."

Charley looked him in the eye. "I'm just doing what anyone else, who has experience life at camp Logan, would do. You'd better get going and keep safe."

The men shook hands again and O'Malley left the office. He followed the connecting corridor to the outside door, opened it and stepped out into the late afternoon heat.

✳

22

The Silo Attack

Banks pulled out his night vision binoculars and surveyed the silo area. The bulk of the structure lay underground but the escape doors of the chamber could be seen in the form of a concrete, square block, about one foot in height and twenty feet across. Two such structures, side by side revealed the positions of two silos, each containing an intercontinental ballistic missile, capable of reaching American soil.

The perimeter diamond-mesh, double-row fencing looked formidable and would take a while to breach. A guard tower stood in the center of the square area which measured one hundred yards, each side. A pair of heavy steel entrance gates on the South and gave entry to the facility. A single hut which served as an eating and sleeping quarters stood about twenty yards from the silos and a light burned in one of its rooms. All seemed quiet. Banks figured that the group of North Korean soldiers they encountered on the path were stationed at the silo, or were on a temporary maneuver from the base at Wiwon, a town further up the river.

The information supplied to him by the client did not mention a squad, only the presence of ten guards, two groups of five working on four hours off and two hours on. The presence of the squad in the area might be a training maneuver of some sort but he doubted they had anything to do with the silo's defense. He decided they would return to the cluster of trees and rest through the coming day until nightfall.

He motioned for the other three men to turn around and retrace their steps. On arrival at the trees Banks posted the Brat in a position close to the path.

"Keep watch here until sunrise and listen for any signs of that North Korean group returning."

The Brat lay down on his stomach and faced the direction in which the DPRK soldiers had departed while the others slunk quietly into the grove of trees. They found comfortable patches of grass and each chose a tree to sit under.

"Get some sleep. The Brat will stand guard until sunlight, then come and wake Ian up. We'll each take a four-hour stint throughout the day and when night falls we can make ready to execute the plan," said Banks.

"When do we hit the silos?" asked Ian.

"At one minute past midnight so, check your gear now and get some shuteye."

*

Hastings loved the feeling of power the presidency gave him. It would be difficult to defer to a council in the future but he knew it would be for the best. Bowman, on the other hand, could not wait for her part in the deception to end. She liked Hastings and felt he was doing a good job of masquerading as President Chambers but Hastings appeared to have some traits which the real president did not have. If these were observed by the other staff members it could place them all in jeopardy. They walked out on the lawn in front of the oval office and chatted. Several yards back two secret service men watched over them.

"How do you find the relationship with the wife coming along?" she asked.

"She doesn't suspect a thing. At least I don't think so," he said.

Bowman steeled herself to share her thoughts. "I know you've studied Chambers down to his finest details, Norman, however, sometimes one does not see the obvious."

"What are you saying, Francis?"

"I'm saying you are so close to the trees you don't see the wood."

"Meaning?"

"You are too quick in giving answers when members of Congress approach you on certain issues. I've watched the video files McHale obtained on President Chambers. He never answers anything right off the bat. It's a small thing but it could make them suspicious of you."

"Bullshit. I think they would see such a change as a positive thing. Everyone wants the president to be decisive, not hesitant and timid," answered Hastings.

"It's just my opinion, Norman. There's no need to get defensive. I'm trying to give you an objective opinion."

"I'm not getting defensive. I'm trying to evolve my performance along the lines of a president's growth in office, a president who is still getting it all together. Chambers is in his first term, an independent who did not expect to win the election and yet won in a landslide. I have obviously also watched all the videos and I think his hesitancy was related more to learning on the job than it was a character trait."

Bowman would not back down. "I read it differently. I think it is a character trait and not related to indecision. I think it's rather a contemplation of facts before making a decision. It's your role, Norman. I'm merely seeing it as I think others will see it. The last thing we want is for the staff, who know Chambers well, to begin wondering why the sudden change."

"Okay, you have a point. I'll throw in a few hesitant moments in the future. Is there anything else you want to discuss? I'm expecting a call from Damian."

Bowman stood to go. "Let us know exactly what day the great event is planned for."

"You'll be the first to know," said Hastings.

A moment later the burner rang and he scrambled to open the drawer to answer it.

Damian Hall's voice sounded jubilant. "The event is planned for the 25th. We have three weeks before all hell breaks loose."

"Did our man take the bait?"

"He took it but I detected a hesitancy after sharing the coordinates. I asked if he was up to the task and it took a few moments for him to confirm—I guess the financial reward dealt a blow to any patriotic sentiments he might have had. In the interests of secrecy, he won't tell his men what we are really doing. They think their mission is to blow up the silo and prevent an imminent attack on the United States."

*

Banks checked his watch and then stood to his feet. His limbs felt a bit stiff after the hours of waiting and he swung his arms in circles to get the blood moving. The other men surfaced from their solitude and did the same.

"Check your weapons. Make sure you have adequate ammunition and that the timers on the explosives are all in good working order," growled Banks.

The men did as he asked and a short while later they left the grove of trees. There had been no sign of the North Korean squad first encountered on the way to the silo earlier. An hour later the four mercenaries took up a position in the long grass close to the perimeter and surveyed the area for any movement. Banks checked the time again and focused his night vision binoculars.

"As I suspected—there are laser-beam terminals on all four corner posts of the perimeter which activates an alarm if interrupted. We can easily get under the beams if we crawl."

The Brat chuckled. "These North Koreans haven't the foggiest idea about security. They haven't even posted a guard in the tower."

"It's 12:10 pm. I see a group of four guards smoking their cigarettes in the far corner of the perimeter, between the two fences. They'll have just started their shift ten minutes ago and appear to be the only ones outside the guard house. The others should be asleep."

"Only five guards at a time? This is going to be a pushover," said Ian.

"Wish I knew where that squad of five goons went. I'm hoping they were from Wiwon but it's also possible there's a circular route which could have brought them back here," whispered Banks.

Ian shifted his position to get a better view. "The client didn't mention anything about them?"

"Not a thing. My guess is they were on route to the base at Wiwon. If not they could be bunked in the guard house—it could easily accommodate at least ten people," retorted Banks.

The third team member plucked a long grass stem and stuck it in his mouth. "We'll be able to catch all of them with one blast, then. It simplifies matters."

The moonlight lit up the entire area and almost every detail of the silo's perimeter could be seen with clarity.

Banks continued to survey the area. "The entrance to the silo is through a manhole adjacent to the missile exit doors. There's a special command center connected to the main chamber by a short tunnel. The center will be manned by an operator who will be locked in behind a steel door. We will deal with him by dropping two of our nerve gas containers down the air duct system. You can see the air intake about ten meters from the entrance manhole. The Brat will deploy these after taking the guards out."

The third member had a question. "What about their communications, Commander? The last thing we need is a squadron of fighter jets swooping down on us."

Banks focussed the binoculars on a post situated within the grounds.

"Do you see the satellite dish on top of that pole? Ian will take it out at the same time the Brat deals with the perimeter guards. That should deal with the communication problem."

He turned to the third man: "You come with me. We are going to blow up the guardhouse and then enter the silo. Use the pencil lasers to let me know when you are in position."

The men checked their M16's and made ready to advance on the perimeter. "You all know what to do—let's get to it," whispered Banks.

The guards, oblivious of impending doom, continued to smoke their cigarettes and appeared to be enjoying a communal joke. Ian crawled off to a section of the fence that offered the shortest distance to the satellite dish while Banks and the third member crawled to a spot directly opposite the guardhouse. When in position the men signalled their readiness for action.

After cutting the outer perimeter fence with military wire cutters the brat crawled through into the space between the outer and inner fences which the guard's used as a patrol area. It took another few minutes for him to get within range. Ian also cut through both inner and outer perimeter fences to make his way toward the satellite dish. The commander and the third team member breached the fence closer to the guard house and made their way to the closest outer wall of the structure.

Banks lay on the grass lawn of the quadrangle in a position where he could see Ian and the Brat. He motioned for the third member of the team to crawl directly to the guard house wall to set the charges. When the explosives were in place the man crawled back to where Banks lay. The leader signaled both Ian and the Brat that everything was ready. They, in turn, returned the signal. The third member held the detonator in his hand and waited for the go-ahead.

Banks gave one more signal with his laser. A second later the peace and solitude of the night dissolved into flames and smoke. A fireball shot into the air above the disintegrating guardhouse, followed by a plume of black smoke which shot two hundred feet into the air. The satellite dish disappeared simultaneously as Ian cut it down with the machine gun and the Brat's M16 spat death at the guards who were taken completely by surprise. An eerie silence followed.

23

O'Malley makes Headway

The delivery truck pulled up at the shelter alongside tank 26. A man with pale skin and long hair that stuck out beneath a blue baseball cap, lowered the driver's window to stare at O'Malley.

"Are you O'Malley?"

O'Malley grinned, walked around the front of the truck to the passenger side and opened the door. "Are you sure you're okay with giving me a ride?"

The man entertained the glimmer of a smile. "Charley told me who you are. Anyone who could escape from thousand dunes has my admiration. Get in, my name's Eric. I'm doing night shifts this week so you can help me stay awake."

O'Malley climbed up into the cab and fastened the seatbelt. Eric glanced into the rearview mirror and pulled away from the side walk, working the clutch and gears with long-term familiarity.

"Tell me why you ended up at camp Logan?" Eric asked.

O'Malley shared the same story he had told Charley and for the next hour, the two men shared experiences of work at the refinery with each other. The question uppermost in the agent's mind came during a lull in the conversation.

"I'm trying to get back to Liberty City and as I have never traveled in this neck of the woods, is there any advice you can give me?"

Eric considered the request for a moment. "I am traveling down the transit one, to San Tormento. The direction to Liberty City is way off my beaten track but I'll drop you off at a station where you will be able to catch a train across the country."

"How long would such a journey take?" asked O'-Malley.

"About two days, if you take the cross-country express."

"Sounds good to me. I'm really thankful for your help."

Eric shot him a quick glance. "No problem at all."

They traveled on through the night, engaged in occasional small talk and anything that came to mind until Eric turned off the main highway at an intersection. The dawn had broken and in the gathering light, O'Malley saw the outskirts of a town.

"There is a huge railway junction in this town and a central station which is used by patrons from all around the area. They have tried to keep the trains away from the main suburbs and city centers. Just remember the cross-country express—platform twelve."

They approached the railway junction and by-passed the shunting yards. A tall building loomed up ahead and Eric stopped the truck in a loading zone.

"This is it. Good luck, Dillon. I wish you well and stay safe."

O'Malley thanked him, pulled on his wide-brimmed hat and jumped down from the cab. He waited for Eric to pull away and then walked toward the station building. On his approach to the entrance, he saw two policemen stopping everyone to check on their identity documents. He had not expected to pass through any security checks. It constituted a complication of huge proportions as he carried no personal identification. He turned away and walked further along the building to a convenience store which had an outside entrance. On entering the store he looked around for any doors which may give access to the station's interior.

A young girl behind the counter spotted him. "Can I help you, Sir?"

"Do you have a washroom?" asked O'Malley.

She pointed to a set of doors at the back. Next to the washroom entrances stood another door with an exit sign stenciled on it. He made a mental note to see where it led after he had relieved himself. Several minutes later O'Malley exited the washroom and tried the door. It was locked. A lineup of people making payment for their purchases had the young girl busy at the till. Behind her hung several keys on hooks, each with a tag and he spotted the one he required.

An idea formed in his mind. He returned to the men's washroom, removed his cloak which he hung behind one of the closet doors and returned to counter area. He waited for the girl to bend down to extract a carton of cigarettes from a large box which she kept under the till. When she entered the price details and removed change from the drawer for the client O'Malley slipped in behind and lifted the key off its hook.

No one took the slightest notice as he returned to the washroom and retrieved his protective gear. The key opened the door and O'Malley followed a corridor which appeared to service the backends of several shops with entrances that opened to the stations exterior. A moment later he found what he had been looking for; a door marked 'station'. Relieved O'Malley opened it and stepped into the brightness of the station interior's overhead lights.

The ticket offices were further back toward the main entrance so he mingled with the crowds of people. He scanned the board and saw that the cross-country express would be leaving from platform twelve with a departure time of 9:30 am. He checked the station clock and saw that there would be time for him to grab a cup of coffee before boarding.

"That will be two-hundred and fifty-eight dollars," said the ticket vendor. "You understand that there will be no compartment with a bed. We only have a few seats in the economy carriage left."

O'Malley nodded. "It's okay, I didn't have the money for a compartment, anyway."

He would have to put up with the inconvenience of sleeping upright, in a seat.

The vendor smiled. "I understand. Compartments are very pricey—here's your pass for the showers and dining carriage."

With two hours to wait O'Malley first went to a pharmacy and bought the few toiletries, he would need for the trip, then found a fast-food vendor. Having not eaten since breakfast the previous day he sat down at a table to enjoy a much-appreciated hamburger and a mug of coffee. Most people had removed their protective gear due to the protection the station's roof cover offered. O'Malley, however, felt safer with the gear on. He knew that with the earlier discovery of his absence the police might be on the lookout for him. He thought about Charley and Eric. The fortuitous meeting with Charley had made his escape much simpler but he knew things would not be that easy when he arrived at his destination. He had two days to think of a plan of action.

The boarding announcement for the cross-country express aroused him from his contemplations and he left the food court to follow the signs to platform twelve. The train, according to the information pamphlet the ticket vendor had supplied, would only stop at five major cities and take fifty-two hours to reach the final destination. O'Malley removed his cloak and took a window seat close to the toilet and shower facility near the back of the coach. At 11:30 am the train pulled out of the station and gathered speed. An elderly man sat in the seat alongside and they made casual conversation until the man pulled his hat over his eyes and fell asleep. General conversation in the coach quietened down as the economy passengers made themselves comfortable. But for a few empty seats across from the aisle, the train appeared to be full.

*

After two nights and almost two days, the train ride had become very tedious. O'Malley had nothing to read and time had passed slowly. The old man next to him had slept almost all the way and only raised himself at breakfast and the previous evening's dinner. Later in the final day of their journey, O'Malley felt a sudden slowdown in pace which woke him out of a daydream. He checked the clock, situated on the back wall next to the exit door: 2:10 pm in the afternoon. The train entered a station, rolled to a stop and O'Malley decided to make a visit to the toilet. This was the fifth and final stop on the line before Liberty City.

He glanced out of the window at the station platform and to his consternation saw two police officers, together with a man in plain clothes, looking directly at him. A sudden fear of discovery caused him to look away and move out of their line of sight. Had he been recognized?

The whistle blew and the train started up again. It gathered speed with every second and soon they were flying along the rails as O'Malley returned to his seat. He looked across the aisle to his right and his heart almost stopped. The man in plain clothes, who had been talking to the two police officers, sat in one of the empty seats. In that brief moment, the man turned and looked directly at him. Their eyes locked for interminable seconds until O'Malley broke it off, stretched out and pulled the hat over his eyes. Without the Glock, he felt vulnerable and had no other option but to wait and see what transpired.

As it turned out nothing happened. The man in plainclothes leaned back in his seat and appeared to fall asleep. The train barreled along and O'Malley felt a sense of relief that the journey would soon be at an end. He went over the plan which had formed in his mind. It would be needful to return to the dock where the Lady Anne under the captaincy of CaptainPenn had brought him and general Mumford from the dimensional link. He might have to wait for the ship to arrive from the Triangle. There had to be a way for him to get on board but how an attempt to stow away would play out seemed uncertain.

He glanced out the window and in the distance saw the outlines of skyscrapers. The train was nearing its final destination and an excitement welled up within him. People were stirring in their seats and some stood to grab belongings from the overhead storage racks. The plainclothes man opened his eyes and stared out of the window for several moments before he too reached up to grab a briefcase. When he sat down again his eyes met O'Malley's and then quickly looked away.

The train slowed down and pulled into the station. Doors slid open and people began to stream out onto the platform. O'Malley put on his dark glasses, donned his cloak and stepped out with the rest of the travelers. He searched the area for signs of law enforcement but saw none, however, the thought of a police check at the station exit did occur to him. He turned to look over his shoulder and felt a chill go down his spine. The plainclothes policeman was following right behind. The man stared at O'Malley and for a brief second the FBI agent thought he saw a spark of recognition in the policemen's eyes.

He spied a sign for a washroom off to the left and hurried past several other passengers to make as though he needed a pit stop. The man followed him into the washroom and O'Malley turned to face his assailant. He found himself looking down the barrel of a revolver.

"Your little escapade is over, Mr. O'Malley. Don't try anything or I will shoot you."

24

Recognition of an Imposter

MacDonald and Martinez sat at the bar counter in earnest conversation when O'Malley's doppelgänger walked in to take the stool next to Martinez. Both men stopped and stared.

"Jesus, Dillon. Where have you been?" exclaimed MacDonald.

The doppelgänger gave him a sheepish smile. "You can say I've been indisposed for a while."

"Everyone's been looking for you. What happened?" asked Martinez.

"It's a long story but before I explain can one of you buy me a beer?"

MacDonald hailed the barman and then suddenly realized that O'Malley never drank beer. He hesitated.

"What beer do you usually drink, boss?"

"You're becoming forgetful in your old age, Roland. Everyone knows I drink A-One Ale."

Martinez grinned. "He's missed you, boss. So have I. Have you seen Janet yet?"

"Not yet—I only just managed to escape those bastards this morning."

MacDonald remembered the password they had agreed on when in doubt about any person's authenticity. He decided to frame it subtly and see if O'Malley picked up on it.

"Things have been in chaos around here since you disappeared?"

The doppelgänger smiled. "It shows you how indispensable I am."

Both Martinez and MacDonald picked up on the lack of response. They glanced at each other and in the moment decided to allow the imposter to carry on with his deception.

MacDonald gave no sign of his revelation. "So, explain what happened after you left Janet's place. When 911 responded to the call they found no trace of you."

The doppelgänger hunched his shoulders. "I never saw the other vehicle coming. It hit my SUV at the intersection and that's the last I remember of the accident. I woke up in a room with two guys checking my vital signs. At first, I thought they were paramedics but the absence of uniforms made me realize they weren't. I then thought I was in a hospital emergency room but again on closer inspection, I saw it was a small, private room."

Martinez continued with the charade. "Who were these people?"

The man shrugged. "I'm not sure. They kept me drugged for the longest time and moved me from one place to another. Then all of a sudden they stopped with the drugs and began to feed me. I asked lots of questions but no one would tell me why I was there."

"How did you escape?" asked MacDonald.

The doppelgänger hesitated, as though he needed to gain more composure. "I managed to overpower the person who brought me food every day. The keys to my shackles were in his pocket and I got out. It was a hotel in Atlantic City."

"Let's go back there and investigate," said Martinez.

"They will be long gone by now," said the doppelgänger. "Can one of you give me a ride to the office? I need to speak to the boss."

"You should call Janet. Here's my phone," said MacDonald.

"Janet can wait. I need to speak to Ingram first," said Wade.

"It's your call. We're just glad you're okay," answered MacDonald.

They finished their drinks and left the pub.

At FBI headquarters MacDonald made an excuse to return to the main office while Martinez called James Ingram, the deputy director, on his cell and asked for a quick audience. He did not mention the reason. MacDonald, in turn, called Ingram from the main office and told him what they had discovered.

"It's definitely not the real O'Malley, boss, however, we thought we would continue with the charade. He may lead us to the people who are holding Dillon's son," said MacDonald.

"Good thinking, Roland. I'll talk to him and see what I can discern," answered Ingram.

MacDonald joined Martinez and O'Malley's doppelgänger in the deputy director's office. After a half-hour of discussion, the vagueness of the doppelgängers story clearly indicated to Ingram that this was not the real O"Malley.

"You had better call your wife. She has been going out of her mind since you disappeared. I have some further bad news—your son has also been taken by these people. I'm surprised you didn't see him being brought in while you were in captivity."

The man feigned surprise. "That's terrible. Janet must be in a state with us both missing. I'll go and see her immediately."

"So, you had no idea they had your son and the Swales boy?" Martinez asked.

"They apparently have several different places in which to hide. They must have taken the boys somewhere else," said the doppelgänger.

Ingram asked the question uppermost on his mind. "Do you know what these people are up to? We have reports of the presence of people's doubles. Your wife Janet was one of them. Your friend Jon Shepherd, the speech writer, says he saw his double in a 7-Eleven store and he was mysteriously killed. Then you go missing after someone crashes into you—can you tell me what's going on?"

The doppelgänger averted his eyes and looked out of the window. "I'm working on it, boss. I'm sure we'll find out the meaning of it all sooner or later."

The deputy director decided to end the interview. "You'd better go console your wife, Dillon. Take a few days off before reporting for work again, and that's an order. I will organize another vehicle for you."

MacDonald, Martinez and the doppelgänger left the assistant director's office and walked back to the main office.

"I'll contact you after I've spoken to Janet," said the doppelgänger.

"We'll carry on the search for your son. Hopefully, we'll find both boys soon," said MacDonald. The man nodded and left. He made a quick visit to the requisitions office to sign the paperwork for another vehicle and a new cell phone. After obtaining a list of key operative's numbers the doppelgänger keyed them all into the new phone.

*

Diego Martinez had a dentist appointment in Downtown DC that afternoon. He booked two hours off and told MacDonald they could meet up at the pub after work. An hour and forty-five minutes later, with teeth cleaned and polished, Martinez exited the dentist's offices and walked over the road to where he had parked his car. The sidewalk overflowed with a multitude of people all in a hurry to get to various destinations. He had not intentionally looked at any of them but would have an eye for any pretty girl who happened to cross his path. In the periphery of his vision a woman with a neat figure passed by as he reached for the car's door handle and he turned to look more directly at her.

He realized the shapely female ass seemed familiar from behind. She wore a baseball cap which appeared uncharacteristic for the woman he had in mind but she turned her head to look across the street and revealed a side elevation of her face.

Recognition came in an instant: Janet O'Malley. He locked the car door with the key fob and turned to follow her. MacDonald had contacted Janet barely two hours prior and she had been at her home in Baltimore. The call was to warn her that a doppelgänger would be making contact and she needed to play along with the charade.

This woman could not be the real Janet O'Malley. It had to be the woman they knew as Vera. It surprised him that she would venture into the city areas where it would be possible for law enforcement to identify her. She had to have known that Janet, O'Malley and their coworker, Gwen Farrell, had all seen her face. He placed a call to MacDonald as he followed on behind her.

"Keep her in your sights. I'll join you in about ten minutes," said MacDonald.

"I'll stay on the phone until you get here," answered Martinez.

After ten minutes Vera turned into a deli which had several tables for customers to sit and enjoy items from their bakery. Martinez followed her in and mingled with the customers waiting to purchase their beverages. She walked straight to a table near the back and sat down opposite a man who held a mug of coffee in his hand. Martinez recognized her companion as the man Beverley Swales had met with in Primrose park.

Martinez ordered a latte and a croissant. He slipped his phone into a pocket, picked up his purchases at the end of the counter and looked around for a place to sit. A table on the opposite side of the room came vacant and he made a beeline for it. He pulled out his phone again and told MacDonald where they were.

"Park outside and wait. There are no vacant tables in here at the moment and they may not stay long," said Martinez."

MacDonald grunted an acknowledgment and kept the line open on his vehicle's speaker phone as he sped toward the downtown area. Ten minutes later he parked the SUV in a loading zone and waited. He could see the deli sign further along, across the street. Martinez kept up a commentary until MacDonald reprimanded him.

"For God's sake, Diego—shut up until you have something useful to say."

Martinez laughed. "You're just sore, Roland, because you're not the one sitting here eating a croissant and enjoying a coffee."

He put the phone down on the table and continued to sip on his latte until Vera and the man stood to leave. He warned MacDonald and followed the couple out onto the side walk. Vera climbed into the passenger seat of a white truck and the man who accompanied her took the wheel. The truck pulled out into the traffic. Martinez spotted Mac-Donald's vehicle and jumped in as the agent pulled out of the loading zone.

"Don't lose them," shouted Martinez.

"Bugger off, Diego. Unlike you, I know what I'm doing."

Martinez chuckled and gave MacDonald a playful punch on the shoulder. He loved to push his friend's buttons. At last, they appeared to have a concrete lead to follow up on.

25

K.D.Martin

The plainclothes policeman held the revolver with a steady hand. He reached into an inside pocket and flashed a badge.

"Name's K.D. Martin—Institute of Universal Investigation. I've been trailing you since you boarded the train. We thought you might try to get to Liberty City so I flew to the last stop and waited for the train to arrive."

O'Malley's shoulders sagged. "How did you know?"

Martin kept the gun pointed at O'Malley's head. "We figured out that the only way you could escape the thousand dunes refinery would be via the pig operation. I managed to get the truth out of the guy who helped you and he will be on his way back to spend more time at Camp Logan."

O'Malley felt a queasiness in his stomach. He mentally measured the distance between himself and Martin but decided the agent would pick him off if he tried anything. K.D. Martin appeared to be a veteran and would not be taken down that easily.

"Turn around. I'm going to cuff you," said the agent.

O'Malley complied and stuck his hands behind his back. Martin snapped on the cuffs and pushed his captive toward the door. As they moved into the main station area Martin pulled out a cell phone to make contact with one of his colleagues. O'Malley stopped and turned.

"Keep moving, O'Malley. Walk toward the station's exit and you will see a police vehicle waiting for us."

The ride to the Institute took forty-five minutes through streets, many which O'Malley recognized but had different names. When they arrived at what would be the J. Edgar Hoover building, he couldn't help being overwhelmed by a feeling of confusion. But for the names on the signs, he could have been back on Earth. He didn't relish the thought of being escorted back to Camp Logan and explaining to his friends that he had failed.

They drove in under the building to the detention area and parked close to the duty office. Martin jumped out, opened the rear door and took hold of O'Malley's arm.

"Do you know what's actually going on here?" asked O'Malley.

"Not really interested. I'm just doing my job," said Martin.

"It's the same job I did where I come from," said O'Malley.

"Oh yeah—and where exactly do you come from?"

O'Malley told the truth. "From a parallel universe which your Council is busy invading."

Martin lifted his chin and laughed out aloud. "parallel universe? My big toe. You don't look like an alien to me."

"Your planet is in danger because the magnetic field is failing. Your government found a dimensional link which connects our two universes together. They are making plans to evacuate only the council and leave everyone else to die."

Martin looked puzzled. "I know our planet is in danger but there has been no mention of an alternative planet. We do not have the means to get to our nearest neighboring star. I think you're talking bullshit, O'Malley."

O'Malley pushed his point. "The dimensional link was only a theory to us. I come from a planet called Earth, in a universe which is exactly like yours in every way—except for the failing magnetic field. Your people found this link which is something like a wormhole."

Martin smiled. "Oh come now, O'Malley. You don't expect me to really believe you. If this was true it would be all over the news."

"The Council is withholding the news because they can't take everyone from Terra. There are too many people on Earth so only an elite few will be allowed through the link and the rest on Terra will be left to die."

"I won't listen to any more of this shit—now, walk," said Martin.

He pushed O'Malley forward toward the duty office. A junior agent sat behind the counter and began recording the details of the arrest. Martin looked at the computer screen while the junior went to call a senior administration official. The details of O'Malley's first encounter with the Institute were on record and his eye scanned down a long list of information. O'Malley watched him make a mental note of the rap sheet and saw the agent's forehead wrinkle. Martin glanced up at his prisoner and then looked back at the screen.

The junior agent returned with the senior administrative officer who put O'Malley against a wall and took a mugshot.

"You've been here before, I see," said the officer.

He turned to his subordinate. Place him in cell 4A and remove the cuffs. The junior agent grabbed O'Malley by the arm and escorted him out of the office. As they were leaving O'Malley turned and caught Martin's eye.

"Check my story and you will find out the truth," he shouted.

Martin stared at O'Malley without expression. The agent walked beside him and a few moments later locked him in a cell. After the cuffs were removed O'Malley sat down on the bench provided and rubbed his wrists. He thought about the next step.

*

K.D. Martin's career with the Institute of Universal Investigation spanned a period of twenty-five years. In his initial year of service, at the tender age of twenty years, he graduated from the academy with honors. Every year since that time his performance had always caught the eye of the institute's directors. The one thing Martin possessed in his resume, a dedicated quest to find the truth, appeared to be lacking in the resolve of his colleagues. There were times when Martin risked reputation and job to put forward the real facts of a case, paying no heed to threats from influential people, in particular, his own superiors.

The words of the dissident O'Malley had an appealing ring of truth to them and he became intrigued with the idea of an alternate, parallel universe. As a kid, Martin's father, a science fiction addict, had believed in UFO's, aliens and alternate scientific explanations. He remembered the argument his dad had brought in support of the parallel universe theory, spawned by an infatuation with quantum theory, a new science which had caused much consternation at the time.

Science fiction, however, did not find its way into his heart as it did his father's. He knew enough about the controversies which surrounded the scientific world on quantum issues but had not taken them seriously. The desperate look in O"Malley's eyes, however, persuaded him to delve into the dissident's case. Martin decided that he would not put it past The Council to withhold certain information from the general public. Their planet, Terra, was indeed in great trouble and no answers had been found to reverse the failure of the magnetic fields which kept them safe from their star's harmful radiation.

He started his investigation into O'Malley's statements by accessing the original incarceration file, the same report he had glanced at in the office that day. Some of the information had puzzled him at the time but nothing came of it as the senior administrative officer had returned to take over O'Malley's reincarceration. As a top agent in the institute, Martin had clearance to access these files. In the confines of his own office, he pulled up the file and began to peruse it with more intent. Something was not right. He pulled up the history on O'Malley and found a total lack of any information about the man's background, his education or work history.

The report said O'Malley had worked for the institute and had been found in possession of a detailed plan to overthrow The Council. He searched for a photocopy of the plan but found nothing. It was as though O'Malley had no prior existence on Terra. He checked the institute's reports on dissident surveillance and again came up empty handed. With his suspicions now raised about the possible validity of what the dissident had told him Martin considered the next question: could The Council be hiding something from the main stream of the institute's leadership?

He did a search on the latest scientific theories which had caused a stir in the public eye and came across a report which claimed the discovery of a dimensional link to another universe. A splurge about the parallel universe theory followed but the final paragraph made Martin raise his eyebrows.

The discovery of a dimensional link to another universe has been denied by the mainstream scientific community and rejected by The Council as false news—just another scientist seeking fame.

Somehow the statement seemed too dismissive and he remembered O'Malley's words: Check my story and you will find out the truth.

Martin made a decision. He would give the dissident the benefit of the doubt and further research the matter. It would not be difficult for him to gain an interview with O"Malley while he remained in the holding cell, however, he would have to act quickly as the authority was making plans to transfer their prisoner back to Camp Logan. The other factor lay in the arrival of the operator, Charley Minx, who had helped O'Malley escape from the storage depot. Martin understood that Charley had arrived under armed escort at the institute's cellblock the previous night.

He had not asked Charley's impressions of O"Malley and although the operator might not have known the dissident's real identity there may be something he could corroborate. Martin placed a call to the junior agent in charge of the incarceration reception and arranged a meeting with O'Malley.

Later that evening he left his office and walked down to the holding cells beneath the building. The junior agent had gone home but access to the area was computer operated and all Martin had to do was place his eye to the camera at the entrance. The computer scanned his retina, unlocked the door and allowed him access to the cell block. He could not enter any individual cell but it would not be necessary. He and O'Malley would be able to converse through the bars. One matter needed to be attended to before the interview could take place; Cameras were situated on the opposite wall to each cell's entrance and monitored the occupant on a twenty-four basis. Martin went to the electrical wall panel and disconnected the video feed. There would be no record of the conversation.

The duty officer would know of Martin's presence that evening but with all the cameras disabled there would be no proof of the conversation. Martin stood at the door to O"Malley's cell and called out to the prisoner.

"O'Malley? Are you awake—can we talk?"

O'Malley who had been dozing woke up with a start. He rubbed his eyes and sat up on the bench. He stared at Martin unsure at first who it was.

"Sure," he answered.

An Hour later Martin left the cell block with a whole new impression of O'Malley. The special agent's knowledge of investigative genius rivaled his own, plus the explanations given about the dimensional link with Captains Penn and Vargas, the two captains who ferried people back and forth. Martin promised to follow up on Captain Penn and the Lady Anne's mission to verify that people were coming and going from a specific place in the ocean.

Of particular interest was the fact that The Council hid the details from the general public and with the deterioration of Terra's magnetic field, were looking to save themselves. This did not resonate well with Martin. He had never married and had no children. His work represented his main interest in life but that did not mean he didn't enjoy being alive. No one wanted to die and if there remained a chance for him to escape the eventual death of the planet he would take it. A plan began to form in his mind.

26

Destruction of the Silo

The four mercenaries stood to their feet and surveyed the scene. The guardhouse had been completely demolished and the perimeter guards lay where they had fallen as the plume of smoke above them began to dissipate into the surrounding air. Banks moved over to check the remains of the satellite dish which lay in many pieces, strewn over the grass lawn of the quadrangle. Olympus had fallen. The smell of burned flesh pervaded the men's olfactory senses as they stood in awe of the sudden destruction.

The Brat removed his backpack and opened the flap. He extracted two cylindrical-shaped objects, ran to the air vent which serviced the underground bunker, and popped them in under the cover.

Banks turned to Ian. "You and the Brat do a quick investigation of those ruins. I want to know how many men were in the building. I am going to blast the door to the command center and make sure the operator is dealt with."

The third member of the team followed him to a concrete apron set in the ground alongside the silo doors. Banks opened the manhole cover and raced down the stairs into the underground structure of the silo. He found the light switch and both men shut their eyes momentarily as the sudden glare lit up the interior. Two gigantic ballistic missiles, at least sixty feet in height, towered over them and a myriad of insulated pipes and cables festooned the inner walls. The mercenary leader searched for the steel door which led to the silo's brains.

The third team member spotted it first and pointed to a steel door set in the wall furthermost from the missiles. "There it is, commander."

He pulled explosive charges from his backpack, set them against the door and both men took shelter behind the nearest missile. Moments later a flash and a bang compromised the door enough for it to be yanked off its hinges. They raced into the low, circular tunnel at a crouch and stopped at another set of doors. Both men donned gas masks, extracted from their pant's leg pockets and more explosives were deployed. The command center's door surrendered its integrity and the mercenaries rushed inside with M16's at the ready. They needn't have worried—the operator lay writhing on the floor under the effects of the nerve gas. Banks pointed the M16 at the man's head and pulled the trigger. He spotted a pedestal fan in the one corner of the confined area and switched it on. In a short, while the gas dispersed down the tunnel and back up the vent, allowing both men to remove their masks.

"Set the remainder of your charges to destroy the Silo and then wait for me," said Banks.

The third member raised his eyebrows. "Won't destroying the silo set off the nuclear warheads?"

Banks chuckled. "Not at all. The fissionable material must be literally welded together to set off a nuclear reaction. Your charges will only disable the bunker launch system and damage the missiles. We will not be in any danger."

The mercenary looked at Banks through narrowed eyelids. "I hope you're right, Commander. How much time must I give us?"

"Set your detonators for thirty minutes. We will be getting company from Wiwon shortly as I'm sure they must have heard the explosions. We're only thirty miles away."

Banks pulled a tablet from his coverall thigh pocket and turned it on. He plugged in a short cable, attached it to a USB port on the missile launch control computer and keyed in a few short instructions. A counter started on the tablet's screen. The tablet's program synchronized with the missile launch system on the control computer and by-passed the password protocols. It then entered the coordinates for missile A.

The program had been developed by one of Banks's acquaintances at the cost of half a million US dollars. The required protocol information had been obtained from one of North Korea's top nuclear scientists in exchange for three-hundred thousand US dollars and a US passport.

Ten minutes later Banks checked on his comrade in the missile bay and the setting of the explosives. His team member had one last charge to set.

"After this one, we are set to go, boss."

"When you're done join me, back in the operations room. It won't be safe for you in here," the commander commented. Banks returned to the control room to check the countdown for the missile launch. Moments later the third member of the team joined him.

"Did you close the door that leads into the tunnel?" asked Banks.

"It's done. Why are we taking cover?"

"I have a little surprise for America," said Banks.

They watched the count down and when it reached zero a rumble started in the missile chamber and the entire structure vibrated, followed by a rush of sound as the missile lifted out of its bay. A few moments later the sound receded as the ballistic projectile took to the air and raced upward into the heavens. Ian and the brat, still sifting through the remains of the guardhouse were caught unawares and could only clap their hands over their ears as the missile escaped its launch pad.

When the sound died down they glanced at each other with wide, open eyes.

When Banks and the other member appeared at the silo's entrance, Ian asked the question.

"Did something go wrong, Commander?"

Banks did not look at his men. "It's a little surprise our client has planned for some political advantage. Don't worry about it."

Ian became inquisitive. "Where is the missile headed, boss?"

"That's a need to know basis. It's above your pay grade," Banks growled.

The Brat saw the look on Ian's face and jumped in to avert confrontation. "There were only five bodies in the guardhouse, Commander. The goon squad must have marched on to Wiwon."

"They could be on their way back by now so let's get going. We have about twenty-seven minutes before the silo blows."

The men donned their backpacks, picked up their weapons and jogged to the perimeter fence where they all slipped through the holes. They were two kilometers up the path when a loud explosion erupted at the silo facility.

The third member of the team glanced at Banks. "You were right, boss—no nuclear explosion on the destruction of the silo."

They resumed their journey to the river.

*

Francis Bowman rushed into the oval office and closed the door. She turned and faced Norman Hastings.

"It's happened. A nuclear warhead has just devastated one of the Hawaiian islands."

Hastings remained seated behind his desk and showed no surprise. "This is something that must remain between you, McHale and myself. The Council must never find out about it."

Bowman sat down and stared out of a window. "They won't. North Korea has been threatening the rest of the world for more than a year now. Ever since they managed to develop an intercontinental missile that can reach America they've behaved like renegade children."

"We have opened Pandora's box but McHale is positive this was the quickest way to escalate our plan. Do we have any news on the loss of life?"

At that moment, the phone rang and the door burst open simultaneously. A squad of White House officials flooded the office, with everyone talking at once. Hastings raised his voice above the rest and they stopped all conversation.

"I have just heard the news. This is awful and our hearts go out to everyone who has lost loved ones in Hawaii. I want an immediate meeting in the war room. Have the joint chiefs been summoned?"

'They're on their way, Mr. President."

Ten minutes later the president faced the joint chiefs and his advisors in the war room where the explosive atmosphere could be tangibly felt by everyone. Hastings knew he would face some difficult questions from the Pentagon generals but he would have to stay the course to bring about the eventual objective of Operation Terra Firma.

Francis Bowman sat at Hastings side and offered moral support as the questions rained down on him. The loudest voice belonged to Hastings's comrade in arms, the chairman of the joint chiefs, being impersonated by Damian Hall.

"We propose an all-out attack on North Korea, Mr. President. I have given the order, in conjunction with my staff, to have a bomber stand by. We will only need to drop one bomb on Pyongyang."

The joint chiefs all chimed in with one accord and agreed with Hall's statement.

The chief of the navy added his own suggestion. "I propose we sink their warships and destroy all their fighter jets first—then follow it up with the bomb on Pyongyang."

There were nods of heads all around as every eye focused on the president.

Hastings braced for a barrage of abuse. "I'm afraid it would be an emotional response to drop a nuclear weapon on Pyongyang. It is what the Chinese are waiting for and could start a world war."

"With respect, that's utter bullshit, Mr. President," shouted Damian Hall. America can't allow that little shit, who runs the show, to do as he wishes. I say we need to drop the bomb and destroy their total military capability plus half the population. That will show them that they can't do as they please."

Hastings remained calm. "I understand your frustration, General Mumford, but if we destroy North Korea it will open up retaliation from both China and Russia. Must I remind you that the Russians are looking for a reason to flex their muscles and rise to super power status again?"

The secretary of defense stood to his feet. "This is an outrage, Mr. President. Are you proposing that we stand down after the DPRK have destroyed one of the Hawaiian Islands?"

Hastings considered the question carefully. "I believe we should have a measured response which does not include the use of nuclear weapons. If we drop a nuclear bomb on them it only means we are no better than they are. I suggest we sink two of their largest warships and destroy their military capability with conventional bombs."

"The people of the United States will want to lynch you, Mr. President. A nuclear attack on one of our states deserves a nuclear response. The rest of the world is watching us and if we show weakness it won't be long before American interests are compromised."

The discussion turned into a shouting match and after ten minutes the president stood to his feet and brought an end to the meeting. The military staff left in a rage but stopped short of a physical assault on the president. Damian Hall went straight to the office of the press secretary.

The next day, after the US military had attacked and sunk two of North Korea's largest warships, every media source throughout the western world carried a similar story: The United States was afraid of North Korea and refused to punish the DPRK with a retaliatory nuclear strike. Every news anchor voiced the same opinion and declared the US president to be spineless; that the retaliatory response was far too lenient. A tangible change occurred in the mood of all US citizens and those on the four remaining Hawaiian Islands called for the immediate impeachment of President Chambers.

Later Hastings called Hall on his burner. "Great work, Damian. The dye has been cast. The American people will do the rest."

*

The four mercenaries jogged along the trail towards the Yalu River. The first signs of daylight had started to appear on the horizon as Banks checked his watch.

"Come on, ladies. Jong Shoo will be waiting for us—we don't want to be late. In a few minutes, the whole of North Korea will be looking for us."

They picked up the pace. The Brat had disposed of the machine gun to make his load lighter and they no longer carried all the weight of the charges, only their M16's. After a difficult trek at the fastest pace, the men arrived at the beach where they originally disembarked for the mission. Banks looked up and down the river but saw no sign of Jong Shoo's vessel. He swore a strip off the Chinese fisherman and wondered what had happened.

"This is strange. Jong Shoo has only received half of the amount promised. I have the other half in one of my pockets, to pay him when he brings us safely to his village."

"He might have decided that the first half was enough," said Ian.

"That's highly unlikely. He pushed me for more money when we first negotiated. I can't see him taking the risk for a lesser amount," answered Banks.

"He may have been compromised in some way," the Brat remarked.

They sat down in amongst the bushes on the river's bank and cocked the M16's. They did not have long to wait. Jong Shoo's fishing boat came sailing down from the North under the power of its small inboard motor and pulled in close to the sandbar. All looked in order and Banks stood up to reveal their presence. The others followed and they waded out to the sandbar with rifles at the ready.

They crossed the shallow bar and started to wade out toward the vessel when two men, on board, appeared from under a tarp. In the early morning gloom, it had been impossible for the mercenaries to see the trap. The two men aboard the vessel opened fire with a machine gun before Banks could react. All four of the men slumped into the shallow water above the sandbar. Blood spurted from the bodies and turned the water red.

The two men on board did a quick check to make sure none of the mercenaries had survived and then turned to the old Chinese captain.

"Well done, Jong Shoo. The United States military thanks you for your cooperation." He handed the old Chinese man a wad of dollar bills.

27

K.D. Martin Comes on Board

O'Malley felt elated that his last-ditch effort to gain justice had succeeded. He believed that Agent K.D.Martin of the Institute of Universal Investigation would delve further into The Council's plans to save their own skins. If Martin managed to verify for himself that people were traveling through the dimensional link to another universe it may provoke the man to form a plan of his own. Martin would need O'Malley to assist in any potential escape plan. From their clandestine conversation, O'Malley assured himself that Martin felt a kinship with his captive dissident due their roles as top agents for both planet's foremost law enforcement agencies.

Two days later Martin made contact again, late in the evening, after the staff had all retired. His entire attitude had changed to one of comradeship and empathy.

"I have been busy over the past two days and rented a motor launch to follow the Lady Anne. I confirmed that the ship headed into the area you had mentioned when we last spoke. I watched through long-range telescopic surveillance equipment. A number of people that boarded the vessel at Liberty City docks did not tally with the count which finally disembarked, back at the docks later this afternoon."

O'Malley relaxed. His intolerable status had just improved a thousand-fold.

"Did you see a lifeboat sail off into a bank of mist and then return a few hours later?"

"It was just as you said. In the beginning, when the crew embarked at Liberty dock I had wondered why the ship had such a fancy lifeboat," said Martin.

"It's the vessel they use to slip through the dimensional link," answered O'Malley.

Martin continued. "I also checked on several communications between my director, Denzil Roshē, and the chairman of The Council. They used a code which we used during a recent operation, not thinking that one of their own would ever look into it. You are absolutely correct in your assumption that the members of The Council, along with certain other prominent people, will leave the rest of humanity behind when the end comes."

O'Malley rubbed his chin. "What have you decided to do about it?"

Martin thought for a moment. "I can't fight The Council or the Institute. All I can really do is inform the rest of the world about what's going on."

"That will put your life in jeopardy," answered O'-Malley.

Martin looked down at the floor for a second. "I will help you escape. You could inform your government that imposters have infiltrated your top leadership and then your military could close down the link."

Martin's reaction amounted to exactly what O'Malley had hoped for. "It sounds like a great plan. At least I know who the main players are but I have a few requests."

Martin raised his eyebrows. "What are the requests?"

"Firstly, you accompany me through the link. It will be necessary to convince the right people on the other side that the imposters are from Terra. My second request is that I need to return for our people at Camp Logan—I made them a promise. I would want you with me."

"Is that everything?"

"One more thing, if I may?" said O'Malley. "I would like to try and save Charley, the guy who helped me escape."

Martin narrowed his eyelids. "That will take some doing. As for me accompanying you, I feel bad about taking advantage of the situation. There are millions of Terrans who are going to die while I get a free pass."

"This is the way I see it," said O'Malley. "You will be preventing a gross travesty of justice by halting a hostile takeover of a sovereign world. We can't save Terra or its millions of inhabitants and Earth is already overcrowded, however, if you orchestrate this escape and help me overturn The Council's unrighteous actions, I believe you deserve to have a second chance."

Martin looked doubtful. "I'm not sure about the morality of such a choice."

"It's not about morality—it's about what you have to offer, I will be able to get you a position with the FBI where you can continue fighting crime. It's a trade off, but will you at least think about it?"

Martin reflected on O'Malley's words. "I will definitely think about it, however, we need to come up with a plan for the escape."

*

The plan came to fruition much quicker than O'-Malley thought it would. The reason for a quick decision on their deliberations came due to the fact that O'Malley was to be moved back to Camp

Logan the next day. To O'Malley's delight, Charley joined them. He did not know the full extent of the reasons except that Martin said it would be explained as they went along. Martin came late that night and disconnected the cameras before opening O"Malley's cell.

"I have decided to take you up on your offer," said Martin.

"I am ecstatic to hear that," said O'Malley. he stuck out his hand to Terran.

Martin continued: "I've hacked the records and entered a transfer form so that the junior agent doesn't find two empty cells and raise the alarm. The administration will think you and Charley have been removed from the holding cells and transferred to Camp Logan during the night."

O'Malley still had some concerns. "What do you propose we do about gaining access to the Lady Anne and getting aboard that link-jumper?"

"Captain Penn has no prior record of who is being transferred and relies on the transferees to give him their files which he keeps as a record. I have prepared the files for the next three individuals who will be replacing some of your military guys. I got all this information from the director's correspondence with The Council."

"We are going to substitute ourselves for three military personnel?"

Martin nodded. "Captain Penn won't know the difference."

"He has seen me before, though. He may become suspicious," answered O"Malley.

Martin pointed to O'Malley's face. "That growth of beard will make a difference, believe me. Captain Penn has seen a host of replacements come through his hands and I doubt whether he takes any real note of their features."

"The hardest part of this will be to take the three imposter generals down before they board the ship which leaves at 6:30 am tomorrow morning."

O'Malley checked the time on the cell block's wall clock. "It's 11:30 pm so I guess we had better get to the docks and find a place to hide."

They extracted Charley and slipped out of the incarceration block to a vehicle in the underground parking garage. Three hours later Martin drove the vehicle into the Liberty City dock area and parked. Martin indicated a group of pallets which contained oil drums.

"We can hide behind those and wait for our targets to arrive. I have brought a few items along to help us achieve our aims."

Martin opened the trunk of the car and removed a large duffle bag. He unzipped the bag and allowed O"Malley to have a peek at the contents.

The special agent gave a low whistle. "Two assault rifles with ammo, rope, and tape—good thinking."

Martin produced two canisters and handed one to O"Malley. "This will take care of our generals. Just spray it in their faces and they will go out like lights.

The three men walked over to the oil drums and hid.

"I'm finished after today if we are caught," whispered Martin.

"You've made the best decision of your life, K.D.," said O'Malley.

"Can someone please tell me what's going on?" complained Charley.

Martin chuckled. "Dillon will explain everything. After all, he is responsible for this."

In a low voice, O'Malley explained exactly what had taken place. "We figured you should be given a chance at life because you didn't turn me in."

Charley's eyes opened wide and he remained speechless for a few moments. Then he grabbed O"Malley in a bear hug. "Thank you, thank you—I've been terrified of dying when Terra finally burns up and have often contemplated taking my own life. Charley teared up and was lost for words. They continued to keep watch until a car drove up and three men got out. The men were laughing and cajoling one another as they started to walk toward the dock. Martin looked at the time.

"It's four-thirty am. We need to take these guys out now and then slip on board—there doesn't appear to be a lookout."

"What are we going to do with them once they have been neutralized?" asked O'Malley.

"I'm hoping there'll be a place on the link-jumper where we can hide them. When we reach the other side we're going to have to take everyone on the transporting vessel prisoner.

Martin and O'Malley moved up behind the men who never detected their presence until Martin called out.

"Hey, you guys—"

The men turned in surprise and the two agents sprayed each man with chloroform. They were so surprised that neither of the three even cried out. They fell to the ground unconscious.

"It will take them several hours to wake up. The ship leaves at six-thirty, so we'll have to find a place in the lifeboat to hide them.

"I'll go and see if the lifeboat hatch is locked. Do you have a lock-picking kit?"

Martin dug into his pants pocket, pulled out a small pouch and handed it to O"Malley.

"Tie the men up and gag them. I"ll be back in a few minutes," said O'Malley.

He slipped up the gangway and boarded the ship. The first rays of light started to streak through the heavens as he made his way to the back of the ship. The link jumper's hatch was not locked and after a quick look inside the vessel, he returned to the dock.

"There's a large empty locker in the bow of the vessel. We can leave the men in there. It doesn't appear to have been used for anything recently."

O'Malley and Martin carried the three men, one at a time, to the lifeboat and hauled their Terran cargo onboard. Charley carried the duffel bag and hid it in a closet inside the vessel. When the tasks were completed the three fugitives had a quick conference. Martin returned to the duffel bag and handed each one a brown manilla-type folder.

"Here are the details of who you will now become. I doubt whether the captain will ask you any details but do quick perusal in case he does."

They heard sounds from within the ship that indicated the crew was waking up and getting ready to prepare the vessel for sailing.

"Let's go back to the dock and wait for someone to come on deck. Each of the generals had a personal bag which the agents had left on the dock behind the oil drums. These were retrieved and they stood at the bottom of the gangway to await the first seaman to come up onto the deck.

28

Mr. President

A hint of a smile played on Norman Hastings lips as he stared out the oval office window. In the distance, he could see the crowd gathered at the boundary on E Street, all in a demonstration of anger at the presidency. Some carried posters, others shouted insults and in consideration of the inclement weather of the day, it showed their resolve in sending a strong message. Hastings turned to Francis Bowman.

"I would say it's playing out pretty well, wouldn't you, Francis?"

"The people are in an absolute uproar," answered Bowman.

"I have just received news that the mercenary group who initiated the silo attack have all been dealt with. There should be no reason to concern ourselves of any exposure. Everyone believes it was the North Koreans, despite their denials. Damian will orchestrate a potential coup with the help of our latest three military replacements and we will be well on the way to set up the platform for change."

"I assume these replacements are the chiefs of the Navy, Air Force, and Marines? When will they be placed in office?" asked Bowman.

"They arrive tomorrow. McHale has the replacements planned for the following day. All three men have trained for several years to take these positions."

"You have certainly made yourself an unpopular figure, Norman. The next few weeks are going to be tough for you."

"All for the greater good, my dear. I expect impeachment to follow and after that, the military will stage their coup. I've been told that our press secretary is so upset with me that he has mentioned to Damian he would gladly see a change in leadership. He's already putting ideas into the minds of the people through the media."

A knock sounded on the door and the president's senior advisor put his head into the office. "I have heard from both the Russian and Chinese ambassadors, Mr. President."

"Come in, Alfred. Tell me what they said."

The advisor slipped into the office and closed the door. He greeted Bowman and sat down next to her on the couch.

"The Russians are saying while they admire your restraint it does show that America does not have the will to go to war anymore. The Chinese are demanding that we stay out of North Korean territorial waters and air space; that any further US aggression against North Korea will be met with stern resistance. North Korea has just threatened to attack South Korea in retaliation for the attack on their silo. They say the US military carried out the attack from South Korean territory and launched the missile in order to provoke the destruction of their country."

"It sounds as though they are the ones who are trying to provoke a world war," said Bowman. "It would make no sense for the US to attack its own territory with a nuclear strike."

The senior advisor had a pertinent question which he felt he needed to ask. "What would you do in the event North Korea attacks its southern neighbor, Mr. President?"

"We will have to deal with the matter if it arises."

"Would it not be the time to take North Korea out altogether? We have an opportunity to totally annihilate the bastards and set up a temporary rule under the South's supervision, suggested the advisor."

"That wouldn't be a good idea, Alfred. The Chinese might decide to take advantage and attack United States interests all over the world. It could also place us in direct conflict with the Russians."

The senior advisor's face turned a deep red. "But we are the most powerful force in the entire world, Mr. President. Neither the Chinese or the Russians are able to match us in military strength."

"It's not all about military strength, Alfred. It's about the lives of people and diplomacy."

The advisor stood and walked to the door. "I would advise you to take action now, Mr. President. Don't say I didn't warn you."

Hastings glared at him. "Your warning is noted, now get out of my office."

The advisor gave the president a malevolent stare and slammed the door on his way out.

"And another enemy is made—well done, Mr. President," said Bowman.

*

Captain Penn looked each of the men in the eye, nodded his head and smiled. "Welcome aboard the Lady Anne, gentlemen. Our journey will take some time and you are welcome to stay in your cabins for the duration.

Martin took the lead as O'Malley looked away from Penn's stare and focused on the bridge instruments. "Here are our files, Captain. I understand you will return them to us when we reach the transition point?"

Penn took the files and opened each one, giving the details a quick scan. "I take a photocopy of the title page for my records. You will get the originals back."

Penn stared at O'Malley. "You look familiar to me, sir."

O'Malley didn't miss a beat. "If you read the newspapers, Captain, you might remember that I served in the coast guard under the name of Lieutenant Bill Riley. I have recently decorated for bravery—It's all there in my file. I have been fortunate enough to be chosen for this assignment because of my look-alike status. I will be impersonating a general in the Earth's military."

Captain Penn glanced through the file titles and opened the one marked with the name Riley. He scanned down the list and squinted at the photograph. O'Malley interrupted.

"Of course I have since grown this beard because we were informed that the general I'm impersonating has recently grown one."

The Captain closed the file and nodded. "I can see the resemblance. Gentlemen, breakfast will be served downstairs at 7:00 am. Please make yourselves at home on my ship but remember to obey the posted rules."

The three men all gave sighs of relief as they made their way down from the bridge to the cabins.

"Just as well you had a quick read through your file or he might have suspected something," said Martin.

The cruise ended thirteen hours later. The three men donned their protective gear and came out on deck to view the area of transition. Miles and miles of ocean stretched out all around them except for a patch of dense fog which hovered above the waters about one hundred yards off the port bow.

Penn came down from the bridge and extended his hand to each of the men. He handed them their files as promised.

"Are you men ready? It won't take long to the other side and you may feel alarming vibrations and noises but don't worry about it. The time capsule has done over fifty trips through the link without any problem. You can climb aboard and take a seat. Two of my men will strap you in and set up the oxygen."

The three men climbed aboard the link-jumper and took their seats. Two of Penn's men entered, checked over all the instrumentation on the overhead panels, strapped the passengers into their seats and attached the oxygen masks. The hatch closed, followed by an eternity of time before the boat started to move toward the heavy bank of fog.

All this was familiar to O'Malley but for Martin and Charley, it evoked a fear of the unknown. The vibrations started up in conjunction with the high-pitched scream that had intrigued O'Malley on his first trip. The vibrations increased in intensity and O'Malley turned his head to look at Charley, seated next to him. Perspiration had broken out on the operator's brow and his eyes opened wide with fright.

Charley turned his head and looked at O"Malley, who smiled but because of the oxygen mask, only the creases around the agent's eyes were a visible sign of his intent. A short while later the journey ended and the vibrations died down as the lifeboat exited the fog bank in the Bermuda Triangle. They were home. The boat bumped against a solid object and O'Malley knew they had moored next to the transport ship, the Lady Gray. Minutes later they heard the sound of feet on the deck above them and the hatch opened. Two men entered and released the oxygen lines first, then the straps which held the three passengers. A strong smell of sea air filtered through into the cabin and O'Malley took several deep breaths. The air bore no difference to Terra's but to him this was Earth.

One of the seamen clapped Martin on the shoulder. "Welcome to Earth, Sir. How are things back home?"

Martin looked him in the eye. "Things are getting worse and I'm really glad to be here."

The seaman grinned. "It's such a treat to be able to walk out in the sunshine and not get incinerated. You, gentlemen, are going to love it. When you're ready you can make your way outside. A ladder has been provided for boarding the ship. Captain Vargas awaits you."

"How many crew members do you have on the Lady Gray?" asked Martin.

"There's only a few of us. Myself and a colleague, who see to all the deck-work—then there's the Captain, his first mate, the engineer, radio operator and the cook—seven of us, altogether."

"Just give us a few moments to regain our composure. That was quite a trip, as short as it was," said Martin.

"Take your time, Sir. We're not in a rush."

The two seamen exited the cabin and climbed the ladder onto the Lady Gray's deck. Charley shook his head.

"I'm glad I don't have to do that again. Are you sure I'll be able to stay, Dillon?"

O'Malley laughed. "I'm positive, Charley. Welcome to your new planet and a new life."

Martin stood unsteadily to his feet and held onto the back of a seat for a few moments. "I'm going to get the rifles. Once we're on board we'll take the captain and his crew prisoner. You can make a call to one of your colleagues in the FBI and they can send someone to get us."

O'Malley also stood up and had to wait a moment to regain his balance. "We need to look at the Captain's files to ascertain exactly who has been transferred from Terra. I don't want to contact my boss if he has been replaced."

"Good point," said Martin. "Are you both ready?"

He pulled out the duffel bag and extracted the two M16 assault trifles. "We can return and release our three bogus generals from the forward storage locker. Their brig's going to be overcrowded."

O"Malley chuckled. "We can lock several of them in a cabin. I doubt whether they can get up to much mischief there."

The three men climbed up onto the deck of the Lady Gray and made their way toward the bridge. The two seamen who had assisted them in the capsule's cabin did not notice the weapons being carried by O'Malley and Martin. They made their way to the bridge where Captain Vargas was busy with his first mate. The captain looked up as they walked onto the bridge. The smile on his face faded when he saw the M16's pointed at him.

"Captain Vargas? Special Agent O'Malley—I am arresting you for your involvement in Operation Terra Firma. You will call your crew up onto the deck."

Vargas turned pale. "This is an outrage. You won't get away with this."

He made the call over the intercom, however, and fifteen minutes later the crew, plus the three imposter generals, were locked up; three men in the brig and four in one of the cabins. O"Malley checked through the captain's filing system and found the relevant files. A quick check revealed that besides himself, only three other people had been transferred to Terra. The three generals, who had not yet been replaced by impersonators, were up for transfer that day on the return of the Lady Gray to New York. O'Malley found the communications room and placed a call to the FBI's radio network.

✳

29

McDonald and Martinez

MacDonald and Martinez followed on behind the white truck in the hope they would not be detected. The driver, however, made a sudden sharp turn into an adjacent road and put his foot on the gas. The two agents continued straight on and called their colleagues on the radio. MacDonald had been charged with the duty of leading agent in the absence of O'Malley. When Martinez had called from the deli MacDonald placed a call to Gwen Farrell and another agent, both in separate vehicles, to join him outside the deli.

Farrell, with her companion in tow, had parked close by and waited for MacDonald to give orders. They had seen Vera exit the deli with a man she recognized from the shootout in the warehouse. Martinez followed on close behind the two Terrans. When the white truck took off with MacDonald and Martinez in close pursuit Gwen and her partner asked for instructions. MacDonald told her to turn into the street which ran parallel, to the left of the one in which they were driving. He told the second agent to do the same thing but with the street running parallel on the right. This way if the driver of the truck turned into any adjacent street he ran the risk of being picked up by another tail.

"Gwen? He will be crossing your street, or turning into it, at any moment—keep an eye open."

She acknowledged and moments later the truck flashed through the intersection in front of her.

"Got him. I"m following, but have to make a turn to the left, against the red."

The chase went on until the truck driver decided he no longer saw the suspicious vehicle in the group of cars behind him and slowed down to a normal pace. By this time the second agent had it in his sights and kept up a running commentary of information which allowed MacDonald and Farrell to follow on in the general direction of travel.

An hour later the truck drove into downtown Atlantic City and carried on through the city center to take a route which led to the suburbs. Gwen followed at a distance and kept the others informed as they found their way through the city. Using their GPS's the agents were able to decide who should follow and who should hang back, or take a different route. The truck pulled in at a residence and parked outside a house. MacDonald checked the address on the computer.

"This house belongs to Beverley Swales, the White House chief of staff. It's an investment she made years ago and is rented out to a tenant."

"I think we may have found the devil's new lair," said Martinez.

They parked their vehicle on an adjacent road and waited for Gwen Farrell and the other agent to arrive. Together the four FBI operatives entered the road, found Swales's property and watched the entrance for activity. They saw the white truck parked in front of the stairs to the verandah and noticed that a short section of road serviced the backyard of the home.

MacDonald spoke to Farrell and the agent who had joined with them in the chase. "Make your way through the neighbor's property and see what they have in the backyard. I would like to get a read on how many people might be in the house. Martinez and I will wait here."

Farrell and her partner entered the adjoining property and made their way along the fence until they could see Swales's backyard. There were no vehicles parked but under a cluster of trees, they spied a container. While they peeked through the hedge on the border of the two properties Vera appeared carrying a bowl and a jug. She walked over to the container, unlocked the padlock and disappeared inside.

Farrell got on her radio to MacDonald.

"I think we've found where they are keeping those two boys. There's a container back here and the woman has just entered it with a bowl and jug," she said.

MacDonald reviewed the situation. "Can you find a way through the hedge without making too much noise?" he asked.

Farrell confirmed there to be a gap between the back wall of the neighbor's property and the hedge.

"We can squeeze through. What are your order's, Roland?"

"Move in on the container and apprehend the woman. If you find the boys, set them free. Diego and I will bust in through the front door and see who's in the house."

MacDonald and Martinez ran down the driveway, up the stairs, and onto the verandah. Martinez tried the door and found it unlocked. The two agents flung the door open and entered the hallway with their guns at the ready. A surprised man, caught in mid-stride between rooms, pulled a revolver from a shoulder holster and managed to get off a round before MacDonald nailed him. A hail of bullets from a shotgun sprayed through an adjoining door which led into a kitchen. The two agents were forced to take cover and MacDonald hoped they were not going to be outnumbered. A flash of light seared his eyes as one of the occupants threw a stun grenade into the hallway.

*

The Lady Gray wallowed in the placid waters of the North Atlantic ocean under a cloudless sky as a Sikorsky helicopter, sporting the FBI logo, hovered thirty feet above the stern like a giant dragonfly. The sound of the rotor's blades beat a tattoo while the surface of the waters around the aft of the vessel rippled under the down-draft.

Armed FBI police in battledress slid down on four ropes extended from the two doors of the helicopter and landed on the deck. O'Malley, Martin, and Charley were there to greet them. The police commander saluted as the rest of his squad lined up behind him and awaited orders. He removed his sunglasses and addressed O'Malley.

"It's good to see you again, Dillon. We thought you were a goner."

They embraced and O'Malley introduced his two comrades.

The commander shook their hands. "Welcome to our universe, gentlemen. Any friend of Dillon's is a friend of mine."

Three of the squad members remained behind on the Lady Gray to sail it and the captive crew back to New York while O'Malley and his two comrades flew back in the Sikorsky. The helicopter approached the helipad at the J. Edgar Hoover building and O'Malley saw a group of people, all co-workers, in a circle around the landing platform, waving their arms. The chopper landed and to O'Malley's surprise, the group of people all surged toward the pad to greet them as they disembarked. At the head of the crowd, he saw his boss, James Ingram.

After the reunion O'Malley, K.D Martin and Charley sat in the deputy director's office and told their full story.

Ingram related the FBI's progress. "We've acted on the information you gave us with regard to the imposters who are in office. A man calling himself Norman Hastings, the president's impersonator, and a woman, Francis Bowman, are both in custody. The man who impersonated General Mumford, chairman of the joint chiefs, has also been apprehended. They had executed a plan to subjugate the military and have the president deposed. The worst part is that Hastings and Hall had devised a plan to commandeer a North Korean Nuke to strike America and have devastated one of the Hawaiian Islands."

O'Malley expressed his concern. "That's terrible—what are the casualties?"

"The missile hit the large island of Hawaii plum in the center, close to Mauna Kea. Fortunately, it was a small warhead and the damage is not that extensive, however, the radiation problem is serious and we have had to evacuate at least half a million people. The astronomy projects on top of the mountain all sustained some damage," explained Ingram.

"Just as well the North Koreans are not that far advanced with their nukes," said O'Malley.

Ingram continued. "The imposters arranged for a mercenary group to attack the DPRK silo and fire off the nuke. They had the mercenaries wiped out by our military who believed the arrangement to be a genuine executive order."

"That must have ruffled the North Korean feathers. Did America retaliate?" asked O'Malley.

"Hastings plan was to show weakness on behalf of the White House. He hoped to start a military coup to replace the entire government," answered Ingram.

O'Malley shared the details of the dimensional link's discovery by the Terrans with its geographic position and that there would be more individuals to apprehend before they could deal a death blow to the Terran Council's plans.

"We substituted ourselves for the three generals who were on their way to take over the Army, Navy and Air Force. They will be arriving on the Lady Gray, the transport vessel used to ferry people back and forth, from the dimensional link."

Martin shared the details about the parallel universe and the problem of the failing magnetic field which had placed their planet in danger.

When all the sharing of information ended Ingram broached a subject he knew would upset O'Malley.

"I don't want to alarm you, Dillon but there is more bad news. Your son, along with young Gerry Swales son of the White House chief of staff, were both taken prisoner by this group who are running operation Terra Firma here on Earth."

O'Malley's eyes showed his concern and his face turned pale. "When did this happen and how?"

Ingram shared the relevant information. "I also must tell you that your double was seen yesterday by MacDonald and Martinez. He joined them out of the blue in your favorite haunt. They knew it wasn't you because of the password."

"What's happened to him," asked O'Malley.

"They didn't let on that they knew he was an imposter, in the hope he would lead them to the boys and the rest of their group."

O'Malley considered Ingram's news. "I guess I was on their list for replacement."

"We have some good news, however. Your colleagues, MacDonald and Martinez, have picked up on a lead and the last I heard they were following up on a possible hideout."

O"Malley stood and walked to the door. "I had better go and see Janet. She will be beside herself with worry. Can you fix up our friends here? I believe they have earned the right to become legal citizens of our country and universe."

The deputy director smiled. "I will see to the applications immediately. You go off and see your wife. You can also try to contact MacDonald and see if they have had any success."

O'Malley shook hands with Martin and Charley. "The boss will take good care of you guys, don't worry about a thing and thanks for everything."

Ingram had one more stipulation. "I have organized a new cell phone and a vehicle for you to use, Dillon. Drop in at the requisitioning office on your way down to the parking garage."

O'Malley thanked him and left.

✳

30

The two Boys are Found

After squeezing between the back wall of the neighboring property and the boundary fence Gwen Farrell and her partner crept toward the container's open door. They could see the back of the house and kept an eye open for any movement by the occupants. Gwen took the lead and waited behind the container door for a few moments to give MacDonald and Martinez time for their approach. Gunfire erupted from somewhere inside the house and she took it as a signal to enter the container.

The two agents stepped through the entrance with weapons at the ready. The occupant had turned to exit the container on hearing the gunfire. The woman, taken by surprise, froze at the sight of the two operatives.

"Remember me?" asked Gwen. Her finger tightened a fraction on the trigger of her revolver.

Vera threw her hands up into the air. "Who are you?"

"Agent Gwen Farrell of the FBI and this time you are not going to get away. I haven't forgotten that you left me for dead in that warehouse."

Gwen's eye moved down to the two disheveled boys who couldn't believe what they were seeing. Steven stood to his feet and a grin spread out across his features. "Agent Farrell? At last, you've found us."

Gerry Swales began to cry. Gwen wanted to put her arms around him but Vera still had to be dealt with. She saw that the boys had been chained to the wall of the container. The sound of gunfire continue to erupt from the house and after a moment's lull, the sound of a stun grenade reverberated throughout the entire premises. Gwen had no idea with regard to MacDonald's status but she knew the two agents did not have any grenades with them.

"Do you have a key for these locks?" she asked Vera. Janet O'Malley's double remained silent.

Gwen turned to her partner. "Search her for keys."

A search of Vera's pockets revealed nothing. "The keys are inside," said Vera.

A voice at the container's entrance made both agents swivel around to face a new threat. Gwen kept her gun trained on Vera while her partner pointed his weapon at a person who stood partially hidden behind the door.

The voice belonged to a man whom Gwen recognized as one of those who was present in the warehouse on the day she had been shot. The man's pistol pointed at Gwen's head.

"Put down your weapons," said the man.

Gwen's partner refocused his revolver. "You put down your weapon."

The menace in the man's voice made it evident that he would not obey any order from them.

"If you don't I will shoot your partner and the two boys before you can pull that trigger."

"You're bluffing," said Gwen.

"Try me," said the man. He turned his attention to Vera. "Walk slowly toward me, love. Don't be afraid she won't shoot you."

Gwen was conflicted. Vera moved slowly between her and the wall of the container until she passed through the door. The man withdrew his gun and slammed the container door shut.

Gwen lowered her weapon in disbelief. Her only hope lay in MacDonald and Martinez overcoming the occupants of the house. The hope began to fade, however, after several minutes of shouting MacDonald's name brought no response. The only light came in through a small square hole which someone had cut into the container's back wall, a few inches below the roof.

The absence of gunfire told its own story. The two agents were trapped together with Steven O'Malley and Gerry Swales, who after several days of captivity, couldn't believe their present plight. So near and yet so far.

*

O'Malley wrapped his arms around his wife, Janet. They had both shared the password to verify each other's identity and the strain of present events had them both shedding tears of tension.

"I'm so glad you're safe. I was worried out of my mind when you just suddenly disappeared. The thought of never seeing you again was unbearable," cried Janet.

"I have been through quite a harrowing experience over the last few weeks and it has given me time to think about our relationship. I thought about you and Steve all the time and realized all I want is that we should be back together as a family."

"There are things we will have to talk about," said Janet.

"Of course, however, it's my first priority to find our son and his friend."

"Are you able to share where you've been and what happened to you?" she asked.

"Not right now, but I will when this whole thing is behind us."

They kissed and hugged for several more moments until O'Malley broke away.

"I have to try to get hold of Roland. He and Diego are on the trail of the group leaders. We hope it will lead to their new hideout and the two boys."

"What is this group's mission and where are they from? How come they have all these doubles?" asked Janet.

"It's a plot by foreigners to subjugate the American military machine and take over the government but as I said, I will share the details with you once we find the boys and wrap the whole thing up."

"Are they responsible for the attack on Hawaii or was it really the Koreans?"

For the moment O'Malley didn't want to answer all her questions. Please, sweetheart,—I'll explain everything I know when I have found Steve."

Janet buried her face in his chest. "I understand, Dillon. Go and do what you have to do and then come home."

He left his wife's house and drove back to DC. Much later, back in his office at the FBI, O'Malley made a call to MacDonald but got no answer. He felt frustrated and didn't know where to start. A quick glance at this desk revealed that a few items were not in their usual place. He always left the desk spotless, with everything in neat geometric spaces but now the desk pad had been moved to another spot. The laptop's screen had also been left in the upright position and a sudden realization entered his mind. His doppelgänger had been in the office.

O'Malley called his secretary in the next-door office.

"When last did you see me, Iris?"

She gave him a puzzled frown. "You were in about an hour ago, boss. Why?"

"What did I say to you?"

She tilted her head and stared at him. "You said you were going out for a while. It was soon after you left Ingram's office. What's going on?"

O'Malley realized that she hadn't been told about his double. "Oh nothing, just forget I asked."

He tried MacDonald's number again but the phone reverted to the answering service. Without warning the handheld radio on his belt, crackled to life.

"Dillon—is that you?" The voice of MacDonald sounded breathless.

O'Malley snatched the radio from its pouch. "Roland, where are you?"

A moment's silence followed and then he heard MacDonald's voice again.

"It's chaos here, Dillon."

O'Malley realized that MacDonald was trying to verify an identity.

"Yes, I understand you have chaos. I have chaos too—it's the real me, Roland."

"Thank God," answered MacDonald. "We are pinned down here in a house in Atlantic City, New Jersey. Diego is unconscious and I'm injured with a bullet in the shoulder. We have found the latest hideout but they had numbers and a stun grenade."

"Are you still in the house?" asked O'Malley.

"I'm outside now. I believe these people were keeping your son and young Gerry Swales holed up in a backyard container. Gwen and the boys went to free them but somehow the enemy got the upper hand."

"Where are Gwen and the boys now?" asked O'-Malley.

"They are locked in the container," answered MacDonald.

"Why don't you just shoot the lock off?"

"Neither Diego or I have any ammo left."

"Give me the address. I believe the chopper is still available. It's the quickest way I can get to you, said O'Malley."

MacDonald gave him the address and ended the call. O'Malley called the chopper's pilot who was still in the flight center's office and then called for a medic to join him at the helipad. Twenty-five minutes later the chopper hovered above the house in Atlantic City and O'Malley, followed by the medic, slithered down a rope to land in the front yard. The two men raced around the back to find a disconsolate MacDonald sitting next to a forty-foot container. The medic gave immediate attention to the injured agent while O'Malley shot off the padlock.

He flung the door open and was greeted by a joyful Gwen Farrell. The special agent rushed past her, however, to embrace his tearful son.

"I will never let you out of my sight again, my boy. I'm so sorry for what you've been through."

Gwen's partner, Morris, shot the locks off the chains which held the boys and set them free. The medic, satisfied that Macdonald's wound was not serious left to find Martinez, who lay injured somewhere in the house. The Terran group had fled the scene and left the body of the man whom MacDonald had shot in the house.

O'Malley called Gwen Farrell to his side. "You and Morris take the boys in your vehicle. Drop Steven off at his mother's place in Baltimore, then take Gerry Swales back to his home. The imposter mother is in jail but Ingram has left a guard who will look after Gerry and his sister. The medic can take Morris's car to ferry MacDonald and Martinez to the hospital."

The medic returned with a disoriented Martinez in tow.

"He'll recover and return to normal within a few hours, but we need to get them both to a hospital," said the medic.

MacDonald protested. "I'll be fine. I don't need to go to a hospital."

"Calm down, Roland. Let the doctor attend to that gunshot wound," answered O'Malley.

He told Morris to give the keys of his car to the medic. "Go with Gwen and the boys. I'll take Roland's car—there's something I have to do."

O'Malley slipped behind the wheel of MacDonald's SUV, fired up the motor and pulled away from the curb but at that precise moment another vehicle pulled up level with his. Its driver peered through the side window at him. O'Malley froze as he recognized the man's face. The driver of the vehicle recognized him at the same instant and stepped on the gas pedal. For a moment O'Malley, in a mild state of confusion, stared after the fleeing SUV, then gave the eight cylinders full throttle. His doppelgänger had a fifty-yard start. ❊

31

O'Malley confronts his Doppelgänger

O'Malley's doppelgänger raced toward Philadelphia at full speed and at times the odometer read one-hundred and forty miles per hour. A shortcut took them onto the Atlantic City Expressway and moments later they barreled passed the vehicle driven by Gwen Farrell. O'Malley spoke to the voice-activated telephone system in his vehicle to contact Gwen.

"I have just spotted my double. He must have come to the house for a meeting with the other impersonators and discovered us there. You keep going and get the boys back to their homes; I am going to follow him."

O'Malley contacted the medic and told him what was going on. "Don't worry about me. Get MacDonald and Martinez to the hospital—I'll be fine."

The medic acknowledged the instruction and did not attempt to give chase.

The doppelgänger veered off onto the 395, toward Baltimore, and O'Malley wondered where he was headed for. The double's destination soon became evident, however, as he approached the city of Baltimore and took the freeway which led to Janet's suburb. O'Malley called on the voice-activated phone service again and gave it Janet's number. The phone rang for several seconds before she answered.

"Jan—get out of the house. My double is on route to your place and I'm in hot pursuit. This could end up in a shootout."

Janet managed a sharp intake of breath. "Be careful, Dillon. I'll go and hide in the shed behind the garage."

"Do that, sweetheart, and don't come out unless I call you. I'll use the password."

The doppelgänger swerved into the road where Janet lived and screeched to a stop outside her property. He rushed into the yard with his revolver in hand and up the stairs of the porch, to the front door. Finding it locked he broke the door with one kick and rushed into the hallway. At that moment O'Malley arrived and stopped in the driveway. He slid out of the seat and pulled the Glock from its holster.

Inside the house, the doppelgänger called Janet's name and made a quick search of the rooms. He ran into the kitchen as O'Malley burst through the front door, took quick aim and fired. The imposter managed to escape unharmed through the kitchen door and fled into the backyard as O'Malley's bullet ripped into the side of the doorjamb. O'Malley wondered if his double knew about the shed behind the garage. The thought caused an injection of adrenaline and he launched himself through the door, into the backyard.

The doppelgänger had disappeared. He must have guessed where Janet would try to hide. O'Malley rushed to the back corner of the garage from where he could see the shed. The Shed's entrance could not be seen from his vantage point so he crept up to the nearest wall and peeked around the corner. The door stood ajar and he feared the worst. A strangled scream rent the air. O'Malley stepped towards the entrance but the doppelgänger beat him to it. Holding Janet around the waist O'Malley's double shielded himself with her body and pointed a revolver at her head.

"Back off, O'Malley. I heard that you had miraculously appeared yesterday. I don't know how you got back to this universe but I will take care of it."

O'Malley felt an ice-cold hand clutch at his heart. "Don't harm her. I'll do what ever you say."

"Put your gun down on the ground and back away—slowly."

O'Malley obeyed the doppelgänger's instruction and waited.

*

MacDonald heard O'Malley's conversation with the medic as they drove down the expressway toward Philadelphia. He felt woozy from loss of blood but the medic had stemmed its flow and he knew he would be okay. He realized that O'Malley might need help to catch his double. They reached the turnpike where Route 42 met with Route 95 and he saw O'Malley, still in hot pursuit of his doppelgänger turn onto the 95 toward Baltimore. MacDonald realized that the doppelgänger's destination was Janet's home.

He told the medic to place a call to James Ingram, the FBI's deputy director. When Ingram came on the line MacDonald used the password to verify his identity and told him that O'Malley might need some assistance. Ingram thanked MacDonald for the call and the medic turned onto the 95 on route to Washington DC.

*

James Ingram and K.D. Martin were in consultation at the time of MacDonald's call.

"I'm deputizing you as an FBI agent until we can make it permanent. I want you to accompany me on a quick venture."

He placed a call to the FBI flight center and asked if the helicopter had returned. On confirmation that the flight attendants were busy refueling the craft he informed the pilot that an emergency required his instant services. The two men made their way to the helipad where the chopper awaited them. Ingram gave a quick instruction and they took off.

"Follow the 95 up toward Philadelphia. We're looking for two FBI vehicles and they will be traveling at speed."

With the sun already setting Ingram worried about the remaining light. The sun's rays had slipped beyond the horizon and they had about an hour before darkness would settle over the entire region. Below them, vehicles could be seen in a two-way flow of direction. Twenty-five minutes later they could see the lights of Baltimore beneath them and moments after that, two speeding vehicles in tandem.

"There they are," said Martin. He pointed to the turnpike where the 95 met with the turn-off to Baltimore.

"They are turning off toward the city. O'Malley figured that the doppelgänger would head for Janet Malley's residence and it looks as though he was right," said Ingram.

He gave the pilot a further instruction and the chopper veered off in the direction of the suburbs.

"The doppelgänger knows he needs some leverage. He will probably try to take Janet as a hostage," said Martin.

"Are you ready for a quick drop by rope?" asked Ingram.

K.D.Martin grinned. "Done it many times."

The chopper came to a certain street corner in one of the suburbs and hovered thirty feet above the ground. Cars stopped and people ogled as the two agents slithered down the ropes to the ground. They raced around the corner toward Janet O'Malley's house and saw one of the vehicles parked on the road and another in the driveway.

"Take this," said Ingram. He handed Martin a revolver and the two men raced into the yard and onto the porch. They found the front door kicked in and proceeded cautiously along the hallway. A quick look in each of the rooms confirmed the house to be empty. The kitchen door stood open which indicated where the others had gone.

"They're in the backyard somewhere. You have the gun, so you go first," said Ingram. They stepped into the backyard with Martin in the lead.

A woman's scream drew their attention to the shed behind the garage and they saw O'Malley slip round the corner and disappear.

"The shed entrance must be around the back. We need to find a vantage point where we can see it and not be seen ourselves," said Martin.

They moved laterally using a grapevine as cover and found a bush behind which they could conceal themselves. O'Malley, now in their sights, moved toward the shed's entrance but stopped when the doppelgänger appeared in the entrance with Janet as a shield.

Martin and Ingram watched O'Malley slowly put his Glock down on the ground and back up. They could hear the conversation and Ingram had a bad feeling about what was about to happen. He knew the impersonator might not yet realize that his cover had already been blown and would seek to eliminate both his captives. There appeared little they could do to prevent it. O'Malley stood in the direct line of sight of the doppelgänger, who also held Janet as a shield.

A shot, in an attempt to take the imposter down, would be a high risk due to the limited exposure of the imposter's body. Ingram glanced at Martin who covered the scene with his revolver and Martin caught his eye. Ingram shook his head.

"I can do it," whispered Martin.

"It's an impossible shot," hissed Ingram.

The doppelgänger pointed his gun at O'Malley's head and time seemed to stand still for everyone.

Martin fired. The bullet singed O'Malley's ear and parted the hair above Janet's forehead. She slumped in the imposter's arm and for a split-second, they held their collective breaths. With a sudden lurch, the doppelgänger fell forward. They saw the blood from his head spatter all over the side of Janet's face and the small visible patch of the imposter's skin looked as though it had been torn away. O'Malley lunged forward and caught Janet as she fell to the ground. He turned her around in his arms to check for signs of life and noticed the burned skin where Martin's bullet had passed on its way. Her eyes fluttered open and she gave O'Malley a weak smile. He kissed her gently and turned to look in the direction from where the shot had come.

K.D. Martin stood there with the revolver's barrel tilted slightly upward while a small curl of smoke drifted away from the muzzle. Their eyes met and O'Malley could not restrain the tears of relief. Ingram rushed forward and knelt down next to the couple.

'Talk about a close shave," said the deputy director.

O'Malley felt the side of his ear where Martin's bullet had scorched the skin. "Yeah, thanks to Mr. wonder-shot." He stared in awe at Martin, who came up beside them.

"Where did you learn to shoot like that?" asked O'Malley.

Martin chuckled. "I was the institute's best shot ten years running, however, I must confess—I thought it was only a fifty-fifty chance."

"If you hadn't taken the gamble Janet and I would be dead by now," said O'Malley.

Martin smiled. "I must earn my new citizenship."

"More like universal-ship," stated Ingram.

Janet opened her eyes again and stared at Martin. "Who are you?"

The three men looked at each other and then O'-Malley intervened. "It's a long story, sweetheart. One which I will tell you later."

They helped Janet to her feet. Ingram pulled out his cell phone and placed a call. When he had given an instruction he turned to O'Malley and pointed to the doppelgänger.

"I called our satellite office here in Baltimore. They will send two agents to clean up this mess."

O'Malley turned the body over and despite the fatal would in the imposter's head, marveled at the sight of his double.

"This is uncanny. I would never have been able to tell the difference between us."

"I think we all need some strong coffee," said Janet.

While they sat in the kitchen the sound of a voice came from the front door.

"Is anybody home."

O'Malley looked at Ingram and Martin, who had pulled out his revolver in the anticipation of danger.

"It's Gwen Farrell. She has the two boys with her," said O'Malley.

Janet rushed to the hallway and embraced her son.

✳

32

A Plan to rescue the Prisoners on Terra

Three days later Alan McHale, Vera, and their helpers were apprehended at the New York docks. The Terrans realized that their mission had been compromised and decided to make a run for the Bermuda Triangle. O'Malley's guess at their final strategy had been correct. McHale confessed afterward that they didn't know about O'Malley's return or the capture of Captain Vargas and the Lady Gray.

With Operation Terra Firma shut down O'Malley had a long discussion with James Ingram as to how they would approach the rescue of President Chambers, Beverly Swales, and General Mumford. O'Malley offered to lead a team of commandos on a raid through the link and across the country to Camp Logan.

"Their Council doesn't know that K.D and I have escaped their universe. They will also be expecting three generals from the Pentagon, as prisoners for Camp Logan. I propose to take a small group of special operations soldiers and commandeer the Lady Anne, the ferry they use to transport people to and from the link."

"How will you get to Camp Logan without being detected?" asked Ingram.

K.D. Martin who had been silent answered the question. "The Lady Anne anchors near the link every week on a Sunday night and waits for the capsule to appear. We can use the ship to sail to a small port, north of Liberty City which the Institute abandoned five years ago. There is a village about ten miles inland where a vehicle can be commandeered for transport and we can then travel by road to the outskirts of Liberty City where the Institute maintains an aircraft at the local airport. A plane leaves once every week, to transport people back and forth from Camp Logan."

Ingram raised his eyebrows. "You are proposing you join in on this mission, K.D.?"

"I wouldn't miss it for anything. If O'Malley is going then I insist—I know the geography, the customs, and the Institute's protocols," said Martin.

"I second that," said O'Malley. There's no one else I would want by my side more. You run the risk, however, of being shot for treason, if we're caught."

Martin laughed. "I know the risks, Dillon. It's the least I can do. Besides, I'm now a fully fledged citizen of the USA and the FBI's newest operative."

Ingram picked up the phone. "It's settled then. You two can make your plans to requisition the equipment you need and I'll make the appropriate arrangements for three special operations men to join you. Be ready to leave by 6:00 am tomorrow morning."

*

The trip through the link took place without any incidents. Captain Vargas had been forthcoming with information on how the contact with his colleagues in the alternate universe worked. In exchange for their lives, he and his men became cooperative and had given O'Malley all the details of his operation. The captains, Vargas and Penn, would communicate with each other and wait for the link-jumper every Monday morning, to facilitate any relevant transfers of people and information.

When the Lady Gray reached the link in the Bermuda Triangle, Captain Vargas used a signal projector to send a communication through the link to the Lady Anne and set up the transfer of personnel. He told Captain Penn that he had three substituted generals to transfer to Terra. Penn returned the communication that the Lady Anne would be waiting to take on the prisoners. O'Malley, accompanied by Martin plus three special ops soldiers, made the journey through the link to the parallel universe.

The assault team took over the Lady Anne and sailed to their point of disembarkation, a small abandoned port north of Liberty City. That night the men locked the crew of the Lady Anne in the brig and proceeded overland to a village where they searched around for an appropriate vehicle to purchase. A drunk, out of work fisherman provided them with an old double-cab truck which they bought from him for an exorbitant price and they made their way toward the outskirts of Liberty City.

At the local airport, Martin led them to the Institute's hanger which housed a small jet transporter, where the team marched unannounced into the flight office and captured the two pilots. After submitting a flight plan to the tower they forced the pilots to fly to Camp Logan. Under duress one of the pilots told them that the security at Camp Logan would be suspicious of the jet's unplanned arrival.

"Radio ahead and tell security that on the authorization of Director Roshē, the transfer of a group of dissidents, due to overcrowding in the institute's cells has become necessary, hence the unscheduled delivery," ordered Martin.

The pilot called up the airport authority at Camp Logan and gave them the information. After a brief wait, they received authorization to land the aircraft. Up to this point, Martin and O'Malley's plan had worked with flawless precision. The transporter landed and taxied up to the reception building. When they came to a standstill O'Malley took charge. He turned to one of his men.

"Keep watch over these two fliers and make sure they don't try to take off until we return."

He handed each of the remaining soldiers a bundle. "The star's rays carry a lethal dose of radiation so wear the protective garb until we are in the building."

One of the pilots opened the door and the assault team stepped down onto the runway.

"All seems quiet," said Martin. The men carried M16 assault rifles and were dressed in military fatigues.

"We must not let our guard down, said O'Malley. "This is the most dangerous part of our mission."

They walked through the entrance and everything appeared normal until a burst of gunfire stopped them in their tracks. A security guard popped up from behind a desk with an assault rifle.

"Stop right there and put down your weapons. You are surrounded," he shouted.

O'Malley whispered to Martin. "I thought it was too good to be true. We can't allow them to take us, prisoner."

"I think the guard may be bluffing about having us surrounded. You dive to the left and I will go to the right," said Martin.

O'Malley gave the two men behind him a quick instruction and they all dived to the ground in unison with their rifles blazing. The security guard also dived for cover as retaliatory fire came from behind the door him. Martin had been correct in his assumption. The four members of the team crawled in different directions to find cover and the guards continued to fire on them. One of the team members sustained a light wound in his right leg but managed to crawl to a line of chairs. It would appear the guards lacked real-life experience as they took cover the moment the team returned the fire.

O'Malley knew from experience that Camp Logan's security operated with four guards. Two accompanied the dissidents to the refinery in the bus every day. He looked at his watch which had been set to Terran time. They had twenty minutes before the camp inmates returned from the Thousand Dunes refinery. O'Malley, lying under a row of chairs looked across at Martin who had taken refuge behind a series of recycling bins and caught his attention.

"They must have called Director Roshē at the Institute to verify our unscheduled visit."

"We have about thirty-five minutes before a jet reaches us from the closest base on the coast—a little longer if it's a transporter with some troops."

"The bus is usually on time and should get here before that. We should be able to round up our friends and make an escape," answered O'Malley.

Martin pointed to the two guards who had hidden behind various items of furniture near the far door of the terminal's passenger area.

"We have to neutralize this lot before the inmates arrive. Any suggestions?"

"Only two guards remain at the camp during the day. Two will be on the bus with the inmates. I'll take care of it," said O'Malley.

He turned his head to look for his remaining team members and spotted them on either side of the aisle of chairs, close behind him. He gave a signal and both men removed a stun grenade from their belts and after a count of three threw the explosives over the top of the chairs toward the place where the guards had concealed themselves. A flash of light, followed simultaneously by two loud explosions milliseconds apart, rent the air and a plume of smoke rose to the ceiling.

Yells of fright and pain emanated from the target area and O'Malley, with his men right behind him, rushed the position with their weapons at the ready to find the guards hunched over and clasping their ears.

The security detail offered no further resistance. O'Malley gave them a few minutes to recover from the percussion of the grenades and then marched the men off to the security office where they were locked in a cell.

He checked his watch again. "They should be arriving any minute."

"I'll tell the pilots to get ready for a quick takeoff. We'll have little time to get our people off the bus and to the aircraft," said Martin. He spoke a brief instruction via their radio communication and a moment later they heard their Transporter's engines fire up.

"Here come the inmates," said O'Malley. He pointed to a cloud of dust following behind the bus as it approached the camp perimeter.

O'Malley touched Martin on the arm. "They'll have no idea what's happened here so we'll let them all disembark and then my two guys can take the guards, prisoner. You and I will see that we get

President Chambers, Swales and General Mumford to the aircraft."

Martin nodded and they waited for the bus to approach. The inmate drop-off point, situated behind the airport terminal building, had ample place for the team to hide and they waited for the bus to come to a halt.

The inmates streamed out of the vehicle and when the last one stepped onto the driveway the two guards followed, oblivious of the trouble that awaited them.

President Chambers, Beverley Swales, and General Mumford all got off the bus together near the end of the inmate group and started to walk away toward their dormitory. O'Malley's two special ops men walked up to the vehicle's door and roughly pulled the unsuspecting guards off the stairs and threw them onto the ground. The inmates all stopped and stared with wide eyes at the two special op soldiers, who held their rifles at the ready.

No one understood the reason for the sudden intrusion until O'Malley called the three inmates from Earth out of the group. Despite the protective gear, the three inmates recognized him instantly and they raced to his side.

"We have to move quickly," said O'Malley. "There's a jet on the runway waiting to take us out of here."

The two special ops soldiers grabbed the guard's revolvers off their belts and told them to turn on their stomachs while electrical ties were applied to their wrists. O'Malley, Martin and the escapees ran around the corner of the terminal building and onto the runway. The jet, parked about one hundred and fifty yards away with its engines fired up, waited for the escapees and the team.

"Run for your lives," shouted O'Malley. As they sprinted toward the aircraft another noise caught their attention. They look up into the sky toward the West and saw a lone fighter jet winging toward them. O'Malley knew its purpose. He mentally calculated the time it would take for them to arrive at the Transporter's door and clamber aboard. It would not be enough. The approach of the jet, at supersonic speed, would be over the airfield within seconds.

Martin had the same thought. "We're not going to make it."

O'Malley lifted the radio and spoke to his man aboard the jet. "All of you—get out now."

Two seconds later the jet swooped down toward the defenseless aircraft on the runway and they saw a puff of smoke as a projectile left the bottom of one of its wings. The vapor trail streamed from the rear of the rocket as it shot toward the target. A flash of light, followed by an explosion, took away the only means of an effective escape from Camp Logan.

33

A Timeous Escape

The Transporter exploded in a sea of flames. There would be no reprieve for the two pilots and the one special ops soldier. They were all instantly incinerated. Pieces of hot metal reigned down on O'Malley and his team as the camp inmates rounded the terminal to view the scenario. There would be no immediate escape for the assault team and the three escapees. The fighter jet circled once to make sure the target had been destroyed and then flew off to the West. O'Malley gathered his wits.

"Quickly—back to the bus. Those poor devils in the aircraft are now beyond our help."

Everyone turned and ran past the open-eyed inmates, back toward the terminal. The three escapees followed the team around the building and they all clambered onto the bus. O'Malley jumped into the driver's seat and took the wheel. A quick glance at the gas gauge revealed the need to fill up and O'Malley remembered the two five-hundred gallon storage tanks on pedestals which were situated behind the dormitories. He fired up the engine and drove the bus around to the back of the complex and parked beneath one of the tanks.

One of the special ops team members jumped out and began to fill the tank. No one other than O'Malley had spoken since the destruction of the aircraft and his rescued friends took the opportunity to make a few comments.

"Are we ever glad to see your face, Special Agent," said Chambers.

Mumford left his seat and placed his arm around O'Malley's shoulders. "I knew you wouldn't let us down. Did you get to the other side?"

"I have not only been to the other side and back—I've managed to make a few new friends along the way." He pointed to Martin.

O'Malley gave a short version of his escape from the refinery and how he had managed, with Martin's help, to escape through the link. By the time he had completed the story the special's ops soldier jumped back on board.

"Tank's as full as I can make it, Sir. We'd better get going."

O'Malley threw the bus into gear and stepped on the gas. "We have to get out of Dodge as quickly as possible. It is likely that a squad of marines will be arriving any minute by aircraft to round us up. With darkness falling soon I'm hoping to put some distance between us and the base. We'll need to find an escape route across the desert."

"I have a compass. If we head in a north-easterly direction we will find hard, flat ground most of the way. We should travel only at night but I need to set up our satellite detection equipment to pick up one of the Institute's satellites. We need a map to find places where gas will be available," said Martin.

O'Malley considered Martin's statement. "I'm guessing at how far this crate will travel on a tank of gas but it could be about three hundred miles. We need to put a reasonable distance between us and the base first—then stop to set up the equipment."

Darkness fell with gradual progression while the passengers kept an eye on the airspace behind them in case a military transporter appeared.

"They are going to know we escaped in the bus but because of the vast distances to civilization, they may leave an air-based search for the morning. I need to turn the headlights on to see what's ahead of us," said O'Malley.

He kept the speed up for about an hour and then slowed down to conserve fuel. The terrain before them undulated in low gradient dunes and the surface appeared to be hard enough as to not impede their progress. Apart from a few rock outcrops, only an occasional bush had to be circumnavigated. An hour later O'Malley brought the vehicle to a stop.

"We need to set up that satellite system and head for a place where there is a supply of fuel," said Martin. The Institute has two satellites that cover this whole area."

They all clambered out and took a few minutes for personal business. O'Malley and Martin then removed the satellite detection equipment which one of the soldiers had carried in his backpack and set it up. Martin connected a tablet and the receiver began to scan the heavens for one of the Institute's satellites.

A ping sound came from the tablet and Martin started to fine-tune the apparatus in an attempt to zone in on the signal.

"I have one of them," he exclaimed.

A minute later a map of the entire desert area came up. Camp Logan appeared in the center and they searched both north and east for any small villages or farms where vehicles might be present. Martin pointed to a village due east of their position.

"Here's one that has contact with the major routes which run across the country. You can see the district roads that link with this major highway which will lead us to the area north of Liberty City, where the Lady Anne is moored."

"What's the distance to the village," asked O'Malley.

"About another hundred and twenty miles—we should be good for that distance," answered Martin.

O'Malley scanned the map for alternatives. "I see there are three other similar sized villages, at least two of which might be closer to our present position."

"That's true but the military will have figured out that we would be trying for Liberty City and they will check for any movement in the desert which could represent a fleeing bus. They don't know that the Lady Anne is involved and berthed two hundred miles north of the City."

"So, we take the route which they would least suspect?' said Chambers.

"It's a gamble but we don't have a better option," answered O'Malley.

Martin looked at his watch. "It's 11:05 pm. We should make the village in two and a quarter hours, let's get going."

They jumped back on the bus and headed off into the night.

*

A high-ranking military officer stood outside Camp Logan's air terminal building and scowled at the inmates. All of them claimed to have seen nothing. The two guards, however, told him about the sudden appearance of a militia group and their escape in the bus. He turned to one of his lieutenants.

"Go into the terminal building and find a map of the area. They will be headed in one of two possible directions: due east or due west. I want to know of any villages that might have a supply of gas and their distances from the camp."

The lieutenant saluted and ran off into the terminal building. The officer further interrogated the guards and discovered that three inmates had been abducted by the group. Neither of the guards knew what had happened to their comrades who had remained at the base that day. A few moments later the lieutenant reappeared with Hilda, the terminal administrator, who told the officer that the remaining security detail was locked in the brig.

"You bunch of immature, badly trained imbeciles were really taken by surprise, weren't you?" ranted the officer.

The lieutenant produced a map which Hilda had given him. "There are three villages ranging from due north to east and one to the West. All are within four to five hours of Camp Logan, Sir."

"It's a huge desert and they might make it to any one of these villages, but they will still be traveling tomorrow and most of the day if they go either east or west," said Hilda.

The lieutenant weighed in. "If I may, Sir—If it's the dissident O'Malley and the Institute's traitor, Martin, they would be trying to get to Liberty City. I would plumb for the shortest route east."

The commander glared at the lieutenant. "You would think that because you're still green, Lieutenant. That's exactly what they would want us to think."

The lieutenant dropped his eyes to the ground and refrained from any further comment.

The officer continued. "I will get two fighter jets in first thing tomorrow morning. We'll catch theses bastards and blow them all to kingdom come."

*

Four hours after leaving Camp Logan the bus arrived on the outskirts of a village. The terrain had changed but fortunately for the team and their three rescued friends, O'Malley spotted a track after passing through a shallow river bed. The track climbed up into more mountainous territory and cut through a dry gulch to approach the rear of the village. They scanned the limited buildings for a vehicle workshop or garage where fuel could be purchased and eventually found what they were looking for on the outskirts. A garage and workshop with a single gas pump.

With the hot, evening air baking the inside of the bus like an oven, the group all climbed out and sat outside under the stars with their backs against the building's wall. A few hours later the first rays from Terra's star began to lick the mountain tops around the village and everyone got ready to climb back into the bus.

At 6:30 am the owner of the garage arrived to open his business. He rode in on a bicycle, stopped under the pump station canopy and stared in wonder at the bus. He never had customers that early in the day and rarely ever saw a large vehicle. Martin approached him and flashed his old Institute badge.

"We need to fill the tank as quickly as possible. Can you help us?"

The owner nodded. "I will need to get the keys from inside."

He disappeared into the building and came out seconds later, unlocked the pump and began pumping the gas.

"We still have a long way to go but I don't think we should risk traveling during the day," said Martin.

"If we can find a place to hide the bus we could stay here and leave at dusk," answered O'Malley.

"Good idea. I would hate to suffer the heat," said Chambers.

Martin asked the business owner if there was a local motel and the man confirmed that a small inn existed in the village's main street. Martin had foreseen their need for cash before their journey through the link and after the Lady Anne had been captured by the assault team he found that Captain Penn's safe contained five thousand dollars, of which he took three thousand, to help with any expenses.

O'Malley asked the garage owner if they could park the bus under some cover and the man graciously allowed them to use his vehicle workshop.

"We don't have many vehicles for repairs because the local farmers fix their own," he said.

That evening the team relaxed in two of the inn's three rooms and drank cold beer which Martin purchased from the local liquor store. Later that afternoon the sound of a jet approaching had them all peeking out of the room's windows. Moments later it screamed overhead, so low that the buildings all shook and the villagers looked to the sky in fear.

"They're looking for signs of the bus," said O'Malley.

Martin turned the TV set on and searched for the news broadcast. The story broke at 3:00 pm that the Institute of Universal Investigation and the military were looking for a group of fugitives who had escaped in a bus and were headed east of Camp Logan. Anyone who had seen the bus was to contact a number which the news anchor displayed on the screen.

A knock on the door of O'Malley's room in which Chambers, Swales, and Mumford were also resting, had them casting nervous glances at each other.

"It's probably one of my men," said O'Malley.

He opened the door to find an agitated garage owner. "Someone has reported your presence here. You will have to leave immediately," he said.

34

The Escapees find an Ally

The garage owner kept his voice just above a whisper.

"I know who you are and I have some sympathy for you. My oldest son died in Camp Logan about three years ago and I have no love for the Institute of Investigation."

"The jet which flew over the village means they were looking for our bus. If we leave now they will spot us," said O'Malley.

"You must leave or you will be surrounded by troops. I saw paratroops being dropped from a transporter plane close by. They are dropping into a field just beyond that dry gulch at the backend of town as we speak."

Martin stepped out into the hallway with O'Malley. "That means they will be here in about twenty-five minutes. Is there anywhere we can hide?"

"I have a better plan," said the garage owner. "Take my truck. It has a canopy on the back so no one will recognize you. I will drive the bus out into the mountains and hide it but we must move quickly."

O'Malley turned and spoke to the other members in the room. "Grab your things—we're leaving."

Martin knocked on the room next door and roused the two special ops soldiers. The garage owner led them down the stairs of the inn and out to an old truck, parked at the curb.

"We don't know how to thank you," said O'Malley.

"You can thank me by not getting caught. Those Institute bastards don't deserve anything."

Martin thrust a bunch of notes into the garage owners hands. "This doesn't compensate you for what you've done for us but it will make up for the temporary loss of your truck."

The garage owner handed O'Malley a bunch of keys. "I must go and remove the bus. Take the road out of the village and keep going until you reach the highway. It will take you to the East Coast."

They climbed into the vehicle, an old double cab, long based truck, with Martin behind the wheel. And the two soldiers on the back under the canopy. Martin pulled away from the curb and raced down the road to the village exit. The road wound around the side of a rocky outcrop on which the village had been established and pro-gressed up a steep gradient. As they neared the brow of the hill O'Malley looked back out the pas-senger window and saw the bus leave the village on a different track which appeared to lead down into a valley below.

They all heard the scream of the jet's engine as it zoomed in from the North, swooped low over the bus and banked for a return run. O'Malley watched in horror as the jet lined up the bus in its sights and saw the puff of smoke emitted from beneath the one wing. The rocket hit its target and exploded in a ball of fire as the gas tank blew. The bus careened off the edge of the track and down a steep gradient, to end up in the valley below. All that remained were burned, twisted metal, shattered glass, and burning tires.

O'Malley closed his eyes. "He was a brave man."

"Those callous bastards—he didn't deserve that," said President Chambers. They drove on in silence and a few minutes later breasted the hilltop and dropped down out of sight from the soldiers who were busily surrounding the village. It would not take them long to discover the lone body in the wreckage of the bus. The dusk began to descend on the flatlands through which they traveled and the district, gravel road stretched out in a straight line ahead.

"They're going to figure out it pretty soon," said O'Malley. "We need to find another small village along the highway and change vehicles as soon as possible."

Martin pulled out a travel map which he had taken from the main desk at the inn and handed it to President Chambers who sat on the bench seat next to him. The president unfolded the paper and squinted at the terrain. O'Malley peeped over his shoulder from the back seat.

"This is where we are." He pointed to a blue line which indicated a highway. And tapped his finger on the map.

"Here's a small town just off to the left where we can look for another vehicle."

"That's about twenty miles from the turn-off," said Chambers.

"I see signs in the distance. We're almost there," said Martin.

At the intersection, they turned right onto the highway. A while later a sign for a small rural town gave the distance of eighteen miles to its turn-off and a larger interstate sign gave distances for the succeeding intermediate towns and cities on the route. Liberty City, as the final destination was nine-hundred and thirty miles away.

Martin turned the truck off the highway at a tee-junction and followed the road into the town, the welcome sign which revealed a population of ten thousand people. Darkness had fallen and the street lights lit up the surrounding buildings as they drove down the main street looking for a potential vehicle which they could commandeer.

O'Malley pointed to a microbus parked near the corner of an intersecting road. "That's exactly what we're looking."

Martin parked the truck behind the target vehicle and they all got out.

"It would appear people retire to bed early in this place," said Beverley Swales.

"All the better for us," said Martin. He tried the door of the microbus and found the vehicle unlocked.

"They obviously don't have a high rate of crime here," said General Mumford.

Martin worked on the ignition wires and within a minute the dash lights came on.

"I will drive the truck and park it around the corner. There's no reason to give anybody clues as to us having been here," said O'Malley.

Ten minutes later they were on the highway again. Terra's satellite, an exact replica of the Earth's moon, had risen in a clear sky as they headed toward the East Coast.

"How much gas do we have?" asked Mumford.

"We hit pay dirt. The owner must have filled up very recently—the tank's between the quarter and full mark," answered Martin.

Two-hundred and fifty miles later they crested a hill to see a host of oscillating red and blue lights on the highway ahead. The lights scythed through the darkness like flashes of lightning.

"It looks like a police stop," said Martin.

"We need to find a way around it. Give me that map," said O'Malley.

President Chambers handed the map to O'Malley who turned the overhead roof light on to examine their options. After brief scrutiny, he switched the light off.

"Stop and turn around. We need to travel back to a turn-off about five miles away. We can bypass the roadblock."

Martin obeyed and returned to the turn-off, a gravel road which served a farming community, and followed it until O'Malley indicated a turn to the right at an intersection. The new road ran parallel to the highway. They continued on for several miles before the police lights could be seen on the highway, about one mile's distance abreast of them, on the highway.

"Nice work, Dillon," said Martin. "It may have been a regular thing but I think it more likely that the Institute would have set it up. They will know by now we weren't on the bus and should have worked out that the garage guy helped us to escape."

"We need to be alert for more roadblocks. They will eventually figure out we are ahead of them," said Chambers.

They drove on and three hours passed without further incident. "We have about fifty miles left on this tank of gas. I'll have to stop at the next town and fill up."

They stopped at the gas station on the outskirts of another small town and Martin filled the tank. A small convenience store sold pop drinks, buns and wrapped sandwiches which helped them take the edge off their hunger. An interstate sign gave the distance to Liberty City as one-hundred and fifty miles.

Martin consulted the map again as they waited for the tank to be filled.

"We need to turn off at a town called, Eastwood, and then head northeast toward the area where the Lady Anne is tied up. I'm hoping against hope that the authorities won't have discovered that we highjacked their ship to get to the mainland. If they have we may have a reception committee waiting for us."

"It's our only way back to the dimensional link," stated O'Malley. "I doubt whether they even know we made it back to our universe so maybe we will be okay."

With the gas tank full they took off again and as the dawn lit up the horizon Martin turned off toward the north-east and made a good time to the village where they first had commandeered a truck for the initial journey to the Liberty City airport. A ten-mile trek through wasteland awaited them as they dumped the microbus on the outskirts of the village and prepared to face the heat of the day with its terminal dose of radiation. The journey on foot would tax all of them, Beverly Swales and President Chambers in particular. It would take most of the remaining daylight hours to accomplish but they wanted to get to the Lady Anne as quickly as possible.

The group donned their protective gear and venture out toward the coast. Four hours later they approached the abandoned harbor and were thrilled to see the Lady Anne exactly where it had been berthed. Captain Penn and his men, still locked up in the brig and one of the cabins were equally glad to see their captors in hope that their misery might be at an end.

Martin addressed Captain Penn. "We are setting you free. If you walk in a westerly direction you will see a small village, about ten miles distant. From there you'll be able to make a plan to get back to civilization."

Captain Penn refrained from comment and soon as he and his men were set free on the derelict wharf they started to walk in the direction Martin had given them. The Lady Anne sailed out of the small protected harbor under the hand of one of the special ops soldiers who had sea-going experience in his resume and made straight for the dimensional link. Eleven hours later they arrived at the coordinates of the links geographical position and the bank of mist.

"Make ready to lower the link-jumper," shouted Martin. O'Malley and one of the special ops men loosed the vessel from its deck mooring. A winch arm swung out and dropped the vessel into the sea where it bobbed up and down next to the ship. At that moment a shattering scream of noise reached their ears and they turned eyes skyward. Two fighter jets appeared low on the horizon and headed straight for their position.

"Get on board the link-jumper," shouted O'Malley. Everyone ran onto the deck and climbed down the webbing onto the smaller deck of the lifeboat as the jets made their approach. Martin, first inside the capsule started the motor, slipped the gearbox into reverse and backed away from the Lady

Anne's side. A shattering crash followed by a heavy vibration coursed though the Lady Anne and transferred through the water to the capsule which began to buck and heave. The Lady Anne started to list as the link-jumper surged away under its own power. The occupants all held on for dear life. O'-Malley, the last person on board observed the ship lean over until the deck they had all been standing on, disappeared under water.

The Jets zoomed overhead and turned to make another run at the Lady Anne but the trawler keeled over and began to sink beneath the waves. The water around link-jumper frothed and churned as it headed into the bank of mist.

Epilogue

The Lady Gray awaited O'Malley and the group as they slipped out of the bank of mist in the Bermuda Triangle. A jubilant deputy director of the FBI waited on deck for the link-jumper to arrive and moor alongside. The occupants climbed on board with huge grins and thanked their lucky stars for the deliverance they had miraculously received.

Waiting for them at New York harbor were Beverly Swales's two children, Janet and Steven O'Malley, a group of Pentagon officials and White House staff members. Roland MacDonald, Diego Martinez and Gwen Farrell, all eager to hear how the assault team managed to free President Chambers, his chief of staff and the chairman of the joint chiefs were also present. That night a party was held at the J.Edgar Hoover building and the assault team was honored for their bravery. K.D.-Martin and Charley Minx, the oil terminal operator who had helped O'Malley in his escape were present and everyone had questions about where they came from.

James Ingram gave instructions to cover up the reality of the alternate universe as the government did not want the news getting out. President Chambers took up his position as president and shared with the press that an unknown foreign power had tried to highjack the White House and the military by using look-alikes as substitutions. He also assured the North Koreans that there would be no further attacks on their sovereignty as it had been discovered by the CIA that a group of mercenaries of unknown origin had been involved in the missile launch. It would take many weeks for things to settle down in both the Pentagon and the White House, but with the right people back at the helm things would soon settle down.

A week later O'Malley took his wife Janet out on a date.

"What about the Clyde-Walker woman?" she asked.

"Tam has been reassigned to another part of the country and it's over," answered O'Malley.

"Does that mean we are a family again?"

O'Malley took her hand and looked into her eyes. "I owe you a deep, deep apology for the way I've treated you and if you will have me back we will be a family again."

Janet lingered before the answer came. "Steven will be over the moon but I'm not sure if I can give you the same measure of trust as before."

"We will take it slowly—one step at a time."

She nodded and squeezed his hand. "Are you staying at my place tonight?"

"If you will have me. I would love to refresh our relationship," he said.

Janet's eyes filled with tears. "I'm looking forward to it."

TheEnd

More Books by Colin Setterfield

The Helium-3 Conspiracy

Love Sweat tears

Subduction Zone

*The A-Mortal Gene

*The habitat Relocation Project

*The Beautiful Planet

The Memory Hunter. Special Agent O' Malley

Merlin's War   SpeciaL Agent O'Malley

The Omega File Special Agent O'Malley

Operation Terra Firma Special Agent O'Malley

www.ingramcontent.com/pod-product-compliance
Lightning Source LLC
Chambersburg PA
CBHW032135190626
46814CB00005BA/1702